The North Tower of the World Trade Center in New York was burning. Everyone gasped when suddenly a second jet appeared on the television screen and plowed into the South Tower.

Jason's jaw dropped; mouth open wide, he was speechless. It wasn't real. It was more like watching a movie. This couldn't be happening. It wasn't real.

Sirens sounded everywhere. Security police, their red lights flashing, were securing Patrick Air Force Base. Threat Condition Delta was declared: a terrorist act was under way. Every American military installation around the world was going into lockdown. Jason couldn't remember when that had ever happened.

"They hit the Pentagon!" a voice cried out over the intercom.

Jason closed his eyes and remembered the night he was at the Khobar Towers in Dhahran, Saudi Arabia. It was a night he'd never forget, no matter how hard he tried. Torn and mangled bodies, some victims so burned and bloody that a veteran combat pilot told Jason he couldn't tell who was who.

Jason lost track of time while he tried to help the wounded. The next day he assisted with the grisly and gloomy task of gathering the remains of the dead. He swore revenge that it would never happen again.

Now it was happening all over again and more innocents had been murdered. From Beirut to now, terrorists had made their cowardly strikes against good and decent people.

The World Trade Center Towers had collapsed while the Pentagon burned. America was at war, but with whom?

Also by Michael Salazar

DROP ZONE
THE LUCIFER LIGHT

THE
WAR ANGEL

MICHAEL SALAZAR

BANTAM BOOKS

THE WAR ANGEL
A Bantam Book / October 2003

Published by
Bantam Dell
A Division of Random House, Inc.
New York, New York

ISBN 0-553-58631-9

Manufactured in the United States of America
Published simultaneously in Canada

OPM   10   9   8   7   6   5   4   3   2   1

ACKNOWLEDGMENTS

But for my fellow travelers and friends, this story would not be. Nita Taublib, John Flicker, Carole Bidnick, Charles Meador, Jean and Julian Leek, Jim Baarda, Peter Pinto, Mike Gorsline, Boyd Lease, Vic Davis, Jeff and Jackie Powell, Russell Wilmot III, Dennis Dayle, Mark Slocum, Oliver North, Art Boyer, Mike Merritt, Dave Nichols, Jeff Clemens, Dawn Collazo, Steve Skipper, Jeff Curl, Doug Kestranik, Ben Codallo, Hugh McFadden, John and Linda Hilliard, and Gary Fraser.

And without fail, many thanks to the unnamed gentleman who encourages me to color outside the lines.

"It is the great battle of the Cross and the Koran, which is now to be fought."

—KNIGHTS OF MALTA GRAND MASTER, JEAN LA VALLETTE, A.D. 1565

"This is not the voice of desire. This is the word of God."

—ISLAM, EMPIRE OF FAITH

"But for the warrior, the seasons are marked not by . . . calendared years themselves, but by battles."

—STEVEN PRESSFIELD, *Gates of Fire*

THE
WAR ANGEL

0615 / TUESDAY / 26 OCTOBER 2001
CHAPLIAR / AFGHANISTAN

"The most deadly thing on the battlefield is one well-aimed shot." —Hathcock

AIR FORCE SENIOR MASTER SERGEANT JASON Johnson lived his life by the motto "So that others may live," but not today. Inch by inch, the PJ, as a pararescueman is called, raised his head from the poppy field where he lay. Then slowly lifting his highly modified M24 rifle, he laid the crosshairs of his sniperscope between the eyes of his target.

The target looked like an old, worn Afghan soldier. He wore a thick, color-worn jacket. The gray turban that wrapped his head blended into his long beard. His shaggy, dusty eyebrows connected above cold, dark eyes and a big nose. His yellow teeth were cracked and split. *Convincing costume, but I know your eyes.*

Jason knew every crease, wrinkle, and hair on the mark's face. There once was a time when the mark even called him friend. *Not today. I know your secrets. You can't hide the eyes.*

The target methodically inspected his troops. They looked loose and ragged, but their well-oiled AK-47s looked ready to fire. And he knew that they could fight because he had once fought beside them.

Glancing at his watch, the target would be "hot" in ten seconds. Slowly moving his eyes to the right, Carl Debaca, his spotter, held up one finger. *No wind.* A straight shot. Touching a button on his Leupold sniperscope, Jason changed the crosshairs to a laser dot.

He patiently traced the mark as he inspected his troops.

Jason and his spotter had crawled through the cold and dusty poppy fields for two days to get within shooting range. Intelligence seemed to be right for a change. Everything was as they had been briefed. But he knew better—this wasn't just war, or a political killing; it was personal, too. *Payback's a bitch.*

Guarded assassination. Captured by the Northern Alliance, the target had been secretly released rather than turned over for an international trial. Now the drug-dealing warlord was being dressed up and posed to become a key member of the Afghan Alliance. That just couldn't happen.

Jason was there to complete the unwritten orders of others: Deliver the message. Return the terror. Take him out. Make *sure* that he's dead, absolutely.

Treachery and illusions. Unless you knew him, Jason would have to agree that the disheveled warlord couldn't possibly be worth billions of dollars, and be able to hold world power. But he was. In a key political position he might become unstoppable, the next bin Laden. Cut him down now and the narcoterrorist world would shake, and take a long time to rebuild.

Concentrate on the job. Almost imperceptibly, Jason nodded. At three hundred yards the shot was easy, almost too easy. He felt that he was dangerously close, but the mission orders dictated it.

"Send it," Carl hissed.

Focus. Get in the bubble. Forget about everything and just draw the sight picture. Nothing else matters in this world. Nothing—it was all about the shot. No sounds. No thoughts. No hate. Just confidence.

Take a breath. Let it half-out. Jason squeezed the trigger of his noise- and flash-suppressed sniper rifle.

The bullet exploded the head into countless fragments as a bloody red mist filled the air. The body flopped around for a few moments, then suddenly stopped. *Dead.* No head. Jason then quickly got off five more random and deadly shots, scattering the surprised troops everywhere.

Jason methodically scooped up his brass casings and pulled the rifle to his side. Nodding, he and Carl backed down into their hide sites and sealed them shut.

Relax. There was nowhere to go at the moment. They would leave after things had quieted down. It might take a while before they could move, but time didn't matter because the extraction unit would wait until they returned.

Pandemonium reigned throughout the village. He could hear shouts and screams, then rapid gunfire as the target's troops shot at everything and nothing. No matter how hard they searched they would turn up nothing. The two sniper teams were ghosts. They knew the territory better than the enemy—they had crawled through lots of exacting scenarios before taking a shot at the real thing.

Wrapped securely in his high-tech, bulletproof cocoon, Jason had time to think about why he was there. Heated political arguments at the highest levels of government ended in a covert decision that no one would ever acknowledge. But someone had to do the shooting. A sniper team guaranteed not to miss—the Brotherhood of Death.

In the beginning it was all about global terrorism, money, and Afghan opium—they turned him loose to go after it. But along the way he uncovered some very dirty things, nasty secrets hidden behind a "top-secret" cloak.

This war was a war fought behind the curtains, a war of the assassin and assassinations. And this *wasn't* the opening round—the killing didn't happen. Nothing would ever be written or recorded. No report of his mission would ever be made. With all the actions, coordination, and finance it had taken to put him in the camouflaged cocoon, no connections to any American agency would ever be made.

While the good people back home in America waved their flags and cried out for justice and protection from terrorism, Jason just shook his head and whispered to himself, "I only hope that I've done the right thing. Just how in the hell did I *ever* get caught up in a war that started over eight hundred years ago?"

CHAPTER 1

0900 TUESDAY / 11 SEPTEMBER 2001
750 RAMP / PATRICK AIR FORCE BASE / FLORIDA

JASON JOHNSON STOOD AT THE RAMP EDGE OF AN HC-130 aircraft giving his PJ team last-minute instructions for a water jump at the Judy drop zone on the Banana River.

"You won't believe it!" cried Rolo Perez, the aircraft crew chief, as he came running toward the plane. "Your flight's canceled. Every flight in America's been canceled! Come on!" he yelled, skidding to a stop. "It's on all the TV channels. You won't believe it. *I* don't fuckin' believe it! Hurry! Run!"

Clueless, everyone jumped off the plane and raced toward the closest television.

Jason shot through the door of the Thirty-ninth Rescue Squadron and into the ops center. "What's going on?"

Everybody was gathered in front of the television hanging on the far wall, all eyes were glued to the unfolding horror.

The North Tower of the World Trade Center in New York was burning. Everyone gasped when suddenly a second jet appeared on the screen and plowed into the South Tower.

Jason's jaw dropped; mouth open wide, he was speechless. It wasn't real. It was more like watching a movie. This couldn't be happening. It wasn't real.

Opinions instantly formed, and the hateful words voiced.

"Damn ragheads!"

"Let's nuke the camel jockeys and turn their desert into a glass parking lot!"

He'd heard all the nasty words before, during Operation Desert Storm. Feeling helpless that there was nothing he could do at the moment, Jason turned from the horror and walked from the ops section and out to the back deck of the squadron.

It was a beautiful sunny Florida day. The sky was blue and a cool breeze blew offshore. But just a three-hour plane flight away hateful murder was happening.

Sirens sounded everywhere. Security police, their red lights flashing, were securing Patrick Air Force Base. Threat Condition Delta was declared: A terrorist act was under way. Every American military installation around the world was going into lockdown. He couldn't remember when that had ever happened.

"They hit the Pentagon!" a voice cried out over the intercom.

"No! Oh my God." Sorrow pierced Jason's heart. The fuckers had struck at the nation's true might: her military brains. And there wasn't a goddamned thing he could do about it! Bewildered, he sat. Confused and lost. It suddenly occurred to him that there was only one place on the base that he could go to for strength. He'd gone there in the past, and he needed to go there more than ever.

Standing in front of the Patrick Air Force Base's memorial for the five airmen murdered by terrorists on June 25, 1996, Jason closed his eyes and remembered the night that he was at the Khobar Towers in Dhahran, Saudi Arabia. At the time he had already been deployed there with the Seventy-first Air Rescue Squadron for more than thirty days.

He couldn't sleep, so he got out of bed and went to work out at the base gym.

In luck, no one was on the Gravitron, his favorite machine, so he had it all to himself. He'd been on it for about twenty minutes and was working up a good sweat. As he was hanging from the machine, first the lights flickered, then there was a low, violent rumble. Before he could blink, a concussion like a giant wave blasted him off the machine and threw him across the room. Instinctively tucking himself into a ball, he rolled, doing somersaults in the air, and crashed into the mirrored wall on the other side of the room.

Glass flew everywhere. He lay there, stunned, for what seemed like forever before he came to his senses. Cut and bleeding from the mirror splinters, he felt nothing as he sprinted toward his building. At first he didn't believe it was possible, seeing massive amounts of smoke but no flames, then he looked to where his room would've been.

He fought to bring out the wounded and the dead, cursing the terrorists who did it and the base commanders, who had known for years that the building was exposed and vulnerable to an attack but had done nothing to protect it.

Everyone from the surrounding buildings worked with the firefighters to put out some of the smaller fires, then helped wherever they could.

It was a night that he'd never forget, no matter how hard he tried. Torn and mangled bodies, some victims so burned and bloody that Matt Winkler, a veteran combat rescue pilot, told Jason that he couldn't tell who was who.

People, comrades and friends, were wounded or dead.

He'd even invited Justin Woods to work out with him, but Woody wanted to sleep. He was gone.

Using all his powers as a medical technician, he lost track of time while he tried to help the wounded. The next day he assisted with the grisly and gloomy task of gathering the remains of the dead. He swore revenge that it would never happen again.

Now it was happening all over again and more innocents had been murdered. From Beirut to now, terrorists had made their cowardly strikes against good and decent people. He'd felt the pain for too damn long.

He softly ran his hand over the picture of Kevin "KJ" Johnson, then touched the pictures of all his other air crewmates. Their mission was to save lives. These men were the good guys, lovers, fathers, brothers, and sons. Once friends, now they were pictures on a granite wall. They had touched a hostile world in peace and paid the price for it with their lives.

He sat on a marble bench and dropped his head into his hands. "Man, it never ends," he whispered. His hands started to shake and his whole body trembled.

Jason tried to calm down, but couldn't. He had escaped death's clutches in many places around the world. He'd saved and taken lives—and he was still standing. Having joined the pararescue brotherhood as a young man, the years he had dedicated to saving lives around the world also taught him about all the hatred in the world.

Used, fooled, and betrayed by others in the name of a greater good left him feeling jaded, cynical, and angry. His nightmares never let him sleep. Mind shaken, but not lost, yet. Now millions screamed out for revenge. He learned that revenge only brought more sorrow. But something had to be done.

He stood in front of his dead comrades, came to attention, and slowly saluted.

Then the tears started, and it felt as if they were never going to stop.

1850 / BUILDING 698 /
PATRICK AIR FORCE BASE / FLORIDA

The World Trade Center Towers had collapsed while the Pentagon burned. America was at war, but with whom?

The section came alive as every PJ in the group began showing up, without being called, and started putting their rescue gear together.

Jason finished packing his gear, then walked into his office and sat at his desk. Lost in thought, he jumped when his phone rang. "Hello?"

"You in or out?"

The color drained from his face. Jason knew well the deep baritone voice. "Look, my team is getting ready to go to New York, or anywhere else we get called. Man, you guys can't call on me at a time like this. I don't work for you anymore, remember?"

"We have no hold over you," the deep voice answered. "Of course, you have a pressing mission."

"But you need me more."

"That's right, Alice."

Jason cringed. He hated his code name and all that it represented. Pissed off with all that was going on, he couldn't hold back. "What? To get screwed by you guys, like usual, and then leave me holding the shitbag, too, right? I'm right, ain't I?"

"Remember who you're talking to."

Oops! The voice on the other end of the phone commanded more power than many world leaders. But he knew what he said was true. "I do, sir, more than you'll ever know."

"Then do you want payback? I know that you care. Alice, *we* know that you care."

"Payback? I'm not in the payback business anymore, sir."

"Get real. And get over your self-pity. You did what you had to do. Right now you can do something that *will* make a difference."

While thousands of rescue support people were headed to the Pentagon and New York City, elite Special Forces would be shipping out to the Middle East, Afghanistan, and central Asia. Jason guessed that the most deadly of them all, the Brotherhood of Death, was probably going in first, and as a former member they undoubtedly wanted him back.

"Look. I'm retired."

"Hey, I don't have time for this shit, Alice, so don't fuck with me. I'm in a hurry. Ya in, ya out?"

That was one thing about General Ben Cadallo—he always came straight to the point.

"Sir, don't you fuck with *me*. You can't try to pin me down like that. I need to hear more before I answer to anything."

"Then read your e-mail." The phone went dead.

Jason dropped the phone back on the receiver and took a deep breath. Checking the e-mail on his computer, there was only one new message: No Subject. He punched the icon.

> *1000. Wednesday. Swimmer's Hall of Champions. Ft. Lauderdale, Florida. You'll know the boat.*

"Damn!" He exhaled.

CHAPTER 2

**0940 WEDNESDAY / 12 SEPTEMBER 2001
SWIMMER'S HALL OF CHAMPIONS /
FORT LAUDERDALE / FLORIDA**

*NATO invokes Article Five of their charter; an attack on
one is an attack on all.*

EVERYTHING MIGHT'VE LOOKED SIMILAR, BUT THE
world had changed. America, the mighty nation,
preeminent world power, had been cut low and
hurt. Rocked back on her heels, her shock and pain reverberated around the world. Freedom was under attack.
How did this happen? Who were the murdering animals
that did it? Where were they? How to get at them? Something had to be done, but what?

One thing Jason knew for damn sure, there were
groups in America who had gotten the green light to
strike back with malice—proven warriors who'd been
"in the shit." They were the men who, at a moment's notice, put themselves in harm's way, crossed over the line,
came back blooded; and kept their mouths shut. The battles that they fought were secret, cold, and dirty.

And they jealously protected their turf. Few ever penetrated their world. Fewer were ever asked to "walk the walk" with them. Jason was one of the few who had.

It was a three-hour drive to Fort Lauderdale. Even though his M35 Infiniti was a luxury ride, Jason always hated the heavy traffic on I-95. *A marina?* He wondered why the meeting wasn't being held at a more secure place instead of some cushy marina. After all, wasn't war business normally conducted on a military base with layers and layers of security? Then again, the Doors never followed any of the established rules. Show the false and hide the real; that was their thing.

Few knew of the existence of the ultrasecret organization. The Doors specialized in dirty deeds that made the CIA look like benign missionaries.

Jason parked his car and walked along the pier. Yacht after yacht bobbed on the water—rich-boy toys. The size and extravagance of everything didn't impress him one bit. He was rich too, but few knew, like his friend Mac Rio. He had no idea how much he was worth, having spent almost nothing of the millions he fell into from Operation Lucifer Light.

Shit, I don't need to be here.

If he wanted to, he could buy his own damn yacht and be out cruising the Mediterranean. But he really didn't give a shit about any of it. His money did him no good because it didn't help him with what he really wanted. But the trouble was, he didn't really know what he wanted. But whatever it was, it would have to wait until he heard what the general had to say.

At the moment he just wanted to get over with the day's business with a secret organization that officially didn't even exist. Its members were named and numbered on a single sheet of paper kept in a top-secret vault somewhere deep inside the Pentagon.

Jason was member number twenty-six of the Brotherhood of Death.

He would've been the first to say that there was no glamour or honor associated with an ultrasecret organization.

Nightmares and betrayals, that's all the Doors had ever given him. Jason wondered why he had even bothered to answer their call. While his combat rescue team back at Patrick was getting ready to deploy to war, here he was, deserting his boys. Still, if someone really wanted to do something about the September 11 homicides, then these were the guys to see. Now, which boat were they on?

"You'll know which one."

Suddenly Jason felt the hair rise on the back of his neck. He stopped walking and assessed his surroundings. A big black bread van blocked any cars from entering the marina. *SWAT.*

Several sleek and fast cigarette boats drifted in the canal. Instead of the usual pretty girls in bikinis lounging on their decks, thick, unsmiling men wearing dark sunglasses and bulging windbreakers kept their heads on a constant swivel.

One of the go-fast boats on the water was a very elegant number. The name **Blue Thunder** was splashed across her hull—*Blue Thunder* belonged to the US Customs Service. Several black Chevy Suburbans with dark-tinted windows were parked around the marina.

Though he couldn't spot them, there was no doubt in Jason's mind that countersnipers had him in their crosshairs. He had ideas of where they might be, so facing a far roof he slowly raised his middle finger to his forehead and rubbed it.

A 150-foot black yacht was tied up at the end berth. Jason couldn't suppress a smile when he saw the name **Dark Secrets** carved on her fantail.

He strolled to the bottom of the gangway and stood waiting until a burly man dressed in a black suit and sunglasses appeared at the top of the rail. With a nod, the man allowed Jason to start up the gangway.

At the head of the gangway the guard motioned for Jason to raise his hands for a pat-down.

Goon. Jason shook his head and turned to leave. With all the firepower and high-zuit toys surrounding him, he had no intention of being caught without his own exit maker. Not now. Not ever.

"Wait," the guard said, and spoke into a small radio. Pressing his earpiece, the man nodded. "Follow me."

He followed the man through a maze of passageways, impressed with the elegant décor. White and black marble with gilded nautical fittings met his every turn. Chrome, mirrors, and a royal motif covered the ship. He wondered if the route was intentional to try and impress. It did, but he tried to stay cool. Even the president couldn't have a rig this fine. No one in the government could afford such opulence, or could they? His mind flashed back to a multibillion-dollar government embezzler named Frank McCone, better known as Mr. Black. But Black was dead.

Jason shuddered. Maybe this was Black's replacement.

Wordlessly, the man led Jason into a large anteroom and closed the door behind him.

In the room four men sat around a large, oval, smoked-glass table. They gave him hard stares and scowls. The black man sitting near the center dominated the room just by his size and aura.

Jason didn't like the scene from the start. Looking like some sort of Inquisition board, it seemed too staged, with too much attitude coming from the men in front of him, making him feel uptight and nervous.

They were all well dressed except for the man in red prison garb. He knew overdressed major players when he saw them. He was no naïve rookie operator. Hell, he knew about the fucked-up kinds of games they liked to play. But then again, even in his jeans and T-shirt, he knew that he could still hold his own with any major actors.

Surprised recognition struck the man wearing the prison jumpsuit. He gasped and tried to stand, but was held to the chair by chains and shackles. Falling back into the chair, he tried to regain his composure.

What's his trip? Jason thought.

"Alice, please sit down," General Ben Cadallo offered.

I got your "Alice" hanging right here. Instead of sitting, Jason leaned against a carved leather wall. He studied the general. While he owed his life to the man, too many bad memories held back a smile or offering of real warmth. "Nice suit. Armani? You asked if I was in or out. What's the deal?"

Cadallo, commander of the ultrasecret Doors, looked quizzical. "Aren't you interested in this vessel, or who these men are?"

"Not at all, sir. I thought I was coming here just to talk to you. *Alone.*" He wasn't there to socialize. A question started nagging at him. What was Cadallo doing with these dudes?

Something clicked inside of him and he was instantly jazzed. All the regret from the day before was gone. "So, what's the deal, sir?" Jason folded his arms across his chest as a chill came over him. *Why am I suddenly so turned on?*

His question had little to do with terrorism or patriotism; was it all about adventure? Was it that he missed something in life if he could not flirt with death?

He remembered how his friend Froto took on a suicide mission just to explode a nuclear weapon. Adventure. Thrill seeking. Somewhere between saving and taking lives, had he grown addicted to the challenge of cheating death? The question almost scared him silly. The answer was probably no better. Common sense screamed that walking out of the room was the best thing he could do. But he knew that he wouldn't do that, not until he listened to what the general had to say. *Eyes and ears open, mouth shut, pal. Look for a way out if the situation gets too deep.*

Cadallo frowned. "These men know of your reputation. I guess I should have added that your manners were limited, too."

He snorted. Cadallo had gotten the better of him. Jason stepped forward and dropped into a plush leather chair. Good manners did count in almost any situation. Besides, the bad-dude act was never his bag. *Oh well.* Ashamed, he shyly grinned. "Can I try this again, sir?"

Cadallo extended his hand. The handshake was massive and firm, almost painful. "I'll bet you're wondering what this is all about.

"*Dark Secrets* is borrowed from the DEA. They've used it as a front for some of the biggest drug stings ever recorded. Jason, let me introduce you to these gentlemen." Motioning to a bald man in a dark three-piece suit, he said, "This is DEA agent Otis Deal, of the Witness Security Program. And this is his *client,* Mr. Willie Falcon."

Falcon was the one in prison garb who had tried to stand up. Jason saw through the smoked-glass table that the man's chair was made of steel and bolted to the floor. Unless he was an escape artist of some kind, there would be no way he could break out from it. How did Falcon take a piss bound to that thing?

Jason knew of Falcon's name and reputation only through the news, but he still felt his hackles rise—he hated dope dealers. Evil predators. He put them in with the same category as pedophiles and terrorists. The bust was big news for one week, then a footnote the next.

Falcon was a Cuban multibillionaire drug dealer who lived a lifestyle that rivaled that of kings and dictators. Busted by the legendary supercop Dennis Dayle, he was now doing life without parole in a maximum-security prison, or so Jason had thought until now. Now he understood why so much armed security was present.

"He's a mortician" was all that Cadallo said about the last man.

The man wore a black Ivy League suit and had a dark complexion. He had a thick, short, black beard. Amber worry beads constantly moved in his right hand. The man looked to be from somewhere in the Middle East.

His intense stare unnerved Jason. "Why are you staring at me like that?"

"I have buried many men. You have good features." He smiled through gold-capped teeth. "You must get your looks from your grandfathers."

Jason's scalp crawled.

Cadallo took over. "No preliminaries, Jason. I'll get straight to the point. We've got ourselves a serious problem. One hour after the attack on the World Trade Center Towers and the Pentagon, mission directives started coming down the line. This operation has been in planning stages for over two years. Now we have less than a month to put it into operation. We're taking on the drug trade in Afghanistan."

"Just who're *we,* sir? And how?"

"Classified. Let me continue. Preliminary investigation led us to a basic major problem that we weren't ready to deal with: There are some very powerful administration big wheels who will try to stop this mission if they find out what we're up to. So we had to come up with a different plan of attack. And you're the key."

Jason rolled his eyes and mumbled to himself, "Great. Where have I heard this crap before?"

Cadallo looked around the room as if he was searching for the right words. "Uhm, see, according to which report you read, its classification level, and which agency filed it, they all conclude the same thing: Afghanistan is a primary opium source. Depending on who's talking, it supplies anywhere from 50 to 80 percent of the world's raw opium that is used for heroin production.

"While we have connections and operational countermethods active in South America and the Far East's Golden Triangle, we're totally lost in the Golden Crescent of the Middle East. Any drug intelligence that we get from the region comes from the Brits and Israelis. But what we have going on here does not include them or the CIA."

"Why not?"

"Too much dirt. This mission has to stay clean. No leaks. This operation doesn't even have a mission identifier or code name."

Jason searched the men's eyes. No one blinked.

Cadallo continued. "With the president's approval and secret congressional oversight, selected agents of certain governmental agencies got together to develop this plan."

"So why me? Who am I? I'm *nobody's* hero. I'm not a trained spook. I'm a guaranteed fuckup. You know that, sir." Jason started smelling a rat. "What's the Doors' involvement in all of this?"

"I've already told you too much, so before I continue." He picked up a sheet of paper on the table and slid it in front of Jason, along with a pen. "You have to sign this. It acknowledges your part in this operation."

Jason took the paper and studied the nondisclosure statement. It was really nothing but a bunch of gobbledygook. Once again, his signature on a piece of paper might sign his life away. The rat smelled worse.

Opium. *What the hell do I know about opium?*

A door opened and two Filipino stewards, dressed in Navy whites, entered the room, pushing a cart piled high with great-smelling food. Conversation stopped until the stewards served dishes and left.

"My lunch, *much* better than that prison shit I eat," Falcon observed, smiling. Glancing at Deal, he said,

"You almost had me. For a moment I actually thought that this guy here was Alex Gomez returned from the beyond. But if that pig Gomez was still around he would've already been all over the food." Even though he could barely move, he tried to look fluid, trying to give off an air of control, but the clinking chains reminded everyone that he was just another thug in a prison jumpsuit.

Jason saw a folder in front of Falcon. He did a double take when he recognized his own name on the header. How could a drug dealer be allowed to read his top-secret personnel folder? That was bullshit! Just what in the hell was going on?

"Who's this Alex Gomez?" Jason asked, picking at his food. It was stupid and ridiculous. A war had started and here he was asking questions about scum from scum, sitting in the middle of a secret meeting, while a gourmet lunch was served.

Falcon eyed Jason. "He's a guy that looks *almost* exactly like you, but fatter. He was one of my *boys*." Leaning forward, he lowered his voice for a moment. "In 1999 he was setting up a connection for me with the Afghan opium traders, but it's my guess that he tried to double deal and *disappeared*. I do know for a fact that the fat fucker set me up and landed me in prison!"

Jason locked eyes with Falcon. "So you had him killed."

Falcon looked indignant. "Look. I said *disappeared*. He can't be found so there's no proof that I did anything. Besides, what can I do from prison? Right?"

Jason shrugged; he wasn't a cop and could've cared less about the disappearance of some shady drug dealer. "General, if you're looking for a hit man, I'm out of that business. Unless you want *this* guy done." He motioned toward Falcon and held out his palms. "So why am I here?"

"That's not open for discussion yet," said the mortician. "Not until you sign the paper."

"I had status. I could go places, anywhere in the world. I had *respect*." Falcon narrowed his eyes, speaking to everyone and no one. "There are worse things than torture. I've spent too much wasted time staring out my damn cell window looking out at a goddamned *brick wall* on the other side. I even know how many bricks are on that fucking wall!" He locked eyes with Otis Deal. "Look. You promised me this deal in the Igloo at the Marshal's Holding Cell in Miami." He pointed at Jason. "You said that if I cover for him, give my okay, and fund you guys for your little war you'd get me into the Witness Security Program. That was the arrangement, *wasn't it?*"

"That's *if* he goes along with the plan," Deal shot back.

"What plan?" Jason asked. He didn't like whatever was going down. "Listen, I'm a part of no one's deal, or plan. I just came down here to see what's what. So forget you and your deals." He had been hungry, but now he had lost his appetite.

"Sign the paper," Deal and Falcon said at the same time.

"Ha! Here." Jason crumpled the paper and tossed it in front of Deal. "Nope." He saw Falcon blanch and struggle to keep his cool by eating, but he choked on his food.

Jason pushed away his plate. It wasn't his idea to drive for three hours just to cop an attitude, but to him dope dealers were the scum of the earth.

Gaining back some control over his outbreak, Falcon could barely move the fork from plate to mouth, but did an outstanding job of making the food disappear. He narrowed his eyes every time he looked at Jason.

Cadallo could see that things were rapidly falling apart. He had to hold it all together. Rising from his chair and walking to the door, he opened it and motioned for Jason to follow. "Jason, can we speak in private?"

"You bet. That's what I came here for in the first place."

In a sumptuous stateroom Cadallo closed the door and faced Jason.

Jason was first to speak. "Ben, sir, just what in the fuck are you doing getting mixed up with sleazy gangsters and ghouls?"

"Look. I ain't gonna bullshit you, Jason. I *need* you. I need your help as bad as I've ever needed help from someone, ever." Cadallo put a massive arm around Jason's shoulder, then slowly ran his hand down Jason's back until he came to the pistol tucked in the small of his back. "You really need this?"

"Hey, I got a lot more back home, plus bullets. You never know when someone's gonna need a few hits of lead to calm them down. Besides, *you're* the one who gave me my insecurities to always go strapped."

"I guess I did." He sighed.

Looking at Cadallo's tailored suit, a question crossed Jason's mind. "Sir, how many buttons do you have now?"

"Three."

"A *lieutenant* general. Christ, even if I get whacked, you'll probably get a fourth star. Oh boy! Then you get to sit at the Big Boy table. Hey, I know how your deals work—shaft the small fry: me. I've been there before. Remember, sir?"

Cadallo grew dark. "Listen to me well. It wasn't like that. After all the fallout from the Lucifer Light operation I was lucky to hang on to what I got. Bottom line, I wouldn't have called on you if I didn't need you."

Jason rolled his eyes. How could he ever forget that operation? A Russian offshoot of the KGB had developed an electromagnetic-pulsed generator and a satellite reflector. It was an ultimate weapon with limitless power. He and his partner, Marine Staff Sergeant Kelly Sherwin, blew the generator with a tactical nuclear bomb and in the act unwittingly killed thousands of Russian civilians.

The Brotherhood of Death was then targeted for death to keep the mission a secret. It took all Cadallo's political power and the calling in of all the favors he was owed to try to keep the Brotherhood alive. But that didn't matter to Jason. Cadallo's Doors had set him up to do the killing, and now Jason could never be sure that one day a government-issued bullet would not find him. *That* was the reason he carried a gun.

Cadallo continued on in an almost pleading manner. "Look. I had you in mind from the first day they came to me with this project, but I didn't want to approach you until the time was right. But yesterday changed all that. Crisis tends to speed things up. I know that this is short notice, and no one's given you any background about what's going on, but you gotta know that these guys in the next room are *major* players in what's going on with this war."

"Wait. Are you telling me that some scummy drug dealers are involved in this situation?"

"We have conventional and nuclear bombs. The terrorists are using the heroin bomb, drug warfare, and someone's got to stop it. We can't call on choirboys to solve this situation, now can we?"

"So, *that's* why the Doors are tied into it."

"This isn't a Doors mission," Cadallo said.

"Huh?" Now Jason was really perplexed.

"Not this one. I'm assigned to this operation as the project manager."

"Is anyone else from the Doors working it?"

"Mike Dennis contracted your bionics. Dr. Art Brownstein has been called in as a medical consultant. That's it."

"Any word on Froto?" His friend and partner, Kelly

"Froto" Sherwin, had been lost on Operation Lucifer Light.

"No."

"So why you, sir?"

"Because I can keep secrets. Plus, I volunteered."

Jason laughed. "So the great general *volunteered* for a mission? I don't believe it. Now you're gonna have to tell me a lot more about what's going on before I sign any paper."

"Stop laughing." Cadallo walked to a huge smoked-glass picture window that overlooked the marina. "Here it is, and it's top-secret. In exactly twenty-five days the bombing campaign in Afghanistan is going to start.

"Afghanistan might not be much of a country to fight over, but for our purposes they don't need to be; they have opium. The Taliban used opium tax to come to power and take over the country after we walked out on them. See, in the eighties the CIA helped make the Taliban by giving them connections to weapons through the Pakistani Intelligence Service. They taught them how to use their drug money to buy weapons and influence from us to fight the Soviets, who'd invaded the country. Then they were secretly trained in the use of those weapons and the art of covert finance."

"An Iran-Contra affair sort of thing."

"Exactly! It's a standard operating procedure that the Company has used around the world since their inception. And since we're out to take down an operation that they set up, I hope you can see why they, and anyone connected to them, are the *last* people we want in on this action," Cadallo said.

A deadly look came into his eyes. "Also, this job goes against how we've traditionally been fighting drugs. No one will get any credit standing on some courthouse steps in front of seized drugs, money, and guns with lots of publicity. There'll be no arrests, no powder on the table, no seizures, and no trials. Cops and bankers aren't running this operation. This time we're gonna burn the source and kill all the players. Everyone's treated this drug war as a joke. Everyone. But I come from the butt of that joke, and it ain't no joke to me."

Turning around, Cadallo faced Jason. "When the Taliban came to power, they said that they were eradicating the poppy trade. They even had video showing them rooting up poppy crops. A lot of countries fell for their lie. They looked good in the press. Real heroes. But what they didn't say was that they had hoarded countless tons of opium. And then they drove up the price.

"Worse than that, while all this was happening, the Falcon organization spread a ton of hybrid superpoppy seeds around the world. Drug goodwill, right? Now it's out of control and we've been directed from the top to stop this drug warfare thing."

"So why me? Let someone else go charging in and be the hero. You know I ain't no smooth operator. I don't even speak Spanish."

"You're a dead ringer for Alex Gomez. And how much Spanish are you going to need to know in Afghanistan? Besides, I already got that covered."

"Gomez. There's that name again. *So?* Do plastic surgery on some other schmuck to look like him. A *trained* schmuck who knows what he's doing."

"This is a tough mission, almost impossible. You're talented like no other. You have the proven abilities to stay alive in the worst of situations," Cadallo said.

"Shit. If you're trying to call that flattery, you could just stop right there and let me walk out of here right now. Hey, I've just been lucky and I don't think I have any more luck to spare."

A look of exasperation flashed over Cadallo. "Look, I didn't call you here to debate!" He fell against a wall and ran his fingers through his gray and thinning hair. "Against my better judgment, I'm gonna tell you why I really volunteered for this operation."

Jason saw a world and lifetime of weariness wash over the general. He looked as if he was being stabbed by old and painful memories. The Superman costume came off. After what seemed like an eternity, Cadallo began to talk.

CHAPTER 3

**1235 / *DARK SECRETS* /
FORT LAUDERDALE / FLORIDA**

DON'T KNOW IF I EVER TOLD YOU, BUT I WAS RAISED in South Central Los Angeles. Watts was my home. Eight kids. No father. I was Blood property from the day I was born.

"My mother lived to get high on any shit that she could get her hands on. The first thing I learned was that the LAPD were the bad guys, and that the Crips were my sworn enemy.

"Dealing with dope, that's what surviving in the inner city is all about. I did my first drive-by when I was twelve. By the time I was fifteen I ran my own crew selling shit for the Bloods. But you know what? By that time I had no more family—everyone in my family was dead, or doing hard time, all over drugs. My mother was so far gone she didn't even know me. Get this. She just recently died, of an intentional heroin overdose. She had full-blown AIDS and throat cancer.

"Anyway, by the time I'm eighteen I got more cash and muscle than I can handle, moving anything that you could inject, smoke, snort, or ram up your ass. I was in a prime position to take over being the Blood Overlord of Watts." Ben stopped and frowned.

"So what happened?"

"One day I woke up to the shit I was doing. See, I was moving *lots* of weight, clocking piles of cash, but I wasn't blind. I saw what that crap was doing to my people.

"Slavery, Jason. I had hundreds, *thousands* of people waiting to get high on my dope. They were *my* slaves. Shit, they would sell their own babies just to get a taste of my powder. They'd kill their own mothers for dope. They would do all that and more.

"Slavery. Think about it. Narcoslavery, that's the real end game of narcoterrorism.

"And here I was helping to enslave and kill my black brothers and sisters with the poison that I sold. I was exterminating them at the hands of the elite rich folks. Call me a fool, but it made me stop what I was doing and try to make a difference. I had to do something, anything.

"Then I became the worst thing in the world to the establishment: a nigger with a cause. I tried to stop it all by myself. Man, I was stupid! By the time I was twenty, there was a price on my head. Then I was on the run, trying to save my skin. The very people I was trying to free were out looking to whack me just to get more dope. I had every nickel-and-dime motherfuckin' dope fiend trying to pop a cap in my ass!

"That's when I learned a lesson that's been with me up to this day: Don't try takin' on The Man until you become as strong and smart as The Man. So I used the dope money I had and hid by going away to college; then I joined the Marines. I never forgot where I ran from, or why. Now we got us a war where I can *finally* make a difference. I'm not running anymore. That's my cut in all of this."

Cadallo leaned over and put his hands on top of Jason's. "If I, *we,* you and me, can take out this drug source, and at the same time take down the terrorists who produce it, we're gonna save *countless* lives, free them. Think about it."

"Nice act." Jason pulled back his hands. "Very impressive, very, but we all have a story to tell. You want to hear mine? You still don't have me, and I'll tell you why. I've been your goat just one too many times. I know you. You *always* have an angle." He saw the frustration return to Cadallo's face.

"How about your country, son? For your *country* that needs you."

"You're forgetting that you've already fed me that BS line before, remember? And look at all the shit it got me into, all those deaths. I still can't get the pictures out of my head. They won't go away. Besides, I got no desire to go alone into Afghanistan and try to take on some crazy drug-dealin' terrorists. You got the wrong man."

"But that's where *you're* wrong. You won't be alone. I'll be with you every step of the way, behind you, watching your back. Jason, I never let you down, and can you tell me how many times I've saved your life? I think you owe me one."

"Owe you one? You're a part of the assholes who put me over cliffs, into death pools, and turned me into a mass murderer! So forgive me if I don't fall under the enchantment of your brilliant scheme. The shit's too deep. I'm outta here." Jason bolted for the door, but Cadallo sprang like a cat and cut him off.

"Jason, all right. *Please.* I'm asking you as a friend, no rank, no tricks, just me, Ben. This is everything I've ever worked for. I need you. You're the only one who has the one chance in a million of pulling it off. Please!"

"Awww, SHIT! 'Jack-it-off' is a better description. I got 30 million *better* reasons for not doing it."

"Look. You can save people's lives, make wrong things right. You could make up for your past and I'll help you."

"*My* past? That's low-down. What about *your* past?" Jason dropped back down in the chair and sighed. However you cut it, even sitting with bad guys, in Jason's heart Ben was still one of the good guys. *And he's right. I do owe a lot of dues.*

He shook his head and chuckled. Call it a major character flaw, but once more he was about to put his life on the line to try and balance out things that he had no control over—because a friend was asking for help. "Shit! All right. I'll help. Go ahead. Tell me about your goddamned mission."

"Thanks." Cadallo finally exhaled. He collected himself and gathered back his military bearing before he continued. "Before September 11 the Taliban was selling their superopium for four thousand a kilo. Confirmed sources tell us that right after the attacks the Taliban suddenly needed *lots* of weapons and money, as much as they could get. This dope is the only material asset they have.

"We have a bona fide report from a mole that they're about to have a fire sale of their superopium—300 million cash for their entire haul, plus a few weapons. We've got to get there and buy it before everyone else, and keep them out."

"How much of that shit do they have?"

"From satellite imagery and estimated figures, our best guess is about two thousand tons, about the size of a two-hundred-car convoy."

"Wow!"

"Wow is right."

Jason sat in stunned silence until Cadallo shook his shoulder. "So why don't you just go in and blow it all up?"

"It's not that easy. First we have to find it, all of it. If that shit gets refined and out on the streets we'll be looking at a heroin epidemic like we've never seen before. We might win the terrorist battle but lose the narcotics war.

Right now we have everything in place but the trigger man."

"So what do I do?" *Hooked again.*

"Sign the paper next door and you'll find out, Alice."

Jason cringed. He hated his code name. He'd lost count how many times he had taken Cadallo's bait. While the name Alice was a legend in the spook world, the name Jason Johnson stood for *sucker.*

Even though there was plenty of food left, Jason still wasn't hungry. His stomach felt worse. He smoothed out and signed the paper, then sat back in a plush blue leather chair and folded his hands in his lap. He saw a look of relief on Falcon's face as the tension in the room vanished.

Gold Teeth, thumbing his worry beads, spoke. "In a little more than three weeks the superopium must be on the open road."

"Wait a minute," Jason said. "Tell me some more about this superdrug that I keep hearing about."

Gold Teeth nodded. "The opium comes from a hybrid poppy that contains a higher percentage of morphine than a normal poppy does. Depending on the altitude, the soil it's in, amount of water given, and how it's grown, a normal opium poppy can contain anywhere from 8 to 25 percent morphine juice. This hybrid yields 40 to 80 percent.

"Further refined, the narcotic yields large concentrations of etorphine, which is a thousand times more powerful than morphine."

Ben interjected, "Think about it, if they can refine it, for every etorphine kilo that gets through here in America, it can be multiplied into a thousand kilos of street-quality smack. Narcoterrorism unlike anything we have ever seen, or can handle."

"We can thank Willie here for this situation; he wanted to run the whole show, a farm-to-arm operation. He wanted to be the Henry Ford of heroin. He wanted to *hook* the whole world," Deal said. "Now it's out of his control. So he's had a change of heart and wants to make up for it. Right, Willie?"

Falcon just scowled and nodded.

Or get back at someone, Jason thought.

Gold Teeth continued. "Since Mr. Falcon supplied the hybrid seeds and set up the base plan, it's our plan to continue to use it. A dead ringer representing the Falcon organization will go to Afghanistan and find Gul Nazari, the Taliban's chief opium trader, and buy their whole crop."

"And I'm that *dead* ringer." Jason saw Falcon slyly nod and smile.

"Not only that," Cadallo added, pleased that Jason seemed to be buying into the plan. "As Gomez, you're going to handle the money transfer and deliver them weapons as part of the deal."

Jason was startled. Drug dealer, bagman, and gunrunner, what in the world had he signed on for? "Shit, I ain't a slimeball. I don't know the first thing about any of this doper-crap stuff." Then he stopped talking, remembering his own small-time drug-dealing mother.

It was a repulsive business. For seventeen years he saw scum come and go, craving the kitchen-made methamphetamine his mother and her whacked-out common-law husband sold. He involuntarily winced, remembering the long scars on his back delivered by that crazed druggie. Yeah, now he could definitely empathize with Cadallo's dilemma.

Once conveniently confined to the bad side of the tracks, drugs had crossed over and permeated throughout all of American society. If only half of what Ben was saying was true, then some very serious shit was going down. Yeah, he could figure out the things needed to know to play a convincing role. A thought struck him. "This is a solo mission."

Cadallo nodded. "Just you. But trust me when I tell

you that you'll have all the support and backup you need. You'll show up at a certain location and time in Kabul, Afghanistan, as Alex Gomez."

"Ah, the famous disappearing man."

Deal slid a photograph across the table to Jason.

Picking up the photograph, Jason did a double take; staring back at him was his own face. But it wasn't quite him. The face and body were heavier and the complexion was darker. "Alex Gomez."

"Alex Gomez," Deal spoke. "He was Falcon's right-hand man."

"But he's *disappeared,*" Jason said with a sneer.

"That's right. Gone," chided Falcon.

Jason glared at Falcon. Guys like him didn't care who they hurt or killed as long as the cash kept rolling in.

Deal continued speaking. "After the superpoppy was developed in Falcon's greenhouses, his horticulturist found that it couldn't survive anywhere except in high altitudes, like Afghanistan. Gomez was going there to set up a Middle Eastern heroin connection for Falcon. It almost happened," Deal continued. "We got names, talked deals, and paid out a lot of money, but then lost Gomez and control of our product."

"You mean that *I* paid out a lot of money, and *you* lost the product," overrode Falcon.

Jason had questions, but kept his mouth shut. What was going on between the two? Just who controlled whom?

Deal scowled at Falcon. "I'll take care of this, if you don't mind." Looking back at Jason, he continued. "It's been a little less than a year since this deal went bad, but we think that with your training and Falcon vouching for you, you can become a convincing Gomez and complete the deal."

Gold Teeth spoke while rapidly flipping his beads. "You must understand that it is very difficult to penetrate these Afghan smuggling clans; there are too many ethnic, familial, religious, and tribal groups to mention. Only one person from a powerful, unquestionable drug organization such as Falcon's can hope to do business with the Taliban. This is the only way we can get at and kill the narcotic."

"Since you have it all figured out. Other than going in and doing it your own bad selves, just how am I going to convince these bad guys to do what I want them to?"

"You know how it works," Ben answered. "Operational planning belongs to the operator."

Jason started laughing. "So, all by myself, I got to figure and plan on waltzing into a war zone and do a zillion-dollar drug deal as someone else, somehow deliver desperate terrorists planeloads of weapons, and then get a trainload of drugs on the road for you to destroy. Oh, and get my ass out safely when it's over. And you tell me you got everything else all *arranged*. You got to be fucking kidding me!" Laughing for a moment, he found that he was laughing by himself. "I can't believe that you guys really expect me to do this successfully. I can't believe that you guys are actually *serious*."

"As a heart attack," Cadallo said. "You buy the load, we track it, attack it, and burn it to hell. Through this deal we will also be able to follow the money trail, uncover their accounts, then seize everything they have. The munitions and guns have a surprise all their own."

"Sure, it's a *brilliant* plan. It all seems very plausible to you guys as long as *I'm* the schmuck goin' in," Jason said. "So how do I get in? Who do I contact when I get there? Ben, I smell rats again, *big*-assed rats. You guys actually think that this gig has a chance of succeeding."

"We've been working on this for a long time," said Gold Teeth.

"What, minutes?" Jason shot back, wondering if he could rip apart the paper he'd just signed. He was already having second thoughts. "I don't need this shit!"

"You'll be well compensated," Falcon added.

"Oh yeah?" sneered Jason. "By who? You? You can't buy me, scum. So you can shove your compensation right up your ass. I don't want any part of you, pal." Now he had a great desire to *really* put a few rounds in Falcon's head.

Falcon sat back in his chair and nodded. "Okay, okay, Dudley Do-right. You get this straight; *I'm* the one picking up the tab for this thing, the 'bad guy.' Do you really think that anyone in your government is smart enough to cough up big cash without drawing any attention, or have my kind of connections? Yeah, motherfucker, while you're out there saving the world, you just remember whose dime you're doin' it on."

"Enough from the both of you," Cadallo barked. "Senior Master Sergeant Johnson, you signed the paper. You will be ready to go by Friday."

"I think I'm already sorry that I did, sir. I need more time than that to take care of my personal shit."

Cadallo groaned. "Okay, you're on my clock in thirty-six hours. I want your best plan drawn up. Your orders have already been cut and delivered. Make the usual arrangements for a Sunday departure."

"Damn! You already had me pegged from Jump Street. It's like I really had no choice in the matter. Did I?" Jason groaned back. "Well, sir, forget about me giving you a plan. I'll figure it out when I get there."

Ben scowled. "You can't do that."

Jason leaned forward and smiled. "Really? Then, by all means, sir, go find yourself another fool."

Ben smoldered.

A thought crossed Jason's mind. "Hey, how are you going to hit the load?"

Ben glanced at the other men in the room, then smiled back at Jason. "Your job is just to get the load on the road. It's my job to attack it." He grinned wider. "See, now no one can beat that information out of you. Just be ready to go."

Sunday morning a C-17 Globemaster III jet would arrive at Patrick's Base Operations to take Jason away to his assignment.

Cadallo pulled out a cell phone and pressed a button on it. "Tell the Baker to get to work, then make the calls and tell everyone that the cake is ready. The party's on in twenty-four hours." He dropped the phone on the table. "So, it's all a go. That's it. Any more questions from anyone?"

"I have two, sir. Who here thinks they're pulling a fast one on me, and just who's really doing this for their country?" Jason looked at each man.

This time they all blinked.

CHAPTER **4**

Selected American counterterrorist groups are activated.

THE RINGING PHONE STARTLED THE MAN SEATED
on his couch in front of his television.

"Ed deLeon?"

"Yes."

"Bake the cake." The caller hung up.

"This *is* good news!" Ed said. Dropping the phone
back on the receiver, he jumped off the couch and ran
from the living room to the bedroom. There he opened
a panel on the inside wall. Behind it were hidden cir-
cular stairs leading to a long underground passageway.
The passageway led to a building located across the
street.

In minutes Ed was inside the building and in his office
sitting in front of a computer, typing commands on his
keyboard. There were a lot of things to do before the
building was up to operational standards.

He paused for a moment to think about where he was

and what he was actually doing. The Party. It made him feel giddy. He was the manager not for a building, but for a top-secret command center that was hidden in plain sight. None of the commands he was inputting would change anything outside the building—it all happened from within.

To look at the building, there was nothing memorable or anything that would stand out—it was designed that way. Passing drivers probably wouldn't remember anything about it moments after they passed, no flashy name, or even be able to recall what color it was.

The building was unassuming in architecture and passive in color. It blended in well with its surroundings, looking like just another high-tech company probably tied to the local Air Force base's contracts.

It was designated as a Green Building. Built to the strictest environmental codes, all labor and materials had to be procured within a hundred-mile radius.

The building had its secrets from the start.

Almost overnight a thirty-thousand-square-foot steel-and-concrete cube appeared. Who put it there? None of the local construction crew could say, they were just there to put up the building around it.

Inside the cube all the walls were made of laminated tempered glass, two inches thick. The glass walls were all on gliding coasters and could move, or were made to be locked into place. This gave one the ability to shift the floor plan to any number of configurations in minutes.

And this was not your regular glass. Manufactured by Laminate Technologies, the membrane that was sandwiched between the glass laminates was almost magic. The membrane was composed of millions of micro plasma pixels, electrically charged, that could make the walls one-way viewing, opaque, or any color of the rainbow.

The glass also had the ability to act as giant plasma video screens. Whole rooms could turn into forests, deserts, cities, or anything else the viewer desired. The screen savers were beyond belief, making wallpaper and paint obsolete.

The floors had every computer LAN drop imaginable. The cube itself was made so that no electromagnetic intrusion device could penetrate the walls. The entrance doors had slats that hermetically sealed when shut, keeping anyone from snooping.

That was inside the building.

The forest behind the building looked healthy, lush, and green. Some of the pine trees were tall and straight—a little too tall, and a little too straight. It was almost impossible to see that those trees were actually radio antennas, or that the vegetation was perfectly grown to camouflage the wire radar dishes.

There weren't any high fences with concertina razor wire that surrounded the building, but that didn't mean that it was unguarded.

Pull into the parking lot, or step onto the grass, and a million and one security systems gave positive identification or sounded alarms in ten seconds. If positive identification could not be made before a person reached the double-glass-door entrance, then a deadly armed response was ready and triggered.

Ed didn't ask why he was getting the command building ready; it wasn't his job to ask. He knew that it most likely had something to do with the terrorist attacks in New York—he would do anything to help.

Ed furiously typed in instructions to his computer. "Visitors are coming. We have visitors coming. Let's get this Party started." He hummed, grinning wide. He knew every inch and design of the building. It was time to bring all the facets and capabilities of the building alive. The host had called to start the Party, now it was time for Ed to pass out the rest of the invitations.

"Drop the gun, stupid. Go ahead; move one inch and you're fucking dead. Go ahead. Hurry! You're wasting my time," said DEA Agent Mike Gorsline, cocking his pistol for added effect. His hand was steady. He was tense, but not scared. The thing was, it really didn't matter whether he shot the creep or not, and that bothered him. There was a time when he was *the* master at the art of the bust, and no one got hurt. But after the endless chases, this shit was old. Nickel-and-dime busts had gotten stale.

Drug crime was out of hand. The media and liberals treated drug addiction like a curable disease. They didn't have to deal with the dope addicts who'd sell their own children to get high, or dopers who cared less if they brushed their teeth, or even if they lived or died; they existed just to get high.

Gorsline pointed the gun between the man's frightened eyes. "Now you got three seconds to make up your mind. One. Two."

The man dropped the gun.

Cops poured in from everywhere.

Gorsline holstered his gun and sat on the hood of his car. Staring at all the young and trim hard bodies on Miami's South Beach, it was easy to understand why hard drugs were so available—immortality. Get out of your mind, live like a god. "You've made it to the Promised Land. Pop this. Smoke that. Snort this. Shoot that. Shove *this* up your ass, it's all good, don't ya know?"

"What did you say? Mike, you should've done him! You had fifteen cops as witnesses backing you up."

Mike glanced at Eric McArthur, his partner. "I guess that God put pity in my heart."

"I know, 'it's a pity that I ran out of bullets.'" Eric was getting to know his partner's sayings.

Gorsline shrugged. "Man, I'm so over putting my life on the line for these street-level busts. It never stops. I think that I'm losing my edge. This ain't crime fighting, it's just toilet cleaning and we're the janitors."

"You mean armed sanitation engineers."

"Yeah, something like that." Gorsline opened the passenger door and climbed in. The big bust was out there, but not for him.

Eric got behind the wheel and picked up the beeping cellular phone lying on the dashboard. "Yeah? Huh? What?" He handed the phone to Mike.

"What's up?"

"It's for you," he said with a perplexed look, offering the phone.

Gorsline took the cell phone "Go."

"Mr. Gorsline?"

"Yeah."

"Your cake is ready."

The phone went dead.

Gorsline opened the door and got out.

"Where ya goin'?" Eric asked.

"Away," he answered, leaning on the door. "Look, buddy, we're still new partners and I'd hate to have to shoot you if I tell you."

McArthur's eyes widened. "You got to be kidding! What's going on? You can't walk out on a smack bust when the case hasn't even started rolling."

"You put him on ice for me. You can do it. You run with it. I can't stay here. I just got called on an emergency to handle."

Eric watched, bewildered, as his partner faded into the crowd of hard bodies.

1430 / SAN DIEGO STATE UNIVERSITY/ SAN DIEGO

Ibrahim al Kalifa was having a very bad day. It started the lousy night before when he was chased from Daisy's, a local haunt where he was eating a late-night dinner. Eating alone, bothering no one, someone called him a sand nigger. Three big guys stood up and walked over to his table.

"What's a camel jockey doin' eatin' a hamburger. I thought you fuckers ate goat," the biggest thug said.

"Yeah, or fuck them first," another sneered.

They all laughed, but there was no humor in their looks.

Surrounded, with nowhere to go, Ibrahim didn't want any trouble. There had to be a mistake. He tried to plead his case. He was a third-generation Arab-American and a professor at the university. But he started growing hotter the more he spoke. His father had fought in the Korean War, for God's sake. "Shit, I speak better English than all you ignorant, fat-gutted, rednecked assholes put together."

Then it was on. They flew over the table to get at him. Their blows were ineffective as they tried to hit him all at once. Shit flew everywhere.

Ibrahim gave back better than he got. It was the first time he'd been in a real fight—he was a second-degree black belt in karate. The stuff worked well enough to get him to the front of the restaurant and out the door. The goons got between him and his car, so he took off in a sprint. The thugs hounded him up College Avenue, but weren't in any shape and quickly gave up the chase.

At a bus stop Ibrahim jumped on the first bus that stopped and grabbed a seat. He'd go back and get his car the next day. Fuming, he was a bloody mess, clothes torn, but his pride was hurting more than his contusions. People on the bus gave him some hard stares. He wanted to give them back, but knew he would wind up again on the losing end.

He got off the bus near his apartment, went inside, closed his curtains, turned off his lights, and sat on his couch. He hadn't given a damn about how he looked until then.

It wasn't fair! He was a third-generation Arab-American. While his mother and father had gone to the mosque, he hadn't. For that, he fell out of favor with his family. Over the years he had tried to get back in favor by becoming a college-level teacher of Middle Eastern culture. Spending years of research, his doctoral thesis was going to be on the history of Afghanistan.

Now it felt as if he was on everyone's hit list. He fell asleep from exhaustion where he sat, and slept until the alarm for class went off.

Looking around his empty classroom, it was obvious that what he had to teach that day wasn't going to be heard. He wrote a note canceling all his classes for the day on the main dry-erase board, then trudged back to his office.

The phone was ringing when he entered.

"Hello."

"Mr. Ibrahim al Kalifa?"

"Yesss," he warily answered. He'd already received threatening calls.

"Your cake is ready."

He hung up the phone and pulled out a blank paper from his desk and wrote a note to his assistant. Ibrahim was secretly grateful for the call.

> Brian,
>   I have to leave. The classes are yours until I re-
> turn. I can't say when I'll be back.
>
>   Ib

STANFORD UNIVERSITY /
PALO ALTO / CALIFORNIA

Brianna Lopez, finished with packing her bags for the long-awaited trip to Mexico, was lost. She was headed there for an archaeological dig at Uxmal in Yucatán, Mexico. She planned on using the material she gathered there for her master's thesis on the Mayans. She also minored in Middle Eastern studies. But now all the planes across the U.S. were grounded. *Now what do I do?*

The phone rang. She answered it. "Hello?"

"Your cake is ready."

Bri was stunned. Hanging up the phone, she stared at it for a long time.

"No way!" she cried. She wanted to get out of the country and as far away from the madness of 9/11 as she could. Now she suspected that whatever they wanted her for at the Party had a direct connection to what had happened in New York.

"Why did I take the money and training from the Party in the first place?"

Because it's paying for all your college and more, she correctly reasoned with herself.

She fished the plane ticket out of her purse, and dialed to cancel her reservation.

While listening to the endless ticket options, Bri understood that she really wanted to escape something that she didn't want to face; she was as scared as the next person that something might happen to her. But now her country called her and now she was actually excited that she might be able to do something to help.

CALLS WENT OUT ACROSS THE COUNTRY AND WORLD until seventy-five people had been notified. They had to drop everything and make it to a building located at a certain location in Melbourne, Florida.

CHAPTER 5

The Senate votes 98–0 to authorize the use of armed forces against terrorists.

STAFF SERGEANT DAR GARO KISSED HIS WIFE, Rita, with all the passion he had left in him. He couldn't tell her where he was going, or when he would be coming back. He was elated and terrified at the same time. Elated that he was going to get to do what he had trained years for, and terrified of leaving his wife all alone. Tagged for the first deployment, he had to go. There was no saying "no," even though Rita was seven months pregnant with their first child.

He had signed up for a special incentive pay to work on a top-secret program. There was a clause in the contract he signed that specifically stated that a spouse pregnancy was not reason enough to be excused from a deployment. He had taken the extra money to cover the arrival of their first child; now it was sort of a catch-22—the money to afford a child was now the very reason he had to leave. Who could have figured on 9/11?

The birth of his first child meant everything to him. His little family was about to grow by one. There was nothing in the world that could take him away from them, until now, and he felt like it was his fault.

The call came the same day he saw the Trade Center Towers collapse and watched the Pentagon burn.

Rita understood; she was from New York City. But she was scared, too. Her man was going into combat. Unlike many of the squadron's wives, she had taken the time to learn about her husband's very dangerous job, Air Combat Control, and it scared the living shit out of her. But she loved him and knew that she married the man *and* his job. He was her knight, love, and all that she ever wanted in her life. There was no way she would try to stop Dar from doing the things that he loved the most.

Her husband wasn't going for combat support—he was headed directly into the mouth of the lion and right under the fangs. She was scared, really, really scared. He was leaving and couldn't tell her where exactly he would be, when he would call or write, or when he would return.

As a combat controller, Dar conducted air battle in enemy territory, on the ground, in a war zone. His job was to control air traffic after seizing an airfield from the enemy, or act as the eyes on the ground that called in airpower.

What she didn't know was that Dar was also part of a pilot program called remote-operated vehicle reconnaissance (ROVR), commonly called "rover." He was getting paid an extra five hundred dollars a month to field-test the system. It was a fantastic reconnaissance system that did great in training, but how would it do in war? There was only one way to find out; send in the guy that they were paying to test out the ten-pound system under actual conditions. So there was no saying "no" when his orders came.

While the rover was uniquely uncommon, it also held secrets known only to Dar. Even other combat controllers were kept in the dark about Dar's extra gear.

The passenger agent announced that the C-5 Galaxy was ready for boarding. It was time for Dar to say his last good-byes and get in line to board the giant transport jet.

"Look at me," Rita sniffed. "I'm a mess."

Red and puffed blue eyes, tears flowing, mascara running, brown hair plastered to her face, she never looked more beautiful to Dar since the day they had first met.

The gum he chewed was worn flavorless hours before. But if he didn't ceaselessly chew, then he'd probably start crying himself.

"Oh, here," Rita said. Reaching into her purse she pulled out a folded paper and a compact disk, then handed them to him.

He unfolded it and studied it for a few moments. "A sonogram picture. Of what?"

"Dar, it's a sonogram picture of your child. I had it done yesterday. The disk is some of your favorite music and some words I recorded for you to listen to."

The gum didn't help anymore. The tears just started flowing.

He held her tight and tried to inhale her essence. "I'll be back. You gotta know that. You *have* to believe it. You have to be strong."

Rita nodded and shook in his arms, clinging to him, shaking, afraid that it might be the last time she held him.

"All passengers will please head to the boarding gate" was announced over the public speakers.

Dar took a deep breath. "Woman, I love you. No matter what, I will always love you. I have to go."

Rita let go and stood straight. She was heartbroken,

but proud of her man. Looking at all the hysterical women and children around her, she realized that she wasn't doing half that bad. She could even muster up her best smile and wave. "I love you, Dar Garo! You go and do the right thing. And I'll be right here when you get back, with our baby in my arms. Think of a name for it while you're gone. Oh, and keep your eyes open and your head down!"

Climbing aboard the behemoth C-5 Galaxy, he found a seat in a row by himself. He wiped away the tears while getting out a fresh piece of gum.

"Oh man," he exhaled as he scanned the cabin, glad that the tough guys he was with were too busy wiping away their own tears to notice his.

As a combat controller, or CCT as they were more commonly called, he was one of the few Air Force men trained to work with any allied military unit. He could "speak Army," and translate it into Air Force jargon on the ground, then communicate it for the pilots above with his forty-thousand-dollar radio.

The radio was an essential element to orchestrate and conduct a concert of destruction such as no one had been witness to in a long time. His orchestra flew in fighters and bombers, moving high above him faster than the speed of sound.

His AN/PRC 117F radio, Mark VII laser target designator, range-finding binoculars, night-vision goggles, weapons, and everything else were somewhere beneath him in the cargo compartment—his compass was in his pocket. Not knowing what to expect, he packed up most of his equipment locker, hoping that he'd be able to find somewhere to store it all once he arrived in-country.

He wondered about the reception he and his rover would receive from the spec ops troops.

He shivered, listening to the engines wind up. Minutes later he felt the giant jet lurch out of its blocks and slowly taxi to the runway. There were no windows to try to catch a last look at Rita. Every foot the jet rolled took him just that much farther from the woman he loved.

In a matter of hours he would be on the ground in a war zone, and worlds away from the loving arms of his wife. It would be his first time in combat, something that he'd trained at for ten years. He had to put "home" in a safe place of his mind and focus on the deadly work ahead.

He was nervous, but not afraid. Like Rita, he had to believe that he would return unharmed; he had to.

A war not of his making had started. Dar could only pray that he wouldn't screw up his first time in combat.

The loadmasters passed out box lunches after the C-5 leveled out at thirty-five thousand feet, headed directly east.

Dar finished his lunch, pulled out the sonogram picture of his unborn child, and studied it for a long time, trying to figure out if it was a boy or a girl. He didn't care as long as it was healthy. Carefully folding the picture, he put it inside Rita's CD case and slipped the case into his cargo pants pocket. He decided that he would listen to his wife's voice an hour a day.

With nothing to do at the moment, he stretched out on the row of seats. Who could tell when sleep would become too precious a commodity to waste?

CHAPTER 6

0900 FRIDAY / 14 SEPTEMBER 2001
PATRICK AIR FORCE BASE / FLORIDA

Secretary of State Colin Powell identifies Osama bin Laden and the al Qa'eda as the primary suspects in the attacks on America's homeland.

THE 920TH COMBAT RESCUE GROUP WAS GOING on a war posture, preparing to send out its HC-130 Hercules rescue airplanes of the Thirty-ninth Rescue Squadron to an undisclosed location in the Middle East. Once there, they would take on a sensitive rescue alert mission. If any American or allied pilots had to eject from their aircraft while over hostile territory, then combat rescue packages were ready, twenty-four hours a day, to go get them.

Out-processed, the flyers and ground crews were issued mobility folders, then they scrambled to get active duty IDs cut, mandatory vaccinations, chemical warfare bags, aircrew bags, sleeping bags, combat arms, survival gear, mess gear, professional gear, and get papers on top of papers signed.

By the time they were finished they were weighted down with well over two hundred pounds of stuff, crammed into six A-3 bags, not including personal things like flight publications, special clothing, shaving kits, towels, cameras, laptop computers, DVDs, radios, and lots of photographs.

Worried family members followed their loved ones around, knowing that their time with them was limited. A spouse's departure would be heartbreaking, and the local television stations would be there to capture the whole tear-jerking event.

Jason had no family to fuss over his departure. When his time came to go, there would be no one to wave to and kiss good-bye. But he was single by choice—the mission seemed to dictate it. Jason's special orders were being processed on base, and this time no questions were being asked.

He walked into the PJ building and into the personal-gear cages. Everyone was going through their equipment, selecting those things they knew they would need in the Middle East: sand goggles, Camelbak water carriers, and plenty of sunscreen.

"You ain't coming with us," Dan Murray said as he packed his gear and checked over the operation of his rifle.

It wasn't a question. There were plenty of rescuers in New York. The unit had received orders to a classified location in the Middle East for the support of anticipated operations. Combat rescue was their mission: The PJs were the men who made the grab on the pilot's pink butt. It took hundreds of dedicated men and women to make this happen.

Wordlessly, Jason shook his head. He wasn't gathering any gear, just closing his locker one last time. His diving gear, climbing apparatus, skydiving rigs, and more would remain untouched while he was gone.

Dan leaned close to Jason, and whispered, "You

know, yesterday there were these guys who came around looking for people to do special missions."

"Did anyone sign on?"

"A couple of guys showed interest."

"You?"

"Hell no. You're the one told me to stay away from them, remember? Besides, I'm married now, and trying to start a family. Putting myself in harm's way for my country's one thing. Suicide's another."

Jason smiled. "Good boy."

"So can you talk about it, or will you have to kill me afterward?"

Jason snapped closed the lock of his equipment cage. "We'll be working in the same neighborhood, just different sides of the tracks."

"Then I'll probably be seeing you over there."

"No. I don't think so. PJ, you take care of yourself and keep an eye on the boys for me. As usual, don't tell anyone I'm gone until I'm gone."

"Yeah, I know the deal."

They shook hands, then hugged. Jason was out of the building before he attracted any more attention, stopping at the Group building just to sign out. His last stop was to Mac Rio's loadmaster office overlooking the Atlantic Ocean.

"I've been activated." Jason smiled.

"Hey, dude, me too," Mac said, always glad to see his best friend. "How's it goin'? I can't believe that we're going back to war again. I can't fucking believe it! I thought that it was over for old war fighter fucks like us. But you know, the call to arms is pretty hard to resist when it sounds."

Mac's mood changed and he became reflective. "You know, I was driving over the Pineda Causeway when word about the attacks came over the radio. I started crying so hard that I had to pull over. Then I started thinking about how many times we've answered that call to arms and the places we've been to.

"We wound up fightin' in Panama, Desert Storm, Bosnia, Somalia, and *everywhere* in the Middle East. Name it. We've been all over the damned world for a peace that always seems to elude us. It never stops and it always turns into more of a 'kill less' policy. And they always put us up in places with names like Butt Fuck Nowhere, with no showers, no booze, lousy food, and no pussy. I just hate it when there ain't no pussy to buy!"

Mac stood up and dramatically poked his finger into the air. "*But* we were there for our country every time that we were called on." Holding out his hands and wiggling his fingers, Mac continued. "And look. We came back with everything still attached. I can only hope that this one lets us keep our heads, and out of body bags."

Jason sat in a chair. "I got the call from 'our friends.' I'm on their dime now."

"No!" Frowning, Mac asked, "When do you go?"

"Sunday. Since it's such short notice without any training, I decided to make a quick drive out to Avon Park Saturday morning to shoot my weapons before I go."

"How can you feel rusty with all the guns you got?"

"I'm rusty enough. You'll still check on my apartment from time to time?"

Sitting on his desk, Mac nodded. "As long as I'm here, but, man, I was looking forward to flying with you." He got up and closed his door. Mac lowered his voice. "What's the mission?"

Jason laughed. "You know I can't tell you."

"Aw, come on, Jason, it's *me*!"

"I'll tell you when I come back."

"That's *if* I'm here. I'm a part of the Show, too, Mr. PJ."

Changing the subject, Jason said, "Listen, you're going to get a letter from me in the mail in a few days."

"Can't you just give it to me now?"

"No. I know all about your penchant for opening things before you should."

"Not another will?"

"No. I'm just trying to tie up some loose ends."

"With all the money you got you don't have to go, you know."

"Try telling that to Department of Defense. Besides, Mac, it's *never* been about the money. This is about payback."

"Oh shit. Payback! Whose payback? This shit is *a lot* deeper than that. Look, pal, all that *payback* bullshit almost killed you the last time, remember? Or did you already forget?

"Don't let those fucks lure you back with that *payback* line. Don't be stupid. You just can't go out like Don Quixote and do it again. You're not getting any younger. Jason, you idiot, walk away from those guys. Hell, run!"

"No. I can't. You know about the dues that I owe."

"I know. I know. But those guys sure as hell shouldn't be the ones who you make your payments to. They'll just use you again and screw you again. Come on, man, you know what happened last time."

They sat without speaking. Like some avenging angel, Jason remembered all the lives he'd taken during Operation Lucifer Light. Only Jason's vow to try to make up for his damning act by saving lives after the mission kept him wearing the maroon beret of a pararescueman.

But now Cadallo used sham emotions to bring him back to the dark side. So where was the payback? Things always seemed to go wrong every time he worked for the general. But Cadallo did have a point: Even though there was no redemption for the dead, there might be a chance to do some good for the living. Stopping the drug terror and taking down those behind it was well worth a try, but what about all those other dangers Cadallo hadn't addressed? There was *always* a price for secret missions.

Jason's jaw tightened. "Sometimes I feel like the only time my wrongs will be right is when I'm covered forever in a dirt nap."

"Oh that's *bullshit,* pal, and you know it." Mac frowned at his friend. "Well, if I can't talk you out of it, the least I can do is offer you this." Leaning over and opening up a drawer, he pulled out a silver medallion and handed it to Jason. "Listen to me well, when you walk the dirt over there in bad-guy land, you *better* remember that there's millions of land mines buried there. You even fart in the wrong direction and you'll get your ass blown off! You wear this on your silver chain and don't take it off."

"What is it?"

"It's Michael."

"Who?"

"Heathen! It's Michael, the War Angel. *Saint* Michael, if you're Catholic. Call it a talisman, or a good-luck piece. My mother had it blessed, then sent it to me. But right now I think that you need it a lot more than me in your search."

"What search?" How did Mac know? But then Mac did seem to have that second sense.

"You've been on it a long time, you just don't know." He pointed at the red-and-blue signet ring on Jason's little finger. "Remember where you got that?"

"Yeah, off a dead kid's hand."

"That may have been only a part of your search. The medallion might help. Fuck it. It couldn't hurt, could it?"

Jason studied the shiny medallion. It was an angel with his wings spread and a sword held over his head, with a shield on his left arm. His left foot was on the head of the devil. The reverse side had a simple inscription: **Michael, defend us on our day of battle.** "I guess the search that this guy is on hasn't quit either."

Mac shook his head at his best friend. "And if this is

another good-bye, then just put the thing on and be on your way."

"Listen, would you mind driving me to the plane this Sunday morning? It's landing here."

"Count on it. I'll use one of the squadron's golf carts. What time?"

"Oh-six-hundred."

"Ouch!"

Jason removed a silver necklace he'd gotten from Seka Miles, the only woman he'd ever loved, slipped the medallion on the chain, and put it back around his neck. "Thanks. Then I'll see you at the squadron Sunday morning." He stood and left the building.

Driving from the base, Jason smiled. In a few days Mac would get a check in the mail. Mac would be a wealthy man, compliments of his best friend. It was the least that he could do for a long friendship and loyalty.

Jason grinned for the first time in days. As a matter of fact, there were several checks in the mail, and with one of them Toby Wiler's family would be set for life.

There was no time like the present to unburden himself of some of his cash and take care of his friends.

The call to arms rang out once more. There would be no saying when or how he'd return, or even *if* he'd return. "Off on another harebrained mission," he spit. He never stayed home. "*That's* why I ain't got nothing, and no woman. Damn! Why do I always do this crap to myself?"

2330 HOURS

Except for the weapons in the trunk of his car, there wasn't much to pack. The rent was paid up for the year. He walked around his apartment, turning off lights and unplugging appliances. Looking in his refrigerator, a shriveled lime and half-empty Corona beer sat side by side. Mac called it a "whore's fridge," no food for an empty life. Well, at least the stale beer was still cold.

He unplugged the refrigerator, downing the flat beer as he went through his closet. He went into the bedroom and began putting together his small leather travel bag. A small gym bag sat in the corner. Emptying the bag on his bed, he was surprised to find his old Paragon automatic knife. He thought he'd lost it years before. It was sharp and still worked fine. Lying at the center of the bed was a miniature Qur'an. He picked it up and opened it. Inside the front cover was a small blue cloth encased in plastic. Under the light the cloth looked closer to green than blue.

"Where'd this come from?" he asked.

Suddenly the memory of a wounded Muslim man he tried to save in Bosnia flashed in his mind. The man turned out to be a terrorist, and it took a bullet to the brain to stop him. Searching the body for anything he could use to keep him going in the frozen environment, he found the little holy book and took it as a war souvenir. He had forgotten about it until then. Jason stroked his chin. "I don't even remember his name. I saved him, then I killed him." He was about to toss it onto his nightstand clutter but something inside him said to bring it along.

Back to war, but what *kind* of war was he going to? He'd been throughout central Asia and the Middle East many times, but never posing as another man. The boundaries weren't defined. The rules of engagement were unclear. He wondered what the war manager planners at the Pentagon were up to, even as it burned.

It was a direct hit that murdered thousands of innocent people; the gloves had come off. Transnational terrorists like Osama bin Laden now had targets on them, but *first* you had to find them. The American people counted on the military for action. He'd been in the action business for too long. But for this mission he wondered if he could handle the role he was expected to play. Trepidation filled his mind. It wasn't the idea that something might happen to him; that he might die was almost a joke if he did. And it wasn't that he wouldn't kill if he had to—it was that he had to do it at all. *I can't believe that I actually let Cadallo talk me into this. Why? What's his real angle?*

He had gone through enough of those eternal moments of paralyzing terror, fright, and rage to last several lifetimes. He only stayed in the Air Force as a PJ to save lives.

Well, if saving a life included keeping a junkie from his or her fix, then so be it. Narcoslavery, that's what Ben called it. If his acts could keep someone from turning to heroin then maybe it would be worth all of the shit he was about to submit himself to. *Alone.*

The big lesson that he had learned in his line of business was that the only things in the world he could count on when the chips were down were himself, his skills, and being flexible to changes. Those were the things that really kept him alive.

It was time to sleep. Picking up his knapsack, he was surprised how light it was; another lesson learned—losing all the gear that he carried at Khobar taught him never to travel heavy again. Material things no longer had much sentimental significance—he had made the shift from immortal to mortal, god to worm.

He dropped the sack next to his boots. "But I still can fight, I hope."

He sat on his bed, then stretched out, and interlocked his hands behind his head. He had no idea when he'd get another chance to sleep on his ultracomfortable king-size bed. His mind wandered over many of the things he'd seen and done, and the things he missed, like family.

Why?

What was it that Mac had said? He was searching for something. Mac was right, but with all his money he still wouldn't find out, or be able to buy it. Maybe he'd never find it—especially in a war zone!

Was it just dumb luck that kept him alive and searching for something? He unclasped his hands and reached over to cut off the lights.

He folded his hands across his chest and addressed the night. "Hey, you just never know, but maybe I'll find out this time, or die trying."

CHAPTER 7

1830 SATURDAY/ 15 SEPTEMBER 2001
AVON PARK / FLORIDA

The president names Osama bin Laden and the al Qa'eda as primary suspects in the attack on America.

JASON LOOKED OVER HIS DIRTY WEAPONS AND FELT good, even though his hands were sore from all the recoil of his weapons. A Thompson submachine gun, M-16 automatic rifle, shotgun, several handguns, and a Barrett .50 caliber rifle lay in his trunk. He'd fired well over five thousand rounds through them. The weapons were still warm to the touch. He knew the guys at the Avon shooting range and they let him have it all to himself the whole day. It was a relaxing getaway, even if just for a short time. With all the gunplay in Afghanistan, if he had any reason to pull a trigger, then he'd better have a sharp eye.

And after all the rounds he had fired, if his eyes and hands didn't work together by then, forget it.

Ben said there'd be no training or rehearsal. It was travel time and minimal briefs, oh, *and a little surgery along the way.*

It'd taken the whole day to fire the weapons, and now the long shadows cast by the tall pine trees obscured his targets. He forgot to bring along night-vision goggles to do some night firing. His plan was to sleep in the car, then drive back in the morning to make the takeoff time at Patrick.

He ate a can of cold chili beans and decided to go for a walk before settling down in his car for the night.

It was the kind of feeling that you get when you're walking in the mall and you feel as if someone is staring at you. You search everywhere, when suddenly you catch the eyes staring at you.

Jason slowed his steps and casually looked around. How could someone else be in this forest?

Jason froze when the eyes from another world stared back at him. They were yellow and ferocious. Long fangs gleamed from a snarling snout. It was a Florida cougar crouching ten feet to his right. Its ears were laid back flat and it hissed and spit, then growled.

Fight or flight?

Instead Jason was rooted to the ground, frozen in time as they faced each other. The eyes said all; the next move would lock them in a life-and-death fight.

The cat's tail twitched, and the body trembled, ready to jump.

Jason thought about all the useless guns back in his trunk. The only weapon that he carried was his automatic knife, puny and feeble protection in this situation against a monster with deadly fangs and claws—it was all he had.

"SSShit," he hissed back while slowly pulling out the knife from his pouch. He held it toward the big cat. He took a deep breath and pressed the button on his knife.

The big cat flinched at the sound of the blade snapping open.

"HOO-YA!" he yelled.

The cat sprang at him and was suddenly gone.

"Oh, man!" Jason twisted around in circles. *Where'd it go? What just happened?*

It didn't matter. Wasting no time, he was inspired to retrace his steps quickly, heading back to his car. Exhilarated and shaky, zooming on adrenaline, he decided that he would forgo sleeping in the car and make the drive to Patrick and get a room on base for the night.

2300 HOURS
UNDISCLOSED LOCATION / MELBOURNE / FLORIDA

Ed deLeon sat in his chair in the security room. With his fingers on the sound and light control board, he felt like the director of a TV show. He could control everything from where he sat and at the moment he was staging General Ben Cadallo's performance.

He also ran a twelve-man security team that was armed to the teeth and ready to respond to anything.

Looking over the assembled crowd through a one-way mirror, he smiled at the routine they were about to see.

Seventy-five people sat silently in the auditorium. They had arrived throughout the day and spent their time filling out their paperwork and getting their room assignments. Unknown to them, the papers they touched were treated to get their fingerprints and DNA samples for verification after they filled them out and turned them back to the Party.

They all knew the rules, and would be rebriefed after the general's speech before being taken on a tour of their surroundings. It was their home now.

From where everyone sat they had an unobstructed view of just how massive a floor they were on. Glass walls surrounded the spacious auditorium. They could even see into the bathrooms. One by one the glass walls turned opaque until they couldn't see beyond the auditorium.

The room was bright, but there was no direct lighting anywhere to be seen. The audience sat in plush theater seats waiting for something to happen.

The lights went out and a low vibration filled the room. A panel of glass grew brighter from the far side of the room. Behind the glass, a silhouette cast by a giant of a man walked along a partition, then the shadow came in through a side door and purposely marched toward the podium on the stage at the front of the room.

They followed the massive figure with their eyes until he stood behind the front stage. The lights came on and the silhouette transformed into a giant black Marine wearing the green gabardine uniform of a general's Marine class Charlie, adorned with lots of shiny medals and colorful ribbons.

"Ladies and gentlemen, I am Lieutenant General Ben Cadallo. You can call me General, or sir." He marched off the stage doing perfect facing movements, and towered over the audience. He was glowering steel with razor-sharp creases. "I am The Man. Don't forget it, whoever you think you are."

Glancing first to his right at the huge one-way mirror, then back to his audience, he continued speaking. "It goes no higher, or farther, than me. You're here because you have talents I can use. You've all been receiving a nice government check every month for doing nothing. Now is the time for you to earn that money." Cadallo walked around, inspecting each person gathered in the main auditorium. "You all signed a secrecy statement, remember that.

"Our country is at war. This is not an army-to-army battle. There are no flags to capture. The enemy hides within a religion whose people are not our enemies. Our enemy believes that everyone not of their beliefs is a combatant, and their battlefield is the world.

"They've targeted America and her citizens for death or enslavement. They have committed acts of war on our land. Well, today we must fight using nontraditional methods and we must now think differently, using new strategies and tactics. You are the result of that different kind of thinking.

"You are not traditional soldiers. But you *will* be warriors. From this building you will assist a frontline covert combatant in his actions against an enemy in Afghanistan.

"You are a part of a new testing ground as force enhancers. Can we bring bright American minds together and support a highly classified mission? Can this set of people with specialized skills handle a fluid and complex mission as it is prosecuted on the other side of the planet? Well, we're about to find out. I have never commanded *civilians*." He almost shuddered. "What happens in the coming weeks remains to be seen.

"You will be split into two forces, Red and Blue. You will act independently of each other, but at no time will you contend with or hide anything from each other. You are split to act as a force multiplier.

"You will hear our operator by his audio signals transmitted from an uninhabited aerial vehicle. You will see much of what our operator is doing transmitted from overhead imagery in near real time. The moment that you see or hear a situation you can help, you pass it forward. Your information will be given to Command staff, and a plan will immediately move forward to our man."

Scowling, an animal power emanated from him—there was no doubt who was in control. He was fierce, an angry warrior god. "Sounds like a game, doesn't it? The payouts are life and death.

"*You.*" He stopped and towered over an attractive young Mexican girl in her twenties. "You get to go home when this operation's over. Fuck this up and the operator we're backing won't. *You* don't want that to happen, do you, Brianna?" His eyes pierced her as sure as an arrow.

Wide-eyed, she shook her head.

He stopped and spun on the balls of his feet. "Ah! A side note, but an important one to remember: Anyone here who compromises this mission will go directly to a solitary federal cell. No trial. No appeal. You waived those rights the moment that you stepped through these glass doors. Any unauthorized person or persons who gets into this area, such as terrorists or spies, will never be seen again. I will personally make sure of it."

The temperature in the room dropped like an incoming Arctic wind.

"While you are here, you will use only your first name. No code names. A small room will be assigned to each of you. All of you have had the initial training in this type of operation. For many of you this will be your first time participating in a real-world operation like this, so I'd like to cover a few ground rules before you get in-processed.

"Keep everything friendly and professional. The walls here really do have ears. Don't ask about each other's background, family, or friends. You're not here to make lifelong buddies, exactly the opposite. Once you leave you will never contact each other again, unless you are brought in for another ops.

"You will not contact, nor attempt to contact anyone outside of this building—that means, family, friends, and *especially* the news media.

"Let me remind you again; *I am* at war. *You* are at war, and you will *follow* orders. I give those orders. I dictate the mission."

"And exactly what is the mission?" Gorsline asked. He'd worked before for autocrats. They didn't bother him as long as they let him do his work.

Cadallo pursed his lips and nodded. "You will get the full details later, but for your general knowledge, our mission is to support one man, thousands of miles from here. Our job is to keep him alive so that he can do his job. We will stop anyone trying to stop our man from doing his mission, including killing them.

"If any of you have any questions or reservations about why you're here, or what you're about to participate in, then now is the time to leave the room."

A hand went straight up.

"Yes?"

"Who's *our operator*?" Ibrahim al Kalifa asked.

"His cover name is Alex Gomez. I put him there. I brought you here. You will keep him alive to do his job, then we all can go home." Cadallo marched back to the podium. "Don't think of me as the boss, just God. Any more questions will be handled by Mr. Ed deLeon, your Party coordinator." He stepped down from the podium and left the room the same way he had come; light panels snapped on, then off, leaving a room full of astonished Party participants.

Cadallo walked to his command center and blacked out the walls until he was isolated with just his thoughts. He studied his master control panel. A lot of time and money had gone into its construction. Millions. Phones and pretty-colored buttons dominated the panel. At any moment he could pick up a phone, punch a button, and ring up the White House, the Pentagon, Central Command, Special Operations Command, Joint Intelligence Center, or any senior leader around the world involved in the war on terrorism.

The radios next to the phones could almost reach out to God. But it was the small black box with a red toggle switch that he was most interested in; it was the one that could talk directly to Jason.

He sat down in the custom-made leather chair and swiveled around. From his position nothing could escape his view. Sitting at the multimillion-dollar command center didn't impress him; it was the knowledge that he carried in his mind that turned his seat into a weapon.

It had taken him a lifetime to get into the position he was in. It had taken persuasion and threats to get the mission off a grease board and into operation. He recruited and stole the best talent available, and spent ungodly sums to equip the Party. If the gamble paid off, only then could he move on to building the Party into a real fighting tool and take it to the next level.

He unbuttoned his jacket buttons and propped his mirror-polished shoes up on the panel. Uncountable deployments, countless covert actions, and several wars had taken their toll. At fifty-eight years old he had gone through two marriages for the Corps. It had been a long road. It really was lonely at the top, but for what?

"For my country," he whispered to himself. After all, he was a patriot and a warrior. But there was more to it. You couldn't buy what he had with money; you had to pay for it with your soul. All the actions and operations he'd been in had brought him to the Super Bowl of crime. There were no questions about his credentials. "For my country?"

Sure, he was a patriot, but did Jason know the real truth? Would he learn that all about power and control of a general stops when the career ends? Control and power, as heady as they were, could be fleeting.

It took all his power to make the mission happen. But could he control it? Finally, after all the time, money, and energy spent to get everything set up and on-line, it all came down to one man being able to play a convincing role. His man, Jason Johnson, out there playing hero of the free world, was undoubtedly doomed. *Will he figure out my plan before the payoff?*

Second thoughts formed, the wrong tool for the right job. The whole mission revolved around his reluctant PJ. Jason had a reputation for saying and doing the wrong things at the worst times. Ben was giving up too much control to Jason and didn't like it one bit; Jason was programmed trouble. He looked up at the ceiling and sighed. "God, I just hope I got the right man, and he can pull it off." It was really a house of cards and Jason was the key card. *Can I control it all and make it happen?*

Mike Gorsline dropped onto his assigned bunk none the worse for wear. The facilities were outstanding, an Olympic swimming pool was the only thing lacking. They were in their own universe; no one could enter or leave.

One thing was for sure—the general was in charge. He had no intention of pissing off the man. The big bust was going to go down and Mike wanted in on it.

He leaned over and picked up the fact sheet lying on his study table. Everything that was said was recorded. *Everything.* There was no discussing personal matters. First names only. No family. No background. They could say what their expertise was, but that was all, not how they came by it. Once the mission was over there would be no contact between anyone. You may not tell anyone of what you did here, or even of our existence. You went to a party, that's all. Any leaks will be dealt with quickly, and severely.

"We want you, Big Brother, Big Brother." He hummed. "Well, at least I don't have to deal with gun-toting crazy crackheads."

He remembered a few years back when he was recruited for the Party. He thought that they were Mormons when they first knocked at his door. Never quite figuring out the game, he went to Homestead Air Force Base and spent two weeks of combat role playing, meshing with spooks, or so he thought. The people who trained him were ready for any calamity, something Mike practiced for on a daily basis.

It was worth it for the government check that came in his mail every month.

He had one hour before the actual mission specifics would be presented. Sleep. It was something he was good at. He set his watch alarm and rolled over. They were at war and he learned one thing from all the action he had been though—sleep whenever you can get it.

CHAPTER **8**

The vice president tells America to "get ready for a dirty war."

THE SUN WAS JUST RISING. MAC DROVE JASON TO the India Ramp at 0545 in a squadron golf cart. He parked on the grass and they sat and watched two specks in the sky grow to an incredible size.

Two giant C-17 Globemaster IIIs were on a final approach to Patrick. Both were from Charleston Air Force Base, South Carolina. Usually the big birds just trained on the airstrips, this time they had business at Patrick. They lined up over the Banana River for an assault landing on Runway 11.

When it looked like a half million pounds of a 240-million-dollar jet was about to crash, it flared and squeaked the tires onto the runway, then the pilot threw the roaring engines into reverse, brakes screaming, leaving just enough room on the assault strip for number two to mimic another perfect combat landing. They both turned left on an adjacent taxiway and slowly made their way to a more secure part of the base.

"That's our future, man," Mac said. "Whatever we put on those beauties will go to the front lines of our enemy, or friends, all over the world." He smiled. "See, it was designed with me, the loadmaster, in mind." He put his hand on Jason's shoulder. "Tell me that moose wouldn't take me anywhere in the world to get me laid."

Jason grinned. "Don't change, buddy." There were few constants in the crazy world that helped him keep a little balance—Mac's hedonism was one of them.

"Wouldn't if I could."

"Hey, mind taking care of my car while I'm gone?"

Mac's eyes flew open. "You gotta be shittin' me, the chick magnet? Hell, now I'm glad to see you go!"

"Well, it ain't done nothing for me." He reached into his pocket and handed Mac his keys. "There's a few dirty guns in the trunk. Hazelwood at the weapons shop said that he'd clean them for me. Can you drop them off to him, and then get them back when he's done and then store them for me?"

Mac nodded. "For sure, anything for the car."

"And do me a *big* favor. Keep cum stains off the seats. Leave the car in the parking lot and the keys in my file when you get deployed."

"You bet, no bangin' in the car at all." Mac held up his right hand and swore, then caught himself and dropped it to his lap. "Well, not a lot, and only on the backseats, with towels. Yeah, that's fair, right?"

Jason chuckled and shook his head. "Just be sure that you stock a case of seat cleaner."

The C-17s turned in their direction.

They watched as the transport jets taxied to park on India Ramp.

"There, tail number 0007 is yours." Mac pointed to the first plane. "I checked with base ops. The plane is holding a classified manifest."

The jets cut their engines at the same time. One was uploading cargo, the other downloading. His plane would leave at 0630, headed in the opposite direction from the other.

The fuel trucks came, gassed up the planes, and went. It was time for Jason's plane to crank engines and go.

Jason stepped from the cart and grabbed his bag. They had been through the good-bye scene too many times before, so it was just a handshake and a quick hug.

Mac started the cart, then called out, "Hey, remember something while you're there; taking down the Trade Center Towers wasn't just a terrorist act: It was a crime against humanity. At no time in history were so many countries attacked at one time, in one place.

"Forget those paybacks and dues, let someone else handle that. Just do your job the best that you can. Don't let the hatred twist you. Keep looking for what you're after. Do what you gotta do to survive, but remember, you're a pararescueman; you *save lives* for a living. That's righteous!

"Jason, keep your head down and your eyes open." He drove off yelling, "Hey, and don't do anything stupid!"

Jason cleared the guard roster, then climbed aboard the C-17.

It was an impressive machine. A work of art made to fly directly into forward-deployed areas, able to land in combat zones, dump the load, turn on a dime, then get the hell out of Dodge, fast!

"Hello, my name is Michelle Tucker, I'm the loadmaster on this mission. Just drop your bag over by ours."

Jason laid his bag on top of the pile of crew bags and shook hands with the attractive woman.

"Pick any seat that you like, they're all first-class."

Jason wandered around the cargo hold. A large white trailer about forty-five feet long by seventeen feet wide was secured to the floor by pallet locks. Chained to the floor next to the trailer was a huge wooden box.

"There's another passenger here waiting to meet you," Tucker said.

He followed her up the flight-deck stairs to where a man stood admiring the fancy flight controls. He turned, smiled, and offered his hand to Jason. "Mr. *Gomez*, my name is Bobby Creel. I'm with the Treasury Department, specially detailed to General Cadallo for this operation. I'll be working with you on your mission planning and specifics, and staying with you until you go in. I hope to be there when you come out. I've been with this operation from the beginning. I helped General Cadallo design and coordinate many *things*."

They shook hands, as Jason studied the man.

Bald, he had deep, penetrating ice-blue eyes. His grip was firm and strong. His smile seemed genuine and warm.

"Where's Ben?"

"The general asked me to tell you that he'll talk to you very soon."

"Great. Good start. He said he'd be with me the whole way. He's not even here to see me off. The fuck."

Creel shrugged his shoulders and quickly changed the subject. "Right now we're the only passengers *officially* manifested on this trip, but I think that you'll find this flight to be very active, and productive." Inspecting Jason's face, he raised his eyebrows for a moment. "Your beard doesn't look too bad for a five-day growth. It should be at least passable by the time you're in-country. Well, let's get this moose in the air." He nodded to the pilot and in moments the engines were turning and the jet was moving.

The plane came to a sudden stop and Jason heard the whines and sounds of hydraulic systems working. Looking toward the rear of the plane, he saw the cargo door open and ramp lower to the ground. A bus stopped behind the jet and people poured off the bus as the load-master guided them onto the jet. They quickly sat on the pull-down seats along the cargo wall.

The ramp and door closed and the C-17 taxied to the runway.

Jason was dumbfounded. The entire operation took only minutes to happen. Who were these unmanifested passengers, and what kind of cargo were they carrying?

WHILE THE JET JASON WAS ON RELEASED ITS BRAKES AND took off over the Atlantic Ocean, the second C-17 back at Patrick off-loaded three RQ4B Global Hawks and their support packages.

Included in the support system were portable trailers, shelters, control modules, maintenance material, and tons of avionic equipment.

The deplaning forty-three personnel had received mo-bilization orders the day before and were packed up and ready to deploy anywhere in the world in twelve hours—their destination was Patrick Air Force Base.

Fast and exact, the load and team were off the plane and on Rescue Road without drawing any attention. In minutes everyone was in a secure hangar. Like a choreo-graphed play, they were set up and ready to fly the Global Hawk in less than two hours.

No one but the base commander, airfield manager, bil-leting, and chief of base security knew that the Global Hawk team had arrived to do their part in the coming battle over Afghanistan.

0630 HOURS
OVER THE ATLANTIC OCEAN

Jason's C-17 was level and at altitude in minutes. The pilot announced over the intercom that the weather would be smooth the whole way. All passengers were clear to unbuckle their seat belts and move around. People stood, grabbed their bags, and started to change into surgical garb.

Jason didn't like what he was seeing. He pointed at the box and trailer. "What's up with those, and all these unmanifested passengers?"

"Don't worry about the wooden box," Creel answered. "I'll clue you in later, but first the doctors and nurses on board here have to prep you for surgery."

"WHAT? What surgery?"

"Cadallo didn't tell you about it?"

"Yesss..." Jason looked wide-eyed at the mobile trailer and felt like jumping off the plane. "But he didn't say *when it* would happen."

"Well, it's happening now. Getting you operational can't be delayed, so this has to happen during this flight. Hey, it's a fifteen-hour flight and you'll be out most of the way."

"Oh, I can't wait."

One man walked to Jason and smiled.

Jason took a deep breath and relaxed. "Dr. Brownstein. I am *real* glad to see you again."

Jason unbuckled from his seat. He stood and hugged Dr. Arthur Brownstein.

"It's really good to see you again, PJ," Brownstein said, then kissed Jason's cheek. "A while back, Ben called me at my practice in Hawaii and started asking me a few medical questions, and your name slipped out. I made him let me in on planning the procedures."

"Wait," Jason interrupted. "You *made* the general let you in on this gig?"

"You're right. I begged him. How could you keep me away? Bionic microimplants." Brownstein grinned wide. "I'm here to watch over you, the neurotologist, and the other specialists working on you." Brownstein studied

Jason's face. "Hasn't anyone briefed you on how radical these new procedures are?"

Jason shrugged his shoulders. "Not much."

"Same ol' Jason. Kept in the dark among the fungus."

"Okay. I'm a mushroom all right. Heavy details were never my bag."

Dr. B had saved Jason's life in 1995. He hadn't seen the good doctor in years, but was more than glad to see him again.

They caught up on old times for a bit, and then Doc B pointed to the big white trailer.

It was a Lenoir Air Portable Hospital. The doctors and nurses were part of a forward surgical team (FST) whose purpose was to give medical treatment much in the way mobile surgical hospitals did during the Korean and Vietnam Wars. Jason would be the first case worked on in the brand-new operating trailer.

"I'm sorry I can't spend more time with you to catch up on things. Once the surgical trailer is ready I'm going to start an IV drip on you and prep you for surgery."

Jason had about enough time to let his stomach settle before Doc B had an IV in his arm and headed him toward the mobile surgery trailer.

Jason felt ice in his guts when a woman in green surgical garb motioned for him with her finger.

"JASON? JASON, CAN YOU HEAR ME? JASON, WAKE UP. Come out of it."

A voice was calling. A fog enveloped Jason. He was floating and had no idea where he was or how long he had been there. "Is that you, Doc?"

"Yeah, everything's fine."

"How long was I out?"

"Five hours."

"It felt like five months." Trying to open his eyes, he

quickly discovered that they were covered. He tried feeling his eyes, but someone stopped him. "Doc, where am I?"

"You're in the recovery room of the trailer. Hey, don't touch your eyes. They're bandaged."

"Why both?"

"If your left eye wasn't also bandaged, then it would move and irritate your right eye. They move together, understand?"

"Yeah." He was coming back to reality. His left arm was warm and his right ear felt thick. "Everything okay?"

"You tell me. Hey, I tattooed my name on your ass while you were out."

Jason knew that Doc B had a perverse sense of humor, and felt his ass for anything unusual. *Nothing.* The only tattoo on his butt was the Jolly Green feet, signifying a PJ's first save. "Screw you, Doc. All right, what got done to me, and what's going to happen next?"

Doc B explained that a microtransceiver, invented by Adam Kissiah, was planted deep in the right ear; the cochlea, to be exact. The revolutionary device was originally invented by Kissiah to bring hearing to the deaf. Now, with major micromodifications, and an overhead relay, Jason could keep in constant radio communication with Cadallo and the Party.

The miniature artificial silica night-vision retina implanted just under his right cornea was almost unbelievable. The optibionic microchip was thinner than a human hair: Thirty-five hundred microscopic solar cells converted light into electrical impulses, and the artificial photoelectric signals were sent through the optic nerve to the brain—the scene transmitted to the brain was received as enhanced night vision.

A rice-sized GPS locator had already been implanted from the Lucifer Light operation. All they had to do to bring it on-line was to recharge the microbattery by an infrared transmitter. The Party would then be able to track him anywhere in Afghanistan.

"I also shot you up with enough good shit that your immune system could eat the plague for breakfast and crap it out by lunch. It's effective for ninety days. Now let me have a look at you."

He lay quiet while Doc B inspected all the procedures that had been done. Trying to shake off the effects of anesthesia, he realized he never questioned the sense or side effects of the things that had been done on him. *Teach my ass to sign my life away for a friend!*

"Are we still flying?" The recovery table where Jason lay wasn't moving.

"We are," answered the surgeon. "This operating room is on stabilizers made especially for midair operations."

"Oh."

It was weird being blindfolded. "How long before the pads come off, Doc?"

"They'll be off before we land. How do you feel?"

"Good. A little sore."

"Great. Creel has to do operational checks with you right now."

Creel helped Jason off the recovery table and onto a bunk locked into the cargo floor.

Jason realized he was wearing one of those damn hospital gowns that was open in the rear. How could anyone be cool wearing one of those things?

Art smiled as Jason reeled. "If you're still woozy, you can dress later."

"How's your ear?" Creel asked.

"Fine, I guess."

Creel led Jason to a seat.

"Then let me try something." Creel pulled out a satellite cellular phone from his jacket and pressed some buttons. "Do it."

Jason yelled, grabbed his right ear, and about jumped

from his seat. "Holy fuck!" Was that Cadallo's voice screaming at him? "Ben?"

He winced when Ben answered. Ben's voice was coming through the Kissiah transmitter.

"Lower volume," Creel spoke into the phone.

"Better?" Cadallo asked.

"Yeah, now I know how Joan of Arc and Son of Sam felt. This is really bizarre!" The sound was as clear as if Ben were standing right next to him. "Where are you?"

"Back in Florida. Alice, from now on we're going to call you Alex, or Gomez. You have to condition yourself to get used to the name."

"Mr. Gomez," a different voice said. "This is your radio tech. We only have a short time. Your hearing device is directional and can be picked up within a fifteen-mile radius of your relay, the Global Hawk, at altitude. At this moment you're within the range of a Global Hawk in your area. You will be out of its range in less than an hour, so I want to run some operational checks before we lose contact."

After going through some simple yes and no questions, Jason did some counting and recited a few sentences. There was a pressure and vibrating itch in his ear, but Brownstein explained that it was to be expected, and that it would soon go away.

Jason was surprised at how quickly he got used to the idea of hearing voices in his head.

Static began to clutter in his ear.

"That's it. Our signal's fading. Everything checks, ops good. We will reestablish communications with you once you are inside of Afghanistan."

Art put his hand on Jason's knee, and whispered. "Jason, when Ben told me about the mission, I thought it was a *very* chancy job. You know that, right?"

"Yeah, I know, *why*? Why are you telling me this?"

"I know you, ready to leap into a raging river to save a life, and only half-aware of the dangers involved."

"Well, I can't stop now. I have to see where this thing goes. I know that it's fucked up, man."

"Well, my friend, that's nothing new to you, but at least you can't say that I didn't warn you."

"It seems like I've heard the same story already." Jason grinned.

Creel was waiting to begin briefing Jason on his role and discuss plans of attack.

"When we land I'm going to be getting off with the surgical team. Know that I'll be on standby. Anytime that you call, I'll come running," Doc B said.

"Thanks, Doc."

"But I can't help you if you get killed."

"I'm hip!"

CHAPTER **9**

0300 MONDAY / 17 SEPTEMBER 2001
PATRICK AIR FORCE BASE / FLORIDA

The Taliban tells Pakistani officials that it will not hand over bin Laden to America.

THE ENTIRE BEACHSIDE HIGHWAY OF A1A THAT ran in front of Patrick Air Force Base had shut down, and armed guards effectively cut off Cocoa Beach from Satellite Beach and the rest of the Space Coast from any prying eyes. The surrounding businesses and citizens were in an uproar over the loss of business; but there was nothing that they could do about it. Federal law prevailed.

Rumors spawned rumors. One story was that three terrorists on a Zodiac boat were killed in the surf, trying to infiltrate the Air Force Technical Applications Center (AFTAC) building and plant a bomb. Those stories did nothing to help improve the economy.

But shutting the highway down did allow a lot of quiet and unobserved aerial missions to occur.

The field was closed. No planes took off or landed.

The automatic hangar door opened and a strange-looking jet with long wings rolled from the darkness and out onto the taxiway. Nothing hindered its eerie progress.

What was strange about the plane's progress was that there was no place for a pilot on the aircraft. Instead, a round dome was at the front of the fuselage, making the jet look almost phallic.

Taxiing to the opposite end of Runway 29 for takeoff, it turned around and the Rolls-Royce engine roared to life, generating over seven thousand pounds of thrust. The uninhabited aerial vehicle (UAV) sped down the runway for twenty-five seconds and took off, heading northeast over the Atlantic Ocean. It would be on station over Afghanistan in eighteen hours, ready to assume a visibly passive, but very active circle over the area of Kabul. Within its frame was almost every snooping and alerting device possible.

The Global Hawk Launch and Recovery Element (LRE) was located in Hangar 750, with the Mission Control Element (MCE) and the maintenance team. They were getting two more Global Hawks ready to alternate with the first bird and provide continuous cover over their area of operation.

The Hawk elements would never meet Jason or the Party. These were active-duty Air Force personnel. The Global Hawk personnel were billeted on base. They were restricted to the base, not because of a terrorist threat, but to keep their exposure to a minimum. No one needed to know why, or what they were on base for.

The Northrop Grumman RQ-4A Global Hawk, a high-altitude endurance surveillance UAV, flew at over sixty thousand feet. It used a host of electro-optical and infrared sensors with synthetic aperture radar (SAR) and other classified systems to monitor and scan the land below for anything that flew, walked, rolled, or crawled.

Able to orbit for over forty hours, it would rotate with

three other Hawks sequestered in the 750 hangar at Patrick Air Base.

Lieutenant Colonel Eric Draper, the Hawk commander, watched the monitors as his bird disappeared into the night. A certified pilot monitored the automatic systems, ready to take over the controls manually in case of an emergency. It would be some hours before it reached its final altitude above Class A airspace.

A lot of organizations combating terrorism were counting on the Global Hawk's cutting-edge technology to help them wage their battles. It was Draper and his team's responsibility to be on their best to deliver the UAV's wide-ranging capabilities.

Once on station over Afghanistan, in addition to all its other automatic actions, the Global Hawk would feed the signals received from Jason's Kissiah transceiver to a MILSTAR satellite. Those signals would be continuously relayed to the Party.

Draper sat in his chair and relaxed. Normally, at a fixed base, the short-notice tasking requirement that came down to move was because someone way above his pay grade said that they needed the system at a more secure location, and up and running, like yesterday. He and his teams were ready to do their part to support all the players on the ground in Afghanistan. Besides, Patrick was nice duty, even if everyone had to stay on base. For some, fighting a war was *always* more preferable at a more comfortable location.

0400 HOURS
SOMEWHERE OVER THE MIDDLE EAST
ON C-17 #0007

The effects of the anesthesia had worn off. All that Jason had to do was sit and listen. The pads on his eyes would soon be coming off.

Creel spoke. "Now I'm going to read to you some more about your role of Alex Gomez. Are you ready, Alex?

"Alex?"

"Oh, yeah," mumbled Jason. He had to consciously make the mental shift. *You're a scumbag drug dealer named Alex, not Jason.* "Hey, am I Alice, too?"

"What? I don't understand."

"Nothing, please continue," he said. *Odd. Cadallo didn't tell him my code name.*

For the next few hours Jason listened to and tried to memorize the history of a notorious drug-dealing slimeball. Gomez was a killer, thief, pirate, and a host of other bad things. But Jason did hear one redeeming quality. The man was supposedly good-looking, making Jason handsome by default.

When they were done, Jason felt as if he needed a steam shower to wash off the slime he would try to replicate.

"Ready, *Gomez*?" Brownstein asked.

"Yeah, Doc B."

The bandages were removed from his eyes. The loadmaster had turned down the cabin lighting.

"Damn! It works." Jason could clearly see every detail around him. The surgical team waved, excited that their new, top-secret procedure was working.

The medical team then spent eternity taking measurements and making Jason do all kinds of weird things. When he closed his right eye everything went dark. Opening it again, he felt a little dizzy.

"You'll get used to it. You've lost a little depth perception, but your brain will quickly compensate for it," Art explained.

The team finished their recordings and decreed that Jason was "good to go."

Looking down at the skimpy cloth he wore, he couldn't wait to go into the lavatory and get back into his regular clothing. He felt the jet descending so he hurried and dressed, then came out of the lavatory. "Hey, what'd ya do, put me in a tanning chamber while I was out?"

"No time," Doc B answered. "Instead, we stained your skin a little darker to match Gomez's complexion." Doc B grinned. "Even your balls. Like your enhanced immune system, it'll wear off in a few months."

Examining his arms, Jason nodded. "It doesn't look half-bad. Where are we now?"

"Just about to land in Kuwait," answered Creel.

The loadmaster instructed them all to take their seats.

Jason felt like the Six Million Dollar Man in a George Hamilton body, about to be thrown into a meat grinder of the worst kind possible.

CHAPTER 10

1720 MONDAY / 17 SEPTEMBER 2001
CLASSIFIED LOCATION / KUWAIT

The New York Stock Exchange opens and drops more than six hundred points.

THE C-17 KISSED THE RUNWAY AND THEN CAME to a dead stop at thirty-five hundred feet. It made a quick left turn as the loadmaster opened the ramp and door.

A huge cargo loader, followed by a bus, was waiting behind the jet.

Michelle guided the driver of the loader to the edge of the ramp, then she ran to her loadmaster station. She threw open the lock switch and in seconds the trailer was gone. Passengers too.

Jason stood with his mouth open as the ramp and door closed, letting the pilots taxi to a well-lit parking spot to clear customs. It was a vanishing act. No one saw anything. On paper, besides Jason, Creel and the three-person crew were the only ones who left from Florida and arrived at the Kuwait International Airport.

It was cold as he stepped from the plane onto the tarmac. Jason looked around and shivered. It was always a little unnerving for him when he arrived back in the Middle East. Ghosts. He had a world full of them, always there, hiding in the shadows.

Creel touched his arm. "This way, please, Mr. Gomez. Throw your bag in the rear of the vehicle. Our box has been loaded onto that semi truck."

They climbed into a gold Chevy Suburban and followed the semi truck, led by a van filled with armed guards.

The small convoy passed through several checkpoints until they were on an unlit, bumpy road.

"We're off base?"

"That's right," Creel answered. "We're going through the Bogron oil fields, which belong to the Kuwaiti Oil Company.

"We start your part right now. I trust that you're getting into your role, Alex Gomez. Right now you're the front man for the money. This gets the ball rolling. You'll get an account and PIN number from a bishop who's acting as our secret banker. After that I'll take you back to the base and you'll get a little rest and a briefing before you go in."

"A bishop in Kuwait? What kind of bishop?"

"A Catholic Maltese. Think you can do it?"

Jason nodded and sat back in the seat. *Why not? Cover is a lie, but I gotta live it sometime.* Besides, he was too intrigued with the mission to think about any consequences.

It was peaceful as they rode through the desert lit by tall pipes burning off natural gas. They passed countless oil wells as they drove. They passed through several armed checkpoints. Looking up at the black sky, Jason remembered that the last time he'd been in Kuwait was during the Gulf War in 1990. *February 25, yeah, that's right.* But it didn't look so peaceful back then—it looked just like hell. A chill came over him as the memories of that night jogged his memory. He relived the events of that war. It was the first time in his life that he had killed men to save others.

He had moved forward from Dhahran, Saudi Arabia, to al Jabail, Kuwait, with fifteen Black Hawk helicopters and teams of PJs and combat controllers. Their mission was to wait on the ground until they got the word to fly, then seize the runway at the Kuwait International Airport (KIA).

Originally tagged to ride a motorcycle, he crashed it in training and went looking for work. It all happened fast when the word came. A gunner got sick on one of the choppers, and Jason quickly volunteered to take his place.

The package mission scenario was for two assault choppers to hit KIA. The lead bird would fast-rope in the Combat Control team to clear the runway and set up a landing zone for four C-130s loaded with combat forces. The second Black Hawk chopper on which Jason flew would provide air cover. Carlos Gonzales, the flight engineer, put Jason to work on the right gun. The miniguns were hot and ready to go.

When the word came for the first launch wave it looked like a biblical plague of the deadliest locusts in history as countless choppers filled the sky. Jason's crew took off with the second wave.

Flying fifty feet above the Persian Gulf water, Jason was ready to open up on anything firing in their direction. Their night vision became almost useless when they came upon the Kuwaiti oil fields—every wellhead burned.

The smoke and heat from the fire created its own weather. Oiled lightning exploded just feet away—combat was more comfortable.

They stayed low over the water until they saw the airport. The lead chopper fast-roped in the combat controllers to clear any runway obstructions and set up communications for aircraft landings. Jason's crew went looking for bad guys to kill. The CCT cleared the runway in record time. The choppers kept up the air cover as an MC-130 Combat Talon touched down.

Cleared off to go hunting, the choppers flew low, trolling to blow away anyone shooting at them.

Jason saw lots of men running away with empty hands over their heads. He wouldn't shoot at unarmed men.

The radios were full of battle chatter when the Guard radio stepped over all others. "Any Rover, any Rover, this is Rabid, repeat, Rabid."

All flight crews had been briefed about the code name on the ground. If called, it was a drop everything and assist the call. Jason was the first person to answer the call. Rabid was in trouble—they flew to his location.

When they found and hovered over Rabid, it was instantly obvious from the muzzle flashes where the bad guys were located. Just like in training, Jason worked his weapon until there were no more muzzle flashes. Cleared off by Rabid, he waved 'bye to the men on the ground and the chopper went back to pick up their combat controllers. He learned later that week that graves team estimated, from the body parts gathered, that he'd killed over twenty Iraqi soldiers.

Body count, he thought. It was the first of many. *And how many saves?* He unconsciously rubbed his angel medallion.

THEY CAME TO KUWAIT CITY AND MADE A PASS IN front of a huge walled compound.

The truck pulled over in an alley and let the Chevy pass and park near an orange brick wall. Creel and Jason got out of the vehicle, walked near two steel doors, then Creel grinned at Jason. "Watch." He stood back a few paces, and said, "Open sesame."

The doors slid up and a forklift rolled out from behind the doors. In almost total darkness it unloaded the big box that had been next to the operating trailer on the C-17, then disappeared back into the cavern as the doors slammed shut.

Jason stood by in total amazement at the operation.

A man stepped from the darkness. The man stood about even with Jason, but outweighed him by at least a hundred pounds. He wore a brown habit. His bushy eyebrows were in constant motion. In his late forties, he looked like a ringer for Friar Tuck.

CHAPTER 11

1900 HOURS
HOLY FAMILY CATHEDRAL / KUWAIT

MR. GOMEZ, I AM BISHOP AKMED MCFADDEN. We are allies in the same encounter. The matter before us is temporal, for the moment. We've been chosen to be your banker for this transaction. Please follow me."

Jason followed the man across the alley and along a brick wall. He couldn't help notice how well the wall was built. It was about fifteen feet high and had open crosses near the top. Or were they gunports? The brickwork had a very intricate pattern. Bishop McFadden took notice of Jason's interest.

"It is part of our design. This church stood during the Iraqi invasion and occupation, but we were never assaulted or molested. Saddam is cautious not to cross paths with the Maltese and their friends."

"I thought that this was a *Catholic* church."

"Yes, it is. The Maltese knights are a Catholic order."

"I don't understand."

"Let's first go to my chambers where we can talk in private."

The bishop took the lead and guided Jason past the thick walls and into a giant, well-lit courtyard. In the courtyard, hundreds of Filipinos, Indians, and other Asians came and went in front of a fenced-off statue of the Virgin Mary at the end of the courtyard. They then went into a huge cathedral. There was no cross atop the cathedral spire; instead, a colossal pentagram atop a separate tower beamed over Kuwait City.

They went into the rectory building and up three flights to the bishop's chamber.

The bishop's quarters were unremarkable. A single steel bed, small bookcase, two wooden chairs, and a writing table were all that were in the room.

Akmed smiled and held out his right hand. He wore a silver ring on his middle finger. It was a Maltese Cross signet ring.

Jason grasped his hand and shook it.

The bishop frowned a little, then smiled.

"You are not Catholic."

"No, sir."

Jason let go of the bishop's hand and sat back in his chair. "I guess I messed that up too, huh, Padre?" Damn, if he couldn't fool the man in front of him, what would happen to him on his first day in Afghanistan?

"No," McFadden said. "Most of the faithful kiss the ring, Mr. *Gomez*."

"Thanks, then call me unfaithful, sir, but I don't kiss rings. I brought you the money. That's all you need to know, Eminence."

The bishop smiled warily. "I understand. Tell me a little about yourself."

"Like what?"

"Tell me about your grandfathers."

"What?" Jason suddenly felt lost.

"Tell me about your lineage. We have a little time while they count your money."

An attendant came in and served tea and Arabic sweet cakes.

Jason could not speak. He had nothing to say because he could not answer the bishop's simple question. He'd never thought about it. *What if some Taliban gangster asks me the same question?* He didn't know who his own grandfathers were, let alone Alex's. *Shit, I don't even know who my own father was.* Raised in an abandoned trailer in Washington State, he had never met any of his mother's family—he had no lineage.

"Are you all right, Mr. Gomez?"

"Yes. I just can't answer your question. I'm sorry."

The bishop nodded with sympathy. "Maybe you would like to see what is becoming of your deposit after you eat."

"I keep telling you, it's not my money, Padre." He wolfed down the paltry snack, then followed McFadden down several flights of stairs until they reached a yellow-brick tunnel.

The bishop explained that they were beneath the church, where the communion bread hosts for celebrating Mass were made. Through twists and turns, up stairs and down, Jason followed the holy man. Then came the doors. There were several rooms. Akmed said that they were once full of people who had escaped the Iraqi invasion by claiming sanctuary and living there during the entire occupation.

Akmed opened one large steel door and they went inside.

Jason tried, but couldn't contain his wonder at the piles and piles of money set out on long tables. In front of each pile a nun, wearing the Carmelite habit of black and brown, and purple rubber gloves for counting the bills, quickly counted stacks of money and passed them down to other nuns operating automatic counting and wrapping machines. Focused, they didn't even acknowledge the men's presence.

Akmed showed Jason out the door and up a small ladder to a trapdoor.

Unlocking the tiny door, Jason was surprised to discover that they were behind the vestibule of the cathedral. Akmed gave Jason a conspiratorial grin, then put his finger over his lips—Mass was being celebrated.

Jason could only enjoy the bishop's boyish glee at sharing in the secrets he showed.

"Kyrie Eleison! Christe Eleison! Kyrie Eleison!" the congregation sang.

The words were beautiful and hauntingly familiar.

"What are they singing?" Jason asked.

The bishop nodded. "It means 'Lord have mercy. Christ have mercy. Lord have mercy.'"

Jason scratched his eyebrow. Right now he sure as hell could use some of God's mercy, and luck, too.

Outside the church and back out in the courtyard, McFadden was not finished with his covertness.

"You see the statue of the Virgin?"

"Yeah."

"Beneath the Lady is the counting room," he whispered.

Jason could only chuckle with a better understanding of why the icon was surrounded by an iron fence.

They went back to the bishop's chambers.

Jason was still a little stunned. While he had his own millions in a bank, he'd never seen 300 million dollars all at once. "Bishop, I have a question to ask you."

"Yes?"

"You've *got* to know where this money is headed. But you're doing the transaction anyway. Why?"

"For me to answer that, you first must answer my question."

"Go."

"Mr. *Gomez,* as you say, you've *got* to know that

where you are headed is very dangerous, suicidal. But you go anyway. Why? Are you not afraid?"

A smile warmed Jason's face. "Terrified, but that's nothing new to me. Why am I going? Well, let me see. I don't know. I don't think I can answer that one. It's like why I can't tell you about my grandfathers—I have no damned idea who they were!

"My best friend told me that I'm searching for something, but for what? I can't tell you that either. The most that I can honestly answer you is that I'm just trying to do the right thing in a very bad time. We're at war with nutzos and crazies, fanatics, you know? And if it means me having to go into a dangerous situation to try to stop the killing, terrorizing, and enslaving of innocent people, then okay, I'll do it, even if I got to whack some people to get it done."

"Today, there are those with simple beliefs who are tasked with extraordinary challenges." The bishop looked at Jason, then out his window overlooking the Persian Gulf to Iran. "A just war does not begin with the presumption against violence. There are no clear questions or answers that can ever bless the taking of sacred human life. But I think that in its simplest measure, the question we can ask is this: Is the good to be accomplished likely to be greater than the evil caused if nothing were done?

"Well, my son, I was asked to do the right thing and I'm using my order, the Maltese, to do it."

McFadden rolled up his sleeves and folded his hands on his small desk. "You are right that this kind of money is going for bad purposes, but we Maltese have been in this battle since the first Hospitaler crossed his sword with the Saracen scimitar in A.D. 1033." He studied Jason's face closely and carefully chose his words. "Our blood mixed with the enemy not only on the battlefield, but also in the bedroom, and many other places. While many may consider this to be a battle of good versus evil, two sides of a coin—it is but *one* coin.

"We are charging but a minute portion of your cash for our banking efforts. It is good to have the power, wealth, and influence for furthering God's cause. I will gladly take from the devil to do good." The bishop reached out and put his left hand on Jason's left shoulder and grasped Jason's right hand with his. "Trust me when I tell you that you are God's warrior. You must believe that He will lead you in your search."

Jason looked in his right hand. The bishop's silver Maltese ring lay in his palm.

"Wear it. This cross has always protected our friends on their journeys."

"Thanks, Padre," he said, trying the ring on his wedding finger. It looked pretty good next to his other ring. He held back a laugh. All he needed was a rabbit's foot to go with all the lucky charms he carried.

A door opened and a nun came in and nodded, then left.

The bishop opened his drawer and took out a tape recorder and held it toward Jason's lips. "Please say, 'Hello, I am calling for a confirmation transaction.'"

Jason repeated the words.

The bishop replayed the recording to make sure he had it, then he wrote down something on a sheet of paper and passed it to Jason along with a pencil. "Memorize that private phone number. Write any word that you like, then a six-digit number, and do not forget them. The word will be your account, use the word somewhere in the next sentence after what you just recorded, then enter the numbers of your PIN. When you call that telephone number, there will always be a voice on the other end, ready to verify your voice and code. You repeat your validation and they will move the money however and wherever you like. If there are any other messages that you would like passed, or services done, the voice on the other end of the phone will do it for you."

Jason listened, did as he was told, and passed back the paper.

The bishop studied the paper a moment, then held a match to it and dropped it in the ashtray. Blowing out the match, he stood. "Then I think our business is concluded." He smiled. "You are a friend of the Maltese. It is in *you* to find your grandfathers. Go with God."

Jason found his way back to the Suburban and climbed in. He was totally exhausted from the travel, surgery, and going operational the moment he landed. It was an effort, but he told Creel, word for word, what had gone on with the bishop. He gave Creel the private phone number to tap, but kept the account code to himself.

"Interesting," Creel said as they drove past the Sheraton Hotel and back onto the highway leading out of Kuwait.

"I'll say. And all that money." Jason whistled.

Creel looked straight ahead. "It was phony money."

"What?" Jason was shocked, and instantly wide awake.

"Yeah. Counterfeit, all of it. You don't think that we would just put our hands on the real thing and give it to the enemy just like that?"

"And you're telling me that you conned the Catholic Church to do it?"

"Not me. You."

"Damn! Now I know that I'm headed to hell for sure. So what's the deal?" Jason stared at the colorful lights festooning the buildings and streetlights, celebrating the emir of Kuwait's birthday.

"Don't feel so bad, we're just giving back to the extremists what they originally gave to us."

"Explain. How is giving millions in counterfeit hundreds to a Catholic charity going to help this war?"

"I'll tell you. But before I do, do you know that two-thirds of American money circulates *outside* of our country?"

"No, I didn't."

"It does. So in the big scheme of things, 300 million phony dollars overseas doesn't hurt our own economy; it doesn't even touch us.

"When the Shah of Iran was deposed in January 1979 by the radical cleric fundamentalists, they scored his material assets, which were worth billions. Included in the loot was an intaglio press and special ink, along with the books on how to operate them. These were 'gifts' that the CIA had given to the Shah. Those presses are the *exact* same kind of presses and inks that we use to print our own currency.

"So the Iranians started making almost perfect hundred-dollar American notes. Those spurious hundred-dollar bills you just unloaded on the Catholic Church came off those Iranian presses. They are such high quality that even our experts have an incredibly hard time telling them apart from the real thing; that's why we've changed the look of our currency. There's no way anybody, outside of our own experts, is going to spot them."

Jason was hooked. "How'd you get the bills?"

"A few years ago we got a confirmed hot tip that a big load of those bills was being shipped on a Liberian freighter bound for Italy. We just didn't know how big, and what a surprise we got! It was never reported that we seized a smuggling ship that contained 500 million dollars of the stuff. Actually, it was closer to 800 million, but no one was counting. Until recently, those unaccounted Super Notes were stashed in a safe spot.

"When this deal you're on was hatched, the only hitch was the money. Falcon put up 300 million of his good money, thinking that he did it all to get better conditions and maybe a chance at escaping—it'll never happen.

"Anyway, any sane person would have to know that we weren't about to give the real goods to the Taliban. Not this time! We kept Falcon's genuine cash to fund this mission. The fake stuff's just been laundered, thanks to you, and now good cash is ready to be moved and traced from an impeccable source: the Catholic Church. And now that the key is in your head, would you mind sharing those codes with me?"

Jason was floored by what he'd just heard. *Suckered again.* "Not today. And no one's the wiser. What if someone catches on?"

"Well, see, there's the beauty of it. There's already a plan on the Big Boys' table to requisition that reported seized counterfeit money from the Treasury Department and funnel it to the Taliban, then trace it and try to seize the accounts. But they're still stumped on how to do it."

Jason beat Creel to the obvious. "Yeah, so you guys are already doing it. If anyone uncovers it, you're ready to come out smelling like roses. And with Falcon thinking that he was in on it, he'll keep his mouth shut just to keep his prison privileges. No one but the insiders will have any idea what really happened."

"Bingo!" Creel looked like a kid seeing an A for the first time on his report card. He continued, "To sweeten the deal, and to make them devour your bait, a secret arms deal with the Taliban has been arranged by the Pakistani Intelligence Service as part of the opium buy. The PIK think they're pulling a fast one on us. But they're all in for a surprise too.

"As far as the money goes, the private phone line that you talk on will be tapped by the Party, and once you transfer the money to the Taliban we will trace the trail of the money transfer from the Pope's annual Peter's Pence Collection. That's where your account is credited. It's the best credit. It is personally controlled by the Vatican, and under very tight reins, to wherever it goes.

"We're going to be following the money as it moves

through a program called Janus. Any countries who coindict with us will be able to seize and split all assets. Once we identify them, we have a stack of rogatory letters ready to serve on the banks holding Taliban and al Qa'eda resources, at our choosing.

"The guns and weapons are just waiting for you to seal the deal with the Taliban. Using your audio input, or the tap, we'll fly in the guns wherever you tell us."

"I don't understand something. Why are you arming these fucks?"

"We have our reasons. Trust Ben."

A thought crossed Jason's mind. "You know, no one's told me just how I'm going to find these dope dealers."

"You're not. They're going to find you. After they do, ask to speak to Gul Nazari. It's a name to use sparingly. Spoken in the wrong circles, it just might get you killed."

"Great. Gul Nazari."

Creel pulled a folder from a briefcase and handed it to Jason. "Here. In it there's ten thousand of the same stuff you just passed to the bishop. It also has your passport, ID, and the last details about your background. Study this cover well. You're posing as a journalist until you meet with Nazari. You have the rest of the evening to familiarize yourself with everything. You have a complete staff located at the base Intel shop to assist you with anything that you want."

Jason flipped through the pages. "From what I've already learned, this Gomez character was one very bad boy. But he was a street thug who did better than most. The role shouldn't be too difficult. I grew up with thugs like this. Nobody over there better speak Spanish to me."

"Not to worry. We got translators at the Party to handle it if the issue arises. You just play your role; walk the talk."

He knew the talk, but he still had questions and knew that there would be no answers until he was right smack in the middle of something very fucked up. "What next?"

"I take you back to base. You eat, sleep, rest, then we drive you to Saudi Arabia. And from the King Fhad International Airport you'll fly direct to Kabul on an Ariana flight. It cost us a fortune, but you got a seat on the flight."

Jason cringed. He was about to jump into a serious game. "Then what?"

"We have no one inside the Taliban or al Qa'eda. It's up to you to make contact with them and make the deal happen."

"Just how? Still no one's told me how to do it. I get thrown into this stuff at the last minute and Ben expects me to be up to speed. What if I get my cover blown and get caught? You got any advice?"

Creel shrugged his shoulders. "You'll figure it out."

"Oh, yeah? Sure. First you have me cheat the Catholics big-time, then you give me nothing for an answer. Shit. I'm doomed. You and Ben gotta be working for the devil."

"Hey, you're the one that put your name on the contract."

"Right. I'm just surprised that Ben didn't have me sign it with my own blood."

Reaching the base, they were put through a bumper-to-bumper bomb search. Creel pulled up next to a modular building and handed Jason a key. "Your room key. You got a few days to learn your role before I'm back here to take you away. Study hard."

"Thanks." Jason grabbed his bag and found his room.

The quarters were plush by comparison to some of the other shit-hole-bare bases he had stayed at. This one even had its own private bathroom. "Oh my God, it even has a *bathtub*." Turning on the satellite television Jason was very surprised to see hard-core triple x pornography playing on something called the Red Monkey Channel.

There in the middle of the Muslim world pornography was on, hot and heavy. "Maybe there's hope for them yet."

Beat, he fell on the bed and studied the folder Creel gave him.

The roar of jets almost rocked Jason off the bed. "I must've fallen asleep," he mumbled.

He got up and opened the door that faced the runway. F-15 and F-16 fighter jets surged and screamed into the cold night. He could see the long blue flames of their afterburners. He guessed they were practice-scrambling for the night that they would jump the Afghan fence and bomb the Taliban and al Qa'eda strongholds. He just hoped that he wouldn't be anywhere near the enemy when it happened, because there was a lot of payback due. A lot.

CHAPTER 12

0500 SATURDAY / 22 SEPTEMBER 2001
CLASSIFIED LOCATION / CENTRAL ASIA

Nation after nation cut off ties with the Taliban.

DAR OPENED HIS EYES AND TRIED TO REMEMBER where he was. "Oh yeah, Shit Hole City." Someone had tacked a note to the alert board that read, "In case you want to know where you are, you're in Shit Hole City. It's located right in the middle of Butt Fuck Nowhere."

He pulled himself up and rubbed his face, then stood up and stretched. His back was sore from the unforgiving cot that he had slept on. The tent smelled of a combination of dirty socks, sweat, and mold. He sat on the edge of the cot, then said a silent prayer for his wife and unborn child, patting the sonogram in his pocket.

The Combat Control tent was about empty. Everyone was gone on assignments. He put on his gym shorts and used a flashlight to find his way to the wooden door. Stepping outside, the sun was just peeking over the desert horizon. "Shit Hole City is cold too!"

He jumped back into the tent and pulled his warm-up suit from his duffel bag. It was a little warmer in the outfit, but not much. He set out to find the gym. Pallets of Dasani water bottles were stacked everywhere. He grabbed one—no reason to dehydrate.

He made a quick pit stop at the "Thunder Buckets," smelly plywood huts, each with a hole cut out in the center for a half fifty-five-gallon drum underneath to catch the waste. Holding his nose, Dar took a few moments to read some of the graffiti penned on the walls. Fornicating disgruntlement by the enlisted against the officers seemed to be the major theme.

Next, he hit the shower tent to get off the grunge of travel. He'd take the morning to get in a little gym time. It'd been nonstop travel and now he was in-theater and filling a levy to fight the war. He was just a warm body with a name filling a slot. "Now go fight," Dar said as he stepped from the shower.

Already checked into the camp, he'd been briefed on the camp policies, and the hazards of the surrounding environment. Finally, he was given the CCT mission and released for isolation time. *Isolation!* What an irony. He was on a closed base, which might as well been located right in the middle of a desert island. It was also a blacked-out base. That meant that nothing unofficial came in or got out. No personal mail, e-mail, telephone calls, television, papers, nothing. And above all else, above war itself, was General Order Number One: NO ALCOHOL. Prisons had more privileges. He understood though.

The camp was established for special operations units like the SEALs, Green Berets, British SAS, Air Commandos, and the No Name Guys, who never divulged who they belonged to. The sole purpose of the camp's existence was, when the word came down, to kill and destroy all Taliban and al Qa'eda assets in Afghanistan. The mission was to drive the enemy from the field of battle. Any other matters had no place in the camp to distract these elite warriors.

Dar couldn't wait to get off the damn base. He was pulled into the command room the moment he saw his supervisor.

"The Big Green Machine normally has us working for them as supplemental force providers," pointed out Chief Master Sergeant Randy Wells, element leader. "I just got direct word from our Special Operations Commander (SOCOM) boss, General Holland. This operation can finally give us our own autonomous command. That's if we don't fuck this up. His orders are get as many combat controllers as we can in the field and be ready to go."

The chief threw his hands into the air. "Trouble is, right now there's only you and me here. Everyone else is detailed, or *already* in the field. I'm three days out from getting in my next rotation of CCT. Are you ready to go operational into a denied area and hook up with an operational team? Do you think you can handle it?"

"I'm there!" He jumped at the chief's offer to go solo.

Dar realized that while he wasn't as seasoned as some of the other combat controllers, he was the only game in town. Besides, if the rover could do half of what it did in training he'd have an edge like no other.

When it all started, the CCT teams' first tasking was airfield seizures in Afghanistan. Then lack of air traffic controllers kept the CCT acting as the airfield control elements. Wells was left with little reserve to detail any of his combat controllers to the work with the spec operators in the high mountains of Afghanistan. At that moment Dar was it.

Dar had to get his shit together, and fast! Being in fighting shape was the key to everything.

Once at the gym, it was no real discovery to find it already packed. "So much for the early bird getting the worm."

It smelled like thirteen years of accumulated sweat. At least he was warm from the body heat everyone gave off and most of the machines still worked. He didn't know anyone so he warmed up as he waited for turns on the weight machines that weren't broken. He listened to the testosterone-driven conversation around him.

Listening to the conversations he could sense that some of the men were glad to be away from home and family, for others it was like a prison sentence every day they were away from their families.

The only thing Dar wanted to do was get on with the mission so he could get back in his own bed, in the arms of Rita. His heart ached for her. He had started playing parts of her CD, trying to follow her program of listening to only ten minutes at a time. It was great just to listen to her voice. But at that moment the conversation that went on around him sure didn't have any feminine tones.

"Man, the first thing I do when I get outta here is drink a cold beer and eat me some pizza," someone said.

"Naw, a pizza ass? Pussy!" another responded.

"No. Eat some pussy *with* pizza."

"No. A piece o' ass, while you're drinkin' a cold beer!"

"That's *when* we get out of here. So *when* do we get out of here?"

It was the age-old warrior question, can't wait to get to a war, and then the moment you get there you want to know when you go can home.

These were all men associated with one Special Forces team or another. What Dar first noticed about everyone was that they looked so damned *young*. Some had cropped hair, while others were hairy all over. He scratched at his itchy, growing beard. Muscles, testosterone, attitude, and a burning desire to settle the score. They were America's answer to extremists trying to enslave the world.

He found a set of forty-pound dumbbells and an

empty spot to move them around. In a matter of minutes he was sweating, working his muscles, mentally going over all the facts that he had to work with. He'd spent hours in the Intelligence trailer, pouring over the Air Tasking Orders (ATOs), and breaking out his specific information from the Specific Information (SPINS) file.

There was one place he could have spent all his time in Shit Hole City, Tent Afghanistan. Inside the tent was a perfect diorama of Afghanistan. For hours he stood and walked around the model, trying to visualize what a pilot would see from above. Then he squatted low, trying to spot places of visual commands. Finally, he crawled around on his belly, looking for the kind of details he might miss in the shadows.

He laid out his map and made notes on his Palm Pilot. There was never enough ground for a combat controller to know in hostile territory.

Even though a combat controller worked with ground forces, he had to keep his head in the air. While the SEALs, Green Berets, and other elite teams engaged the enemy on the ground, he had to understand and master the bigger picture of battle. He had to precisely bring in airpower to command and destroy the enemy, then let the ground team close the scene.

His body felt great! Electric. Even though, at thirty, he was one of the older guys in the tent, he was all fired up to get on with the action. While everyone else's weapons fired bullets, his put out radio signals. With his 117F radio he could call on and direct more firepower and explosives at one time than many entire armies throughout history.

He was excited to try the rover system. If it worked, there was a bonus in it. The money would come in real handy after his baby was born. His mind roamed back to Rita, and he silently prayed that she was doing well. She had to, but who could tell? There was no way that he could pick up a phone and call her—he had to concentrate on the job at hand.

He shivered with nervous anticipation. Afghanistan and war were only hours away.

1445 HOURS
THE PARTY / MELBOURNE / FLORIDA

Everything was being set. The people at the Party were about to man their posts. They had gelled in a very short time. There were no prima donnas. Ben whipped that out of them the first day. They were virtual-combat warriors. Expectations were high. The place looked like a war room.

Charts, maps, personal notes and records were taped and tacked around and on each Party station. Computers of all types and brands were fired up and ready to access anything at a moment's notice.

Like excited actors right before showtime, everyone was getting ready for curtain time, putting on mental makeup, getting clear about any last items that might not have been "what iffed?"

Cadallo was pumping up the Party, all over them, letting them know what they meant to the mission. They were Jason's intellectual bank. Their job was to pool together everything that was ever known, classified or not, about Afghanistan and the Middle East.

They were also going to record voices, take overhead pictures, and identify each and every person that Jason came across. They hoped to build a definitive encyclopedia of the who's who of terrorism.

They had scoured the classified Internet protocol routing network (SIPRnet), and any other source, open or secure, to gather intelligence and knowledge about Afghanistan and Islamic extremists.

But at no time could they have contact with anyone

they knew, including family and friends. The lines were monitored at all times. Any personal communications and you were gone. It'd already happened to two people. No one asked about it.

Cadallo sat at his command center watching every move anyone made. "One mind, people, our man's in bad-guy land. Be on your toes. Be ready for the unexpected. We have to watch and guide his every move."

The fight was on.

CHAPTER 13

**2240 TUESDAY / 25 SEPTEMBER 2001
KUWAIT / SAUDI ARABIA**

The streets of Kabul, Afghanistan, are in chaos.

HE DRIVE FROM KUWAIT TO SAUDI ARABIA WAS uneventful. The highway they traveled on had once been called the Highway of Death. At the end of the Gulf War thousands of fleeing Iraqi invaders jammed up on the road leading to Umm Qasr, Iraq, with their stolen loot. It looked a lot like Los Angeles at rush hour. They were bombed and napalmed in their vehicles.

That had been the Allied coalition's chance to get in their last and very lethal licks on the enemy. It was also their last chance to clear out their inventory of dated munitions. Cleared of the charred vehicles and bodies, the four-lane highway was modern and smooth.

Guards waved them through all the checkpoints, and at the Saudi Arabian border crossing. Jason just dozed as they drove through the desert. Camels, sheep, and the occasional late-model, crashed car dotted the barren desert. The smell of gas permeated everywhere until they got close to the city of Dhahran, and the King Fhad International Airport.

"Wait," Jason said to the driver. "Can you go by the Khobar Towers? Creel, do we have the time to do it?"

"We don't have a lot of time," Creel cautiously answered.

"No problem." Jason guided the driver until they were in downtown Dhahran and next to the local prison. The shortcut from the prison to the towers was still there. The road was full of sheep and sheep dealers. It really stank, even with the windows up.

Through the shortcut and past a park they arrived at the Khobar Towers, a sixteen-square-block collection of apartments. It had once housed the coalition military units from core nations during the Gulf War.

Building 131 had been *nice,* huge rooms and great air-conditioning. At the time the Seventy-first Air Rescue Squadron and fighter maintenance were billeted together in the building. Jason had done several rotations at Khobar after the Gulf War for Operation Southern Watch (OSW).

It wasn't such a bad deal. The apartments in the eight-story buildings were huge and well made. There was plenty of room and marble bathrooms for everyone. Plush. Jason loved turning on the bidet in his bathroom to make a fountain effect next to his toilet. Very soothing.

There was no booze though. To drink, you had to sneak over to the French or British section. Even though he wasn't a big drinker, he did it a couple of times just because the brass said "no." The only place they could "officially" drink liquor was on R&R in Bahrain, but that cost an arm and a leg.

"Stop," Jason ordered the driver.

He got out and looked around. It took a second to get his bearings, but there it was, or wasn't. Where once stood an eight-story structure, there was now an empty lot. Some of the other buildings were gone, probably too damaged to stand.

As he got closer, he saw that the big bomb crater was covered and paved over. Other than that, it didn't look much different than before, when he had been there. He stood and looked over the empty lot. It wasn't that big.

The building had been modern. The roof was a great place to get naked and get a tan. There was a great workout room the PJs had built right next to his. He did the most pull-ups and sit-ups of his life on that spot. Memories.

He smiled, remembering that he was standing right where some Arab kid tried to jack off in front of Ida Wallace, the hot blond Life Support supervisor, who roomed on the first floor. Only a flimsy fence and twenty feet separated them. Ida threw a pilot's helmet at him. It flew over the fence and hit the kid square in the dick. Clutching his pecker, he ran away in pain.

Yeah, Khobar had been good duty. After the Gulf War, combat rescue personnel actually looked forward to doing rotations at the complex. Jason had studied the Qur'an under a mullah at the Culture Center, which was right next to Baskin-Robbins. It was fun. Friday was his "Islam and ice-cream night." But that all changed the night terrorists set off a tanker truck containing fifteen thousand pounds of explosives from right where he stood. The blast was so powerful that it was felt on the island country of Bahrain, a forty-minute drive away.

The American military had been at the Dhahran for over fifty years and all it took to get rid of them was one terrorist bomb—one night attack of mass murder.

Guilt rode him for years because he felt that he should've done more to save lives that night. How much more, he didn't know.

It was unreal. He never thought he'd ever see the spot again. But here he was, and about to go on a mission that didn't even have a name.

Looking around, there wasn't anything to commemorate what had happened, not even a marker. Knowing the Saudis, Jason figured they didn't want to attract any attention to the fact that they had supported America in a fight against their Islamic brothers.

At that moment he felt empty. It was like being caught in a never-ending vicious circle.

Countless lost roads and lives had been crossed to bring him right back to this place. If only he could retrace the path of just one of those destroyed lives and put it back together, bring back the love and joy ripped away by hatred, then maybe he might be able to find himself, too.

Well, a fight was on and he was in it. Maybe he was supposed to have died here but God had kept him alive just for this battle, who could tell? He knew that he needed to pass this spot one last time. It had taken twelve years to bring him back to hallowed ground on an empty lot; now he'd come full circle.

"Mr. Gomez, it's time!" Creel called out from the car.

"Damn," he said to himself as the driver headed toward the highway. Sitting back in his seat, Jason just stared at nothing.

"You okay?" Creel asked, handing Jason a pouch.

Jason nodded. "It's game time." Jason went through the pouch, making sure that his will, military ID, passport, checkbook, credit cards, orders, and the like were in order. Satisfied, he locked it and spun the combination tumblers, then handed it back to Creel. Sanitized, he was no longer Jason Johnson. He was now Alex Gomez. He would get the pouch back once the mission was over.

They got to the airport and Creel kept feeding Jason information that only made him wonder why he accepted the mission in the first place.

There was no rescue plan. He wasn't covered by any force protection or Geneva Convention rules. The only out he had was that there were a few code words he could pass on to identify himself if he was on the run and picked up by allied troops, providing they had SATCOM capability.

"And don't make contact with any Westerners before you do the opium deal. Good luck, *Alice*. What I know about you came from General Cadallo. From what I've learned, you are some kind of operator." Creel shook Jason's hand with almost a starstruck look about him.

"Oh, I'm *some kind* all right. The stupid kind," Jason muttered, walking into the terminal.

He checked in with Ariana Airlines. The ticket agent acted very discreet after he brought up the name of Alex Gomez on his screen, telling him that there would be no boarding announcement. "Keep an eye on the gate. The sign to board will be when the door is opened. When it closes, the plane leaves. Please do not wait around the door until it is open."

Jason walked around wearing sunglasses, trying to avoid any attention, keeping an eye on the boarding door. The King Fhad International Airport was new, and world-class. Looking more like a mosque, it was full of incredibly huge Islamic works of art. Giant geometric mosaics blended into huge waves of colored glass. Gold domes gave an almost sacred ground effect. No expense had been spared on the architectural wonder.

But it was just a modern Islamic airport, a gateway for Jason to enter into an ancient Islamic land of war.

From a giant picture window he watched the military action across the tarmac with interest. C-5s, C-130s, and other military transports disgorged hundreds of American soldiers and military equipment. To anyone else watching it was obvious that they were staging for a probable move to the same areas that he was headed to. A pang of guilt rumbled in his stomach. He should be with his boys doing his PJ job, something that he understood and was good at, instead of trying to play the part of a sleazy doper. But he'd committed to the operation, wherever it led.

The Ariana door opened and several people headed for it.

In less than fifteen minutes he was on board the blue-and-white Boeing 727. He took an aisle seat. The window seat had a huge box on it. The flight carried only a handful of passengers, mostly European men dressed like journalists: khaki pants, safari jackets with lots of big pockets, and some sort of shirt—same as him. Nobody talked. The rest of the seats, aisles, and anywhere else were full of boxes and bags. Unmistakable ammo and explosive boxes took up a lot of space. At that moment Jason no longer worried about anything bad happening on the flight because he knew that he'd be blown to smithereens in seconds if it did.

This was an unpublished flight, one of several in the coming days. Only those with the right connections knew of these flights. It took connections, power, or money, to get aboard the Ariana jet.

Jason carried press credentials of the *San Diego Union Tribune*. Any call or e-mail to the newspaper coming from the Middle East or central Asia would automatically be routed through to the Party in Florida.

It was a rough ride in bad weather, and three eternal hours before the plane began descending. Jason felt his stomach rise, not from lost altitude, but from the butterflies that hatched in his gut.

It was Wednesday, and the sun was about to rise. Kabul, Afghanistan's capital, could barely be seen, as it was enveloped in a thick, brown fog.

Once again Jason was stumbling into something he had no control over, or any real idea what to do, hoping that luck and ingenuity would carry him through. "Damn you, Ben Cadallo, if I get killed on this thing I'm gonna haunt your soul forever," he swore.

The Ariana jet touched down at the Kabul International Airport right at dawn.

The moment the cabin door opened Jason knew that he was in a failed country. It smelled like burning shit. The smell wafted through the cabin. And it was thick, too.

Turbaned and bearded men with AK-47s came running aboard yelling and waving their rifles to help motivate everyone off the plane. It worked great.

Their baggage was thrown off to one side as a fuel truck hooked up to the jet. At the same time the plane was rushed by a mob. More screaming and yelling, it was insanity. Jason wondered if the fall of Saigon was something like what he was witnessing. A stranger thing yet, it was only men who were trying to get out. Where were their women and children?

Grabbing his bag, he followed the other journalists to the Customs and Immigration gate. Everywhere everything was shot up, especially the bombed carcasses of Soviet jets and choppers. Walking past one of the forever-grounded aeronautical skeletons, he saw something that wasn't right: Men appeared to be working on it. Then it hit him. "There's guys booby-trapping the wrecked planes."

"Roger," Ben said. "We got you overhead. We're passing the info to our war-planning liaison, now. What's the code to the money?"

Jason was relieved to know that the Kissiah transceiver was working. "I ain't telling you."

"What?" Ben screamed.

"That's right. If anything happens to me you'll never know what happened to the cash. So don't let anything happen to me, pal."

"This isn't part of the deal!" Ben fumed. "You can't do it that way."

"Can't I? I'm doin' this just like the way you conned me into this fuckin' mess. Well, this is part of *my* deal, and insurance. I better not just have words backing me up. You better be ready to spring me if the shit goes bad, sir. Now shut up while I clear customs."

All the windows of the buildings at the airport were blown out and some windows were covered in black plastic or cardboard.

Clearing customs was a joke. It was one table with two men standing at it. They stamped passports for five, American one-hundred-dollar bills. That was the going rate for entry. Not twenty-five twenties, but five Benjamins—they made smaller stacks. Too quick to grab the greenbacks, they didn't even glance at the ones Jason gave them.

He then wordlessly followed everyone onto an ancient bus held together by wires and prayer. It was cold and dreary leaving the airport, but the roads were already packed with locals not wanting to be caught on the ground when the bombs started falling—Taliban rules were over.

The ride was slow, bumpy, freezing, and dusty; then, for a few minutes after sunup everything turned purple and the area was breathtaking. For a very short period it looked like the southwestern desert of Nevada. Jason got a tug on his heart. Nevada was free, and it didn't have carcasses of Soviet tanks, dead goats, and rusting hulks cluttering up the scenery, and mines, lots of buried mines.

When they reached Kabul he understood the fog—it was dust churned up by chaos. All the movement stirred up layers of dust that covered everything.

Jason knew war zones well. A lot of killing could quickly happen. This time he was unarmed and *nervous*. The only weapon he had going for him was his wits, plus a building full of people—thousands of miles away.

The city of Kabul—it barely passed the definition— was a city in panic. Most of the colorless, run-down buildings were boarded-up, or empty, bombed-out shells. Knowing that a very large target had been placed on the city on September 12, the normally calm Afghan citizens were looking for a way out, a quick exit.

The streets were swarming with people in Russian cars, small trucks, Japanese motorcycles, donkeys and horses pulling carts, and bicycles. All were piled high with all sorts of things. They were getting the hell out of Dodge.

The bus pulled up in front of the Ministry of Foreign Affairs. It was one of the few buildings with minimal damage. The rest of the buildings were either half-standing, or total rubble—there were blocks and blocks of ruins.

They were led into a big empty room with a blown-out picture window. The only decorations adorning the walls were hundreds of bullet holes.

"Passports! Passports!" a black-turbaned man yelled as he came out from behind a wooden door. He collected all the passports, then said, "I am Aziz. You wait here. I call."

The moment the man was out of sight, moneychangers assailed all the passengers, trying to trade huge stacks of Afghan currency for American dollars.

"You're a fool if you change it," one journalist called out. "It's counterfeit. All of it."

Everyone nodded as if they already knew.

Jason watched as one by one, Aziz called everyone, handed them back their stamped passports, and directed them to get back on the bus with their in-country identity cards, except him.

"Gomez!"

Jason jumped out of his chair and followed Aziz.

Through a side door, and he was pushed out of the building and into a side alley.

Aziz tossed Jason his bag, then called a boy over and whispered in his ear, pressing some cash into his hand. Frowning at Jason, Aziz said, "You not stay here. You follow boy." He slammed the door shut.

"Hey, dude, give me back my damned passport!" He banged on the steel door. Nothing.

Jason didn't like it one bit. "Where am I?" A panic rose in his stomach.

"You are headed east on International Road," the Party said.

"Where?" He was relieved that the transmitter was on-line and working, but he still felt lost. Looking up he saw nothing but gray sky. They might be able to see him but were helpless to come to his aid.

"Stop," the transceiver buzzed. "You are not where you're supposed to be."

"What? Who's talking? Where am I supposed to be? Where? Where in the hell am I?" A map sure would've helped.

The boy motioned with his head to follow. He looked to be about twelve years old or so. He had a pretty face, but his eyes were cold and hard.

Jason could do nothing but follow the boy.

The moment he entered the street, children mobbed him as Ibrahim translated their words into his transceiver.

"No mama. No papa."

"Money. Give me money."

"Matches! Cigarettes! Gimme smoke!"

"Back away, fuckers," the boy said.

They ignored him and kept assailing Jason with their tiny hands and pleas for help.

They backed away when the boy pulled out the biggest handgun Jason had ever seen.

He pointed it at the biggest kid and cocked the trigger. The look in the kid's eyes read true that he would kill anyone who faced him.

Jason saw that the children had weapons, too. They were not toys. This was not a children's game they played. The boy's gun was steady. He would shoot without blinking.

"First one who touches him again gets it. Go away," he said.

In moments they were alone.

Jason was speechless. It would take generations of peace before these people got the stone-cold killer out of them.

The boy tucked the gun away, motioned with his head again, and was off at a trot.

On the streets, weaponless, Jason had never felt so naked and vulnerable as running after the kid.

Through countless alleyways and across bombed-out lots he followed the boy.

The high altitude and lousy air quality had him wheezing in no time. "Hey, kid," he gasped. "Slow down." Then the kid was gone.

The Party desperately called out where he was going, but they could only stare at the overhead imagery of a maze of collapsed buildings. No one had any idea of what was going on.

Jason moved around bomb craters that were all over the place; the voices in his ear were driving him crazy. "Hey, kid, come back here! Where are you?" he yelled. He was alone in a sea of panicked city dwellers.

That's when the whistling began. Unsure at first, he began to follow the sounds and soon had no idea where he was, or what was what, even though the Party continually pinpointed him in the middle of chaos. The whistles eerily bounced among the ruined buildings and bomb craters.

"Come on, guys, where am I headed? I have no idea what's going on. You guys are totally useless! What the hell should I do?"

No one could answer him. With all the combined talents, no one had a clue what was happening. The boy reappeared, then smiled, turned, and ran. Jason raced after him.

"Override!" the voice of Ibrahim cried out in Jason's

transceiver. "Alex, turn around. Run. Get out of there, fast! The boy has led you to, to, look! It's the Taliban headquarters at the Pol-e-Charkhi Prison!"

"Oooh, fuck me," Jason spit, frantically looking around for a way out of his situation.

They came running at him from everywhere he looked, guns pointing at him from every direction. Jason ran toward the only empty street.

Sprinting, a pack of stray dogs came out of nowhere. Howling and barking, they snapped and nipped at his heels. He didn't think that he could run any faster, but he did.

Something hit him. He pitched forward and rolled onto his back. It felt like a wasp had stung him. Looking at his left shoulder, blood was pouring down his arm. *Shit!* He had been shot, but was too hyper to know how bad it was.

All he could do was put his hands over his head and curl into a ball as the dogs tried to tear into him.

The dogs yipped, howled, and scattered as a crowd of men kicked and beat them away, then the men pounced on Jason from all sides. Someone threw a bag over his head and he was flung to the ground. He heard a ripping sound, then felt something being wrapped around his feet. Fighting to look down at his feet, he saw that it was tape, strong duct tape. His hands were taped behind his back. The hood was tied shut and he was picked up and roughly dragged through the streets.

"Jason, we've lost electronic track of you. A crowd of people is going through the front gates of the prison. Are you their prisoner?" Ben asked.

CHAPTER 14

1030 WEDNESDAY / 26 SEPTEMBER 2001
POL-E-CHARKHI PRISON / KABUL / AFGHANISTAN

Osama bin Laden calls on all Muslims to kill Americans all over the world. Kabul citizens riot in the street against America.

THEY DRAGGED JASON INTO THE PRISON AND threw him roughly to the floor. A rag was crudely taped on his wounded shoulder. He had to hope that it wasn't a serious wound and that the bleeding would soon stop.

His tape bonds weren't giving, so, moving to a sitting position, he tried to get as comfortable as possible. He couldn't see a thing through the hood. Screaming and yelling filled his ears. He felt a claustrophobic panic rise in his throat.

He heard a door opening and boots stomping. He was yanked to his feet.

"Who are you?"

"Alex. Alex Gomez. I'm an American journalist."

"Lie!"

Jason saw stars from a vicious slap.

"Who are you?"

"Alex Gomez." Tears of pain stung his cheeks.

"Lie!"

The crushing kick to his stomach put him on his knees. He fell over into a fetal position.

"Don't tell them anything!" the transceiver buzzed.

Kicks and fists rained down on him. He tried to protect his shoulder and genitals the best he could.

"Your name!"

"Puddin' Tain, ask me again and I'll tell ya the same." He grimaced.

"Who?"

"Fuck you."

There was silence in the room, then someone spoke, and Ibrahim quickly translated the cold words.

"He is mine. I fuck him first."

"Oh, no you're not! You guys can forget it." It wasn't happening. Nohow. No way.

There was no stopping all the hands on him. He was lifted and then bent over something. The tape on his legs was cut, his pants were ripped down to his ankles, and then his feet were spread. For the first time since he'd accepted the mission, a familiar foe jumped on his back—panic. On his own, no one from the Party was coming to his aid.

"You sons of a bitch motherfuckers. Touch me and I'll kill you! I'm not playin' around here. DON'T YOU BAS-TARDS TOUCH ME!"

"Shut him up!" someone in the Party translated.

The hood was ripped off his head, and for that instant, Jason got a snapshot of hell. He was in a torture chamber. Blood was everywhere. Pieces of bodies and bones were on tables. Dead bodies were hung on hooks. Dark red blood dripped everywhere.

A rag was stuffed in his mouth and the hood was pulled back on. The room became quiet. He could hear

insane screams coming from other rooms. His body
jerked when gunshots rang out.

The men laughed, and then became quiet as Jason felt
rough hands spread his butt cheeks.

His eyes flew wide open. The gag muffled his scream
as something pierced his anus.

The room erupted in laughter.

"If my finger makes him squeal so, just wait until he
gets the real poker."

The room erupted in laughter again.

"Go, call everyone to come and take their turns on
this infidel."

The room became quiet again.

Hands pinched his butt. He could hear heavy, uneven
breathing behind him. Hands pried apart his cheeks. He
wanted to cry in shame.

Do something! Jason spit out the gag. "Gul Nazari!
Gul Nazari!"

There was movement, as something was happening in
the room.

"How did he know the name?"

"Maybe we should call him."

Whoever spoke was agitated. "Mustafa, go call him.
Strip the infidel naked! An infidel will never meet the
Ismali clothed."

The clothes were cut from him, boots yanked off and
jewelry taken.

"Rashad! Look!"

Jason could only hear silence. Yanked to a sitting position, the hood came off and he was staring, face-to-
face, at a gorilla holding his miniature Qur'an.

Uh-oh.

"Where you get this?"

Jason kept silent.

Someone leaned over and whispered to Rashad, just
loud enough for his words to be translated. "You cannot
keep it, Rashad. Too many have seen. The Ismali will kill

us, our friends, and all our family, if he finds out we did not turn the book over to him."

Rashad stared hard at Jason, but did not hit him.

He was doing well, so far. Jason did his best to keep his mouth shut and not smart off or make a stupid face. All that he wanted to do was avoid being the center of attention in a gang rape.

The hood was tossed back over his head and he was pushed back down to the cold floor. But the hood was loose this time and he could see a few feet past his feet.

"Jason, what's happening?" Ben asked.

Jason worked out the gag back out, but wouldn't speak. There was nothing that anyone could do for him. He couldn't believe that something like this could be happening.

"Here he comes," someone warned.

Jason heard a commotion as feet rushed to get away from whoever entered the room.

Through all the screaming and sounds of torture, he could clearly hear the sound of taps. The sound became a sight when he saw a pair of polished black riding boots circle him, then stop in front of him.

"What is your name?"

Jason was surprised to hear someone speaking English. "I said it already, Alex Gomez. I'm a recognized journalist. There has to be some sort of mistake. Let me go and give me back my clothes, jewelry, and money, please," he replied, trying to give off an air of dignity in his precarious situation.

"The money pays for your *visit* here. Now tell me the truth, or I will leave you for Rashad and all his men to continue with their buggery. Who are you, and why are you here?"

"To buy opium."

"From whom?"

"Gul Nazari. Are you he?"

"*I* will ask the questions."

There were so many people talking at once on the transceiver that nothing clear came through.

"Everyone shut up!" Ben ordered.

"Sorry, you asked for the truth," Jason said. At least no one had cut his throat for asking, so things were cool, for the moment. He saw a pair of sandals stand next to the boots.

"What is it, Rashad?"

The boots gasped. "Where did you get this?"

The sandals faced Jason. "Him."

Jason saw the boots disappear and heard the taps circle him. They stopped at his back. He felt fingers tracing over scars on his back. Some were pretty deep. He winced, remembering the crazed methamphetamine addict who had put them there. The boots reappeared back in front of him. "You are not Alex Gomez. You are someone's slave. It has been brought to my attention that you have come here with something very, very valuable. Who sent you?"

Jason froze, waiting for someone at the Party to say something. *Say something, somebody. Anything!* "Well, I was wrong to think that this would be an easy deal to do, but I think things have gotten a little more complicated. I am a messenger. Is there someplace we can talk, privately?" He braced for a strike.

"What is your name, messenger?"

"I cannot say it but to Gul Nazari."

The hood was ripped off his head. Someone grabbed his hair and pulled him face-to-face with angry eyes, fierce and penetrating. They searched Jason's eyes, looking for secrets, answers, or any hidden weakness.

"Well, messenger, if you survive the journey, we shall speak again." He turned around. "Tape him and bring him." Taps faded into the screams and howls of the prison.

Once again he was tossed around, then held on the ground. He felt duct tape being stuck on him. In just a few minutes he was wrapped up just like a mummy, unable to move an inch.

Someone held his nose closed as a nasty-tasting liquid was poured down his throat. The world began to spin.

The Party kept up a line of useless dialogue. "Jason, Jason, what's happening?"

"Mmmmffff!" he choked. He was trying to say "motherfuckers."

Jason's head was taped, leaving just a slit to breathe through and a hole to eat through.

He felt himself thrown onto something hard, and felt movement. He was in some sort of car, or truck. "Mmmffshhhbbb!"

"Jason, a truck is moving. Are you in it? We're losing visual contact with you. We've lost you. Are you all right?"

Jason was as pissed off as he ever could remember. How could he ever think that some stupid bug in his ear could protect and guide him in a hostile environment? The tape across his mouth was ripped away.

"No! I'm not all right. I think I'm in some sort of land vehicle," he angrily gasped. "You cut me free, or so help me God, I'm going to kill every last one of you motherfuckers!"

A stick was forced between his teeth, forcing his jaw open, and more of the bitter drink was poured down his throat. He had to swallow or he would gag. The world began to swim and grow dim. Someone was saying something.

"There! That should shut him up," Ibrahim translated.

"Jason, we're losing our visual contact. Can you hear? Give us some sort of sign."

"Yeah, lose me, General, and say good-bye to your big cash." They were the last words he said before it all went black.

CHAPTER 15

0430 WEDNESDAY / 26 SEPTEMBER 2001
THE PARTY / MELBOURNE / FLORIDA

Iran says it will not help America with their attacks on Afghanistan.

HE NEVER CRIED FOR HELP," IBRAHIM MUTTERED.
"What happened?" Bri asked. "We froze, everyone, including the general."

"Because of us, one of the good guys, with 300 million bucks, just got clipped," answered Gorsline. "We lost our man. If we lose the dope too I'm going on the warpath. And that's for *anybody's* record."

Don't sweat it, Ben wanted to say. Planning.

Suddenly all the visual feeds from the Global Hawk began to spin wildly, then the screens went blank.

Everyone could see the rock that was General Cadallo, but they couldn't see his hands under the control board as they clenched and unclenched. The pressure of the contractions could probably bend steel. This wasn't planned for.

"Hey, what's happened to the screens?" Gorsline asked. "Talk about your bad fucking day!"

0435 HOURS
PATRICK AIR FORCE BASE / FLORIDA

Lieutenant Colonel Eric Draper, the Hawk mission commander on duty at Patrick, asked the same question at the same time. "Just what in the fuck is going on here?" he asked the pilot.

"It looks like she's going into a flat spin. It won't fly straight." Working the joystick on his panel, he gave instinctive cockpit body English while he kicked his feet on imaginary rudders that weren't there. "Christ, I can't bring it out of its spin. I think something's wrong with the ailerons," the pilot said.

"Override and fly it," Draper ordered.

"Negative response. Shit. I'm losing it!"

"Confirm that it's out of control."

The pilot quickly ran his emergency checklist and agreed. "We can't let the gomers get their hands on it."

"Autodestruct," Draper commanded. He felt his body turn to ice. Not because he was losing a thirteen-million-dollar airframe, but for all the duties, functions, and missions it handled for the units about to fight the war in Afghanistan. He looked at the FLASH phone, praying that it wouldn't ring. Of course it did.

0436 HOURS
THE PARTY / MELBOURNE

Roars of confusion reigned as the all the screens went blank.

"People. Be cool!"

Everyone froze at Cadallo's command voice.

"Kill the local feeds," he said. "Then bring up all the live satellite feeds from the Combined Air Operations Center from Saudi Arabia. Now!" What was happening wasn't in anyone's script.

Ben picked up the phone and punched the button that connected to CENTCOM at Homestead Air Force Base, Florida. "Get me a Predator headed to Kabul," Ben ordered. "Where's the U-2?"

"On its usual course," came the answer.

"Divert its command to us. Send it over Kabul, NOW!"

Everyone froze for a moment. The general was pissed.

"Damn," Bri sighed. "We lost our man, our money, and now we lost our visual."

Gorsline slammed his palm on his desk and glared up at Cadallo. "This ain't like losing a petty bust. What's next?"

"We continue on with the mission, that's what's next. We find our man. We start an overhead imagery sector search of the whole fuckin' country, inch by inch. We'll direct any spec ops teams on the ground to be on the lookout for our man. Keep your eyes and ears open. Stay focused and find our man." Cadallo had to hope that Jason could cover for himself. He punched the room blocker on his control board.

The panels around Cadallo went black. He picked up the phone and punched a green button. It was time to squeeze some big balls, maybe even crush them.

0115 THURSDAY / 27 SEPTEMBER 2001
SOMEWHERE OVER CENTRAL AFGHANISTAN

War. This time it was real. Dar unconsciously ran his hands over his pistol belt and all the equipment attached to it. This was the first line that carried his 9mm Beretta, M9 bayonet, first-aid kit, and other items that could mean life or death if everything went to shit. He reminded himself that he could get rid of everything else if he had to, but *never* to drop the first line.

Dar Garo swore that if his knees could touch they'd be knocking. He could barely think with twin engines thundering overhead and the sounds of rotor blades slicing through the thin air.

He had missed all the previous wars. This would be his introduction to combat. He tried concentrating on the mission, but his heart raced just too damned fast. It wasn't just the fighting or dying that made him nervous—it was all of it. For the moment all he could do was hang on to the strap that held him to the chopper floor while the bird bounced all over the place as they raced through the sharp Afghan mountains.

The two MH-47E special operations helicopters cleared the mountain's ridge by only inches. Army Chief Warrant Officer Five Jay Goetz, the lead pilot, flew white-knuckled on night-vision goggles, listening to every input of the crew. If everything worked out, then just five miles ahead was a dropoff and a long, narrow valley.

"Landing environment should be in sight, three miles," said the copilot.

"Confirm," agreed the flight engineer. "And the ground radio squawks, identifies good."

Goetz said, "But that don't mean that the bad guys aren't around, close by, and drawing a bead on us. Let's get this over with."

The chaff and flares were armed, ready to automatically dispense flaming decoys or aluminum streamers at the first sign of a missile attack. The gunners were steady, ready to open up on anything hostile with their M-60-D automatic machine guns.

Everything fell away as they entered a river valley.

Dar was about numb. *Holy shit! I can't believe we're here.*

They were over a long valley—and very exposed if the Taliban used night vision.

Everyone surged forward as the pilot quickly bled off the forward speed and slowed to a hover. In moments they were on the ground and the ramp lowered. The engineer motioned for Dar to move—they didn't want to be on the ground and exposed for one second longer than they had to be.

The second bird circled, ready to fire on any hostile receptions.

Dar released his safety belt and ran off the ramp as the flight engineer rolled off a thousand-pound supply pallet and unceremoniously tossed out his gear.

"Hey, asshole, that crap costs a lot of money," Dar yelled, but he couldn't be heard over the noise of the chopper rotor blades spooling up.

Goetz waved good-bye to Dar and pulled up on his collective.

Dar couldn't see well in the dark, even less when a whirlwind of dust enveloped him as the Chinook lifted off. In seconds the big choppers were gone. It felt like the last link to home, warmth, and safety had just deserted him.

It was quiet as he unpacked his night-vision. Only the rustle of the frozen wind whipping through his gear could be heard. No one at Home Plate could tell him exactly which spec ops team he was hooking up with, or anything about them. The request through secure channels seemed legitimate; if it wasn't, then the enemy had cracked a billion-dollar code. Dar would soon find out, one way or another. He chambered a round in his M-4 rifle.

Turning on his night vision, he scanned the area. "Looks like Iceland on a bad day," he said to himself. Desolate snowcapped ridges lined up to infinity. Down the valley, frozen plateaus dropped off into bottomless ravines. "No. It looks more like the moon," he corrected.

The cold wind unmercifully pummeled him. Bad-guy country.

It would be his home for the coming months. Letting his NVGs hang from his neck, he opened his pack and donned his warmest overgarments. Suddenly a beam of light reached out and almost blinded him.

"Don't move," a voice from the night commanded in English.

Dar froze. He heard the sound of hooves, then he smelled the horseflesh, and something else: human sweat from unwashed bodies.

He stood still as silhouettes of mounted men surrounded him. It reminded him of the wraith riders from the *Lord of the Rings*. There was no doubt in his mind that he was facing a lot of guns and that he was in the sight of someone's weapon.

Code words were exchanged before the bright light in his face was turned off.

"It's the Air Force guy we're looking for and, thank God, food and supplies!" a voice cried out.

Shadows dismounted and attacked the pallet like ants until nothing lay on the ground.

With little ceremony, someone motioned for a horse to be brought. Reins were put into Dar's hands and everyone started riding away.

"Well, Air Force, load your shit on the horse and let's get moving."

Dar could only do the best that he could, seeing how he had never been near a horse in his life. There was no way he could balance his 170 pounds of gear and ride a horse at the same time. After forever, and looking like the tenderfoot that he was, he finally climbed onto the horse, precariously balancing his heavy pack on his back. He had no idea what was next, until he found himself flat on his back, wiggling like an overturned turtle. Laughter surrounded him. It seemed as if the horse had intentionally dumped him.

"Air Force, you're *supposed* to hold on," someone said. "Haven't you seen how they do it in the Western movies? Do like they do, cowboy."

He said nothing and struggled back onto the animal. His ego was bruised more than his ass. Whatever he was expecting, this wasn't it. He hung on to the reins and did his best to match the horse's gait. *Be adaptable.*

There was nothing to see in the dark, following the horse's ass in front of him, so Dar just tried to stay focused and on the animal. Everything bounced and was out of balance. He cradled the radio, his most valuable piece of equipment, in one hand, while putting a death grip on the horse's mane. If they had very far to go there was no way he'd survive the ungodly ride. He mentally composed a short letter to his wife.

> *Dear Rita,*
>   *I've landed on a COLD moon and the moon*
> *people here are assholes!*
>
> > *Love,*
> > *Dar*

The horse he rode seemed to be in a bad temper. Dar was surprised the first time it turned its head around and nipped his knee. He let it pass the second time, but he was ready on the third, and he timed it, smacking the horse with his fist before it could bite him again. "Look, sucker, *you're* the locomotive and *I'm* the engineer. Got that? I might not be a cowboy yet, but I'll have you for lunch if you try to bite me again." The animal seemed to get the message and there were no more bites.

Soon they arrived at a camp surrounded by mud walls. Dar's ass ached from the rough ride. The Afghan men started fires and turned on electric lights using a belt around a jacked-up truck's turning tire that kept an ancient generator moving.

They all tied up their horses, set out feed, and busied

themselves with grabbing their gear and heading off to sleep. Dar just mimicked what everyone else did, making sure to stay away from the horse's rear when it tried to kick him, then peed on his boots. There was no doubt in Dar's mind that the nag was an al Qa'eda plant.

"I can see that we're not going to be the best of friends." Dar didn't like the looks of the animal. With a swaybacked mangy hide, and nasty teeth, Dar understood the "why?" of the animal's bad nature—he'd be miserable too if he looked like that.

No one had said anything to Dar, so he just followed everyone's lead. He could hear explosions in the distance that sounded like thunder, or was it thunder? "Taliban?" Dar asked an Afghan.

A wide, bad-toothed grin broke out on the man. "No Taliban here. They all go to the caves."

Dar was a little surprised to find that a few Afghan fighters spoke some English.

"Welcome to Afghanistan," one said.

"Are you an American, brother?" someone else asked.

Nodding, after all the briefings he still had no idea what to expect of these people. He had landed in another world that was *way* in the past.

"You trade boots?"

Dar smiled and shook his head.

The fighters were clearly amused and in wonder of all the gear.

"You have much," a man said to Dar. "We have little. Many families could live years on what you have." They all trudged away into the night.

The Islamic night prayers began. Dar had heard them many times on rotations in Turkey. Five times a day, things in the Middle East would stop and everyone would pray. Everyone. Here, the Taliban would kick the shit out of you and throw you in prison if you missed a session; they kept a list of offenders. They had a lot of bad habits that needed correction, which was one of the reasons Dar was glad he was there.

His vision had adjusted to the night and he could see men getting ready to sleep. The Afghans didn't bother posting sentries. In the cold night they just lay down on the ground and covered themselves with their *pattus,* a cloak that served many purposes—blanket, cloak, prayer mat, and burial shroud.

The spec ops guys camped and slept against a mud-brick wall in their sleeping bags. They each had fighting holes set up and ready to go. Perimeter guards stood alert, waiting for their turn to rotate into their own sleeping bags.

Filthy, smelly, and grubby, Dar was only too happy to crawl into his sleeping bag, but he still shivered in the dark. The night was clear and a million stars were out. It was hard to believe that a war raged on the land. It was always strange and a little scary the first nights in unfamiliar territory, no matter whose land it was. He wondered how Rita was doing, and ached to hold her in his arms. He patted the pocket that held his unborn child's sonogram and closed his eyes. Somehow it made him feel a little safer and spiritually closer to Rita.

The sound of a nearby explosion had Dar instantly scrambling out of his sleeping bag. He jumped to his feet, rifle pointing in every direction. He was stunned to find himself standing alone.

The sounds of laughter reverberated throughout the camp.

"It's happening over in the next valley, Air Force," someone said.

"Maybe you should try sleeping standing up, like your nag."

More laughter. Even more laughter when the quip was translated.

"At least it's good to see you're ready, my guys might get dead," one voice said.

The laughter quickly stopped.

Dar just lowered his weapon and crawled back into his sleeping bag. His first night in the war hadn't gone well. He just hoped that the next days would go better.

CHAPTER 16

SOMEWHERE IN THE AFGHANISTAN MOUNTAINS

JASON WASN'T SURE IF HIS EYES WERE OPEN OR not. He reasoned that there must've been some sort of material covering his face. He ached everywhere. *Where am I?* Everything had blanked out after all the thugs jumped him.

His head still swam. He vaguely remembered being tossed around, and hearing engine noises. He'd remained in a dreamlike state, in and out of consciousness. "Can anyone hear me?" he tried to say. "Mmmmmm" was all he could vocalize.

How much time had passed? There was no way of telling.

There was no response in his ear. Maybe he was out of hearing range for the Global Hawk, or possibly his hearing device was out. The only thing that mattered then was getting himself out of his predicament, but how?

The more he regained his consciousness, the more he regretted it. He had been out *cold*. Fully alert now, he realized his body was very numb. Taped like a mummy, he couldn't move. Panic surged through his body. *Maybe I'm paralyzed!* Try as he might, he couldn't move an inch of his body. There was no way he was going to bust loose from the tape that bound him like a mummy.

It was worse than any straitjacket, and he'd pay millions to be free.

He tried to reason out what was going on. The only consolation he could take was the fact that he was still alive. But the longer he was a mummy, the better chance was that he might suffocate if they left him in the wrong position.

Relax! Maybe somebody was watching.

What was going on? This was no way to treat an opium buyer, especially one with big-time American cash. What went wrong, had Falcon betrayed him?

There were scraping sounds.

Don't move. Be Novocain, his inner voice cautioned.

Suddenly the tape across his mouth was ripped away.

Jason might've been trembling with fear but he was too numb to feel it.

A soft finger ran across his lips. Then a fingernail softly scraped away the crust buildup around his lips. He could smell flowers. They were sweet. What kind of flowers were they?

A straw was gently placed between his lips. God above, the water was cold and pure! He sucked in the water with every part of his being. The straw was pulled away and something sweet-smelling was put under his nose. Jason slowly opened his mouth.

He didn't know what time it was, or day for that matter, all he knew was that he was starving. Nothing ever tasted as good as whatever it was he chewed on. Was it dates? He didn't care. He kept on eating as long as the dates kept coming. Then it stopped. What next?

Nothing happened, and then tender lips began to kiss him, a tongue slowly tried to part his lips. He tried wrenching his head away, but it was held fast. He pressed his lips together, but the lips were soft and sensual, passionate and hot. For a moment the lips made him forget the bind that he was in.

A horrible thought struck him. *What if this is a guy? Oh no, I'm gonna be some dude's sex slave for life!*

The lips were gone and Jason wondered what was coming next.

Things started getting woozy again. The dates he ate must have been spiked. Damn, drugged again!

A soft and very feminine voice whispered precisely clipped English in his ear. "Treachery and illusion. Secrecy is permissible for one who serves against the Evil One."

The lights in his mind dimmed, then went out.

0600 FRIDAY / 28 SEPTEMBER 2001
HINDU KUSH MOUNTAINS / AFGHANISTAN

The morning came gray and cold, and Dar saw figures warming themselves around a fire built in a small bomb crater. He pulled himself out of his sleeping bag, grateful for the Polartec underclothing that left him just stiff, rather than frozen.

The first thing he did was turn on and set up his combat radio to the frequencies and codes he would be using. Everybody was there, ready to work. Radio checks good, he put everything into standby. "Just give me targets," he said to his surroundings.

The rover would stay packed until he understood his surroundings.

Then, after Dar took care of the calls of nature, it was time to reconnoiter his surroundings.

Scrawny dogs roamed around the camp sniffing and barking, looking for scraps of food. The camp had only men. He was probably in a frontline stronghold near the forming battle lines. In one of the mud huts he saw a woman covered in a yellow burqa tending a cooking fire. At least he assumed it was a woman. Intel briefed that the enemy might use burqas as a cover for escape or assassination. From time to time he heard the sounds of gunfire and artillery in the distance. No one seemed to take notice, so he didn't get too excited.

Buckets of water for washing the extremities had been set out, so he washed himself and brushed his teeth, doing his best not to swallow the water, and dried himself with a rag. It was still colder than hell. The blowing dirt already had him grimy before he even got his clothes back on. Stoicism, that was part of the price it cost to be there, but nothing could uplift his spirit from the painful ride the night before.

"Damn horse," he muttered.

He found a spot between two Afghans and started massaging his butt and legs, surreptitiously observing the men around him. They grinned at Dar and whispered. The first thing that Dar noticed was that the spec ops guys looked very young, while the muhajadeen fighters looked old—they all had hollow eyes and a haunted look.

The spec ops guys still had beards to fill in. Their faces were soft and white. They weren't outfitted in the Department of Defense general-issue battle dress uniforms (BDU). Dar figured that they probably bought their gear out of a *Brigade Quartermaster* magazine. They wore slick desert camos, custom-fit Kevlar helmets, tan body padding, and lightweight bulletproof vests— they had the latest in combat fashion. But they had all sorts of weapons, including AK-47s. He even saw one of the operators carrying a gangster-looking Thompson submachine. It was beautiful.

Dar wore standard gear that was Air Force issue, including his M-4 rifle. It was adequate. Functional. As long as he had his big radio with him they could fire their popguns while he dropped pure hell from above.

The one thing that they all had in common was a gas mask. Dar could only pray that Osama bin Laden and his ilk didn't have, or wouldn't use, chemical weapons. The Afghans carried no chemical-warfare protection.

The Afghans wore a mishmash of dirty uniforms, rags, and regional clothing. On their feet they wore anything from boots to flip-flops. They all carried AK-47s. Some had rocket-propelled grenades or bazookas. They seemed friendly enough, easy to laugh.

"You want kill Taliban?" one fighter asked, then pointed at the man next to him.

The man pointed back. "Him al Qa'eda."

That brought the first chuckles of the morning as they sauntered off to their morning prayers.

Dar was getting tired of being the butt of everyone's humor.

"You want some chow?"

It was the voice that had shut everyone up the night before. Dar turned around to see an American man in tan desert fatigues. No rank was on the uniform. The man smiled and held out a meal ready to eat (MRE).

Finally, a friendly face. "Sure. My name's Dar Garo." He looked at the label. "Ham." His breath was all frost.

The man grinned. "Yeah. It's my way of rebelling. No booze. No women. But where you gonna find any of that shit around here?" He held out his hand. "Vance." ·

"You the team sergeant?"

"We're not Army."

"SEALs?"

"We're not them, either." Vance smiled like the Cheshire cat. "Just consider us something like an intelligence special-activities division. Think of us as more of a cloak-and-dagger outfit. But we're not the bow-tie guys from downtown, we're sheep-dipped graduates of Knuckle Dragger U. I'm the translator here. I speak Dari, Pashtun, Tajik, Farsi, and I understand some of the other dialects."

Dar nodded and smiled with understanding; he was

with the No Name Guys. There were special operations units, and then there were *special,* special operations groups. *Go figure.*

"You got any combat experience?"

"Not yet." Dar shook his head.

"Trust me, you're gonna get some. I did Panama and the Gulf War. I did all right. So will you. It's the first time in combat for most of my guys, too. We'll all do fine. I'm here to make sure that we do. And don't let my guys get to you. It always takes a little time for them to warm up to newcomers. They're still a little sore; our asses ain't adjusted to these damn woolen saddles yet either.

"Rene is our team leader. He's one bad Puerto Rican, former Delta, but you'll get used to him and his Army ways."

There was an aura about Vance that Dar liked. Full blond beard and long hair, he looked like a Viking, or one mean biker, but he had a comforting and secure attitude, for a spook.

Vance went on to explain that they were at base camp. The six-man team had been in-country for a little more than two weeks. They had come with cash. Millions. Their first assignment was to meet, then buy off, all the warlords in their area of responsibility. Their orders were to shadow, locate, and map as many enemy locations as they could, then relay back the intelligence and targeting information. Their mission was to prepare the area of responsibility for later direct actions.

He pointed out the six members of the team and their specialties: weapons, engineering, intelligence, communications, and field medicine. "We all fight as one tight fucking unit. But our job here is to get these Barneys to pull the trigger when the time comes, not us. You're here because we're about to get the green light to engage." He pointed to the overcast sky, looking pissed. "But we haven't been cleared to authenticate with *them,* the Zoomies, for air strikes. That's why we called in a request for a combat controller. You, Mr. Air Force."

Vance told him that their Afghan guides and shooters hadn't been too reliable, and that the rest of the hundred-man unit was treating it like a holiday. "To them, the al Qa'eda and us are the foreigners. Right now I'm not sure if they care who lives or dies.

"There are a lot of rivalries going on around here, turf battles that we can't sniff out until it's too late. They have this very nasty habit of mutilating their rivals, cutting off their heads and such. We're trying to break them of that and other bad habits. But you know; some clans are better than others. Unfortunately, we lucked into the Barney Fife clan. Their leader is named Ubu. They're really not so bad. When they have to be, they're great fighters, but they're all spirit and no tactics. It's part of our tasking to teach them battle logic. They'll get better—or die."

Vance concluded Dar's in brief. "So that's our work. Oh, we also have to be flexible for any priority tasking that hooks us. It's the ol' 'expect the unexpected, stay flexible' routine, but now it's war. Last item, but very essential. If we spot ol' Osama, or any of his lieutenants, we take them, dead or alive."

"Got it. Thanks for the MRE. I'm gonna go and get my gear together." The sun was up and Dar could clearly see the area. They were near a road bend just beneath yet another mountain pass. The Barneys controlled a checkpoint at the pass.

He pulled out his laser range-finding and targeting binoculars, and scanned the area. Dar could see trucks full of men coming and going. Most groups of men flew colored flags, identifying them as one group or another. Men drove camels, little donkeys, horses, and carts laden with everything. He spotted one cart that included a sink of some sort.

There was no describing the kinds of bizarre vehicles he looked at. Through the binoculars, the whole scene looked like Lawrence of Arabia meets Mad Max.

Vance's horse was close to Dar's own, which the

Afghans called Iblis. It looked as if Vance's horse actually smiled at him, then nodded. It was almost as if it was ridiculing him and laughing at him for having Iblis as his mount.

Dar got near Iblis to tie his gear to the saddle. "I swear to God, horse, you mess with me and I'll shoot you."

Vance came to his horse.

"Can I have another horse?"

"It's all they got, until someone here gets killed."

"I hate this horse."

Vance laughed out loud. "So does everyone else, but he was the only one available." He knew a little about horses and explained basic horsemanship, then showed Dar how to saddle and bridle a horse. Mounting and dismounting, Vance demonstrated the fundamental skills of controlling his horse.

Of course he used his own mount to instruct Dar. The moment Dar tried the same techniques on Iblis it all went to hell, leaving everyone but Dar bent over in fits of laughter. Dar swore that Iblis was not a horse, but a demon.

Eventually Dar was able to maneuver the animal enough for the rest of the group to prepare to move out from camp.

Vance gave Dar his last instructions. "When we're riding, try to ride in the same trail as the horse in front of you, the same goes for when you're on foot. Follow close, but not *too* close—mines."

Dar had all his gear ready, grateful that he didn't have to shoulder much of the stuff himself. All he had to carry on him was his first-line gear, and the radio in a backpack. The frequencies for radio calls that he would make through his two-way earpiece would be typed on a cigarette-pack-sized keypad in his BDU pocket. He was ready to ride. "What's up with all the flags that they fly?"

"We're still learning. These guys look so much alike, even to each other, that they use flags to distinguish themselves.

"Mostly, you'll see variations of the red, black, and green flags," Vance pointed out. "They're a variation of Afghan's national flag; they belong to the Northern Alliance. And then there's all sorts of other colors that belong to this tribe, or that, or some warlord. But, we're looking for the white-and-green flags, them there's the Taliban and al Qa'eda. We track them, or the ones our guides point out, and relay their position back to our people."

"I see." Dar pulled out his map and GPS and located his position.

He tried to picture in his mind just how the scene before him compared to the diorama back at the launch base. Yeah, the model was good, but damn, the rises and angles of the snowcapped mountains looked incredibly tough, fun only if you were a mountain goat.

Rene, the team leader, waited until his radio operator received a SATCOM Situation Message, then rallied the team together. He said that the Mission Order was to continue shadowing, identifying, tracking, and targeting the enemy and his hideouts. They were setting up kill boxes for arriving A-teams to engage on D-day.

"Just so you know, Air Force," Rene said, "I'm not interested in the statistics or sorties that the Zoomies fly. When it happens I only care about your ability to get the bombs on target. You do that and you're in the club. Can you do that?"

"That's what you called me here to do." Dar took a deep breath. It was time to go to work.

1620 HOURS
THE PARTY / MELBOURNE

No one spoke in the cafeteria. Their minds were wandering, lost in their own worlds. They had started out as an all-star championship team, unlimited resources, led by a real gladiator general, ready to take on the world—then froze and lost their ball. How'd it happen?

"I liked the guy. He didn't cave in," Gorsline said to Bri. He didn't care about anyone listening in. Cadallo may have been king, but that didn't mean anything to Gorsline when it came to a free opinion.

"You're right," Bri agreed. "I feel bad that we lost him because we didn't work together. We've been through everything about *us,* and forgot about *him* at game time. He's just disappeared."

Ibrahim nodded.

The three had naturally gravitated to one another.

"I'd just like to know who Gomez really was," Gorsline mused.

"*Is,*" Bri corrected.

Ibrahim frowned over his coffee at Mike and shook his head. Discovering the identity of their operator was digging *too* deep. The whole purpose of the Party was to maintain an effective operation through what was called Triple Cover: a complicated strategy that essentially boiled down to a "nobody knows anything" situation if the cover's blown.

"I know," Gorsline said, shrugging. "I'm just saying that the guy had balls. Hell, did you hear him bust the old man's chops about the cash!"

The three chuckled together.

"I'll say a prayer for him tonight," Bri said. "Let's hope that he's not hurting too bad, wherever he is."

Gorsline stared into his coffee. "Well, if we can't find our man, and soon, Cadallo's problems will soon become the DEA's problem no matter how secret he wants to keep this thing. There's tons of heroin out there that's threatening to make it here."

"How will the DEA know?" Ibrahim asked.

"Someone real close is going to tell them."

1700 HOURS
PATRICK AIR FORCE BASE / FLORIDA

Frantic and directive calls were made for help to the technicians at Global Hawk Production Plant 42 in Palmdale, California. Every blueprint and all flight data were inspected, then each of the three remaining Global Hawks was inspected nose to tail by technicians flown in from San Diego. The designers concluded that the most probable cause was "an improperly installed nut plate bolt, which placed undue stress on the flight control rod." The Hawk ground teams checked and changed all the control nut plates on their birds in record time and were cleared for flight.

CHAPTER 17

SOMEWHERE IN AFGHANISTAN

JASON LAY IN A HALF WORLD, TRYING TO BALANCE his sanity. He knew he was under some very heavy sedation. From time to time he was aware of being moved; otherwise, he was unaware of anything. But things weren't that bad under sedation. He actually began to understand some things about the junkie's world; he didn't give a fuck about anything.

The nightmares of his past came and went without him caring a thing for them until they vanished. He didn't care about who he was or where he came from. He didn't care about shit; it could go on forever, too. They could kill him for all he cared; he was unfeeling to anything and everything.

He felt himself being strapped to something moving, supple but pungent. A horse? He could barely breathe. He wanted to just stop breathing . . . .

Stop. Don't give up, his inner voice yelled. *Wait!* He couldn't just give up and die. Not like this. It all would have been worthless. Fight back. He had to do something, but what? *Think about it!*

But he couldn't quite get over to the conscious side of life. He was in the biggest fight of his life and was losing. He began to drift away again.

2000 SUNDAY / 30 SEPTEMBER 2001
BACTRIA / AFGHANISTAN

It'd been cool, at first, being in a medieval world, riding on the descendants of horses that could've come from the times of Alexander the Great, or Genghis Khan, but the novelty of being in the saddle quickly wore off. Dar's ass was numb. His legs ached from hanging on to a horse that seemed to take great pleasure in trying to pitch him off at every crevasse or gorge they crossed.

But at least he was getting the hang of it. He had no idea what kind of horse he was on except that it was male and beat-up and mean. Ilbis had a bad temper, and Dar was sure that at the first opportunity, it would try and toss him off in the middle of a minefield. As long as Iblis just followed the other horses things were cool. He trusted the animal like he would a snake.

As they rode, Vance and his Afghan guide gave Dar more rudimentary instructions on how to use the stirrups and reins to start, stop, and turn the animal. The friendlier Afghan fighters showed him how to keep his gear tied to the saddle.

The flat land was okay, even pretty at times, but the higher elevations were pure frozen hell. Dar understood Iblis's toughness after one particular high crossing. Mean as he was, the horse had a survivor's will to match it. They crossed over in waist-deep snow, with wind lashing everything. The horse never stopped once.

Now the horse was in flatland and more than kept up with the herd. They were riding hard. They couldn't stop. They were tracking prey.

The enemy was hightailing it to the mountain's caves,

not looking back to see if anyone was tracking them. Once identified, it was a simple matter for the team to keep out of sight and follow the dust clouds stirred up by the enemy, or the mud tracks that they left. When the dust settled, a peek over a rise was usually all that was needed to nail the concealment site, then turn around and head back to camp.

It was twilight and the horses were just walking on a paved road; it was far safer than minefields, possibly inches from the level road. But life still went on.

It seemed to Dar that it was pretty crowded for a war. A war fought in a land trapped somewhere in the Middle Ages. Farmers plowed their fields with horses and plows made from tank tracks; stones weighted the track to dig into the dry earth.

Children appeared at any time, begging for anything. Goatherds would lead their animals a short distance, then squat and let them wander. Armed parties of men would pass on horses, walking, in vehicles, and on camels. Their tribal or warlord flag would identify men who all looked the same.

"Who's the enemy?" Dar asked no one.

The sun had set. Up ahead the lead Afghan scout suddenly stopped at a road crossing and got off his horse, then hunched over and away from an approaching group of riders. The rest of the Afghans did the same thing, leaving the mounted American soldiers in confused wonder.

Dar watched as about a hundred riders, each on either a pure white or jet-black horse, passed. The riders wore clothing colored to match their horses. They passed like wraiths. The lead rider carried a black flag. A golden arrowhead was the emblem at the center of the flag. Tied over the back of one horse was a body wrapped like a mummy.

When they had passed, Dar saw that all the guides were still turned from the road.

"We wait," Vance translated the headman's words.

They waited until the black riders had passed. Suddenly it seemed as if Ubu's men couldn't put enough ground between them and the checkered band.

Several hours had passed when Peyton, the communications operator, urgently rode up to Rene.

"Hey, Rene," he said. "We just got a flash message to intercept and stop the riders that crossed in front of us back there, but as always, they wouldn't say why."

Vance translated Rene's words to Ubu, the headman, whose eyes grew big. He shook his head, then stopped his horse and refused to move. Vance continued to talk with him.

"They might be Taliban or al Qa'eda," Peyton said.

"They are neither," Vance corrected. "Ubu says 'no' because 'they are the ghosts of death.' He won't go anywhere in their direction, and neither will his men. Look at them, they're scared shitless."

"What do we do?" Dar asked.

"We go," said Rene.

Word quickly spread to the rest of the Afghans and from their looks a mutiny would happen if they carried out the message.

Rene did a quick reassessment. "You know, I think that we have to let this one pass, we can't jump into their country and start barking orders at these guys. Peyton, give me the radio."

He spoke on the radio, then pressed his earpiece and listened for a few moments. He nodded and replied, "I want you to understand something. This was just a formality call. I am not in your chain of command. You take this tasking back, or get someone else to do it. My men aren't here to die for you. Out!" He looked at his team. "We're here to do a job, not play at heroics. Without these Barneys scouting for us, we'd get ambushed."

"What about us going it alone?" Peyton asked.

"Get real," Rene answered. "This is our first time

operating on horses. These mountain goat roads have too many fucking passes and choke points where we'd get ambushed. We stay with the mission as planned. Anyone say different?"

Silence. Rene was the leader. He took care of his men.

Dar liked Rene's thinking. If they didn't have to go chasing after an ambush then that was fine with him. He could've offered the rover, but the time didn't feel right. Besides, staying alive was his highest priority.

Just a couple of weeks before Dar had been in the luxurious arms of his wife in a very green Florida. Now here he was on a horse that was stirring up ancient dust on a ghostly gray moonscape. He was in a world where ordinary rules of life didn't apply. This was a land of war, a place where killing was the easiest answer for everything. Pain and suffering was free for everyone. Death permeated everything. And somehow he found that being there had a taste all its own. And it was sweet.

Back at base camp Dar felt relatively safe, so he unpacked his CD player. He crawled into his sleeping bag, put in Rita's disk, turned it on, then put only one of the earphones into his ears—he wanted to keep one ear listening for trouble.

Closing his eyes, he was back with Rita through her words of love and the music she chose.

His body relaxed and every part of his being was in love with the love of his life. For a little while he could escape to home and all the love. Rita had recorded hours of his favorite music, and took time in between songs to read poems, tell jokes, and speak words of love.

Damn, how long had she been working on it? He kind of felt stupid for not doing something of the same. *Oh, well,* he thought, and fell asleep listening to his wife's loving words.

CHAPTER 18

SOMEWHERE IN AFGHANISTAN

THE FIRST THING THAT JASON NOTICED WHEN HE came to was that he could move. It was still pitch-black, but he could move again and was back in the real world. *Great!* But before doing any celebrating, he slowly felt his naked body for any injuries and did a self-assessment.

His left shoulder was crudely bandaged. He slowly moved it. Nothing was broken or bleeding. *It's only a flesh wound.* But there was enough missing flesh to assume that his locator had been shot out or destroyed, and it still hurt like hell. It was going to leave a big scar. *Nothing new.* He hoped that the enhanced immune therapy Dr. Brownstein did on him covered infections from gunshot wounds, too. *Free. Man, it feels like heaven just to be able to scratch my butt again!*

Where was he? He lay motionless, enjoying for a moment the luxury of being unbound. Everything was black around him, to be expected. How long had he been out?

Being a pararescueman, he had a pretty good handle on medicine and pharmacology. But he couldn't quite nail the drug or drugs his captors had given him. It hit fast and knocked him out. But for how long had he been out? No telling. Mercifully, there were no more bad dreams or lag time associated with the effects. Recovery was quick. It was undoubtedly opium-based. Whoever was dosing him must be a real professional. It was time to do something about his situation.

He slowly stretched and massaged himself back to life. It was still pitch-black. His night-vision implant was no good in absolute darkness. He suddenly heard movement all around. The air got thicker and smelled bad. How big was the place he was in?

The sounds stopped.

"What is your name?" a deep voice asked.

Christ, here it goes again. "What's yours?"

"*I* will ask the questions and *you* will answer them. Now, what is your name?" The voice boomed in Jason's ears.

The scene reminded him of Dorothy meeting the Wizard of Oz for the first time. "Alex Gomez, Mr. Wizard."

"The only thing I know for sure is that your name is not Alex Gomez. You said you were a messenger."

"Yeah. Can anybody hear me?" *Shit.* No Party contact.

"What are you talking about?"

"Nothing. I'm sorry, but you've drugged me so much that I'm having trouble making sense, even to myself. What's in that shit you're giving me? Do you mind stopping? I ain't no junkie."

"Not yet." A candle was lit. Jason's NV implant went to work. He could see that he was in a large round room. The room was filled with men, smelly and sweaty. He was glad that the candle's shadows covered his privates. He could see no doors or windows.

"I want to show you something, messenger."

He heard the sounds of taps. Getting closer, Jason saw a character step right out of Scheherazade's *Arabian*

Nights. He wore black felt boots with the toes turned back. A golden arrowhead crowned his black turban. His jet-black mustache and goatee were waxed. He started to take off his black robe.

Jason trembled.

The man crouched in front of Jason, raised his left arm, and pointed at an arrowhead brand made by a hot iron on his inside biceps. "This is how we recognize each other."

"Each other?"

"You will find out, *if* you live long enough. Now what is your message?" He stood and began pacing around Jason. "Who are you, and why are you here?"

"Alex Gomez. But I'm not a journalist. The message is that I'm here to buy Gul Nazari's entire opium crop. Are you he?"

"I am not sure of which parts of which truths you are telling me, but to say that you are Gomez again will insult me. There are those here in this room that understand your tongue. I will cut it out if you again say that you are he."

He wagged his finger, and a box was slid in front of Jason.

"Open it."

Jason flicked a latch and the box fell open on all sides. His skin crawled. A severed head was frozen in its last painful grimace. Through the dried, dead features, he could tell that it bore a strikingly familiar resemblance. *I'm in a world of hurt!*

"*That* is Alex Gomez."

"Oh, right. You mean that this *was* Alex Gomez," Jason corrected. So Falcon was telling the truth back on the yacht, or maybe Falcon had sold out Gomez.

Nazari looked confused for a moment, then nodded. "Oh, I understand. You like questions and games? Then we will have much fun while you are alive. Now, who are you, and why are you here?"

Keep him talking. The interrogation felt just like the resistance schools he'd been through over his career. He silently thanked all the survival escape resistance and evasion (SERE) instructors who'd knocked the crap out of him in training. "Well, this head is certainly compelling, but you said you had other reasons not to believe me. What're some of them?"

"*You* question *me* again? Your insolence will cost you."

Another candle was lit and set in front of Jason. Two sources of light were more than enough for Jason to operate. Still, he couldn't see any exit. The room was a tomb.

An arm reached out and three objects were dropped in front of Jason—the bishop's ring, his own, and Mac's Saint Michael's medallion.

"Why were you wearing these? Just whom do you belong to?"

Staring at the ornaments, his mind raced, looking for any edge that he could get. *Damn!* The stuff he wore had actually caught someone's attention, but whose attention? "Why can't I own jewelry?"

"No one wears rings like these unless they are a part of something." Picking them up, he examined each piece. "Your rings, the Maltese Cross, and God's eye. The angel Michael is your medallion. Why?"

"A friend gave it to me."

"Who is your friend?"

Jason kept his mouth shut.

"What about this one?"

The man called it God's eye. He'd gotten it off the hand of a murdered child. "I found it."

Walking behind Jason, he paused for a moment. "The scars that you bear cannot only come from the life of a slave, but an order of extreme discipline. *We* give scars like that. And then there is your mark."

"What mark?"

The man crouched next to Jason and moved the candle to Jason's butt. The light glowed on two green feet tattooed on his right butt cheek.

First Jason just smiled, and then started laughing low. In a few moments he was roaring with laughter.

The laughter was contagious, and soon the whole room reverberated with laughter.

"Silence!" The man quickly stood and the room stopped laughing, except for Jason.

"Tell me what is so funny."

It would have taken a lifetime for Jason to say how he came about having green feet on his ass. Also, Jason completely forgot about the obvious giveaway. He had gotten the green feet over twenty years ago lying facedown in a Philippine tattoo parlor and whorehouse. It was a ritual PJ act for his making his first save. The Jolly Green feet was a story all its own. There was no way that his interrogator would ever understand. It was a "rescue thing."

How could he ever think that he could actually just walk into the Den of Forty Thieves and expect to pull off a gazillion-dollar dope deal? The laughter left him weak and relaxed, with a better understanding of his precarious situation. "All I know is that anything that I say can be the right or wrong thing, and I'm dead, right?"

"I am glad that you see this as a game and that you find this all so, so amusing. Well, my funny friend, I like you, and that is dangerous. It is dangerous because my amusements run to the extreme, and you make me feel *extremely* amused.

"My better senses tell me that I should kill you now, funny man, but I believe that you actually do have information. I want to know how you came by *this*." He held out Jason's miniature Qur'an.

Jason thought for a moment, then remembered something he learned at the Cultural Center at Khobar.

A young Sunni scholar had once shown him a passage

in the Qur'an that said if you capture an enemy and he
wants to convert, you must spare him and treat him as a
brother. It was something he'd stored in the back of his
mind—*you never know when it might come in handy.* "I
want to learn Islam."

The man frowned, then smiled and laughed. "Good,
very clever. Before we continue, you *must* tell me your
name."

"Are you Gul Nazari?"

He nodded.

"Then I go by the name Alice."

Nazari looked astonished for a moment, then gave
Jason a feral smile. "You have to tell me your secrets and
tricks. I myself know many. I will show you one." He
flourished his finger at Jason. A bright light flashed, almost blinding him. His men were gone.

Jason tried to look surprised but he had seen the secret
of the trick through his night-vision lens. *Trapdoors.*
That was how the men vanished. Now Jason knew how
they came and went.

Gul had a jug of water and plate of flat bread placed
in front of Jason. "For you. Go ahead. Eat. It is nan, our
bread."

Jason drank and ate like the starving man he was.

Nazari smugly smiled as if he controlled a magical
power. His face turned serious. "It is only you and I now,
Alice. How is it that you have the Cloth of the Prophet?
Do you come from *our friends*?"

Jason could see a few men lying flat on the ground,
just waiting for Jason to make a move. *Say something.
Anything!* "Yesss, I am from our friend's messenger. But I
can't reveal it, yet."

"Buying time. Excellent answer. I go. If you really are
a messenger from our friends, then you already have
been trained, all that remains for you is to be tested.
There is not much time. As a matter of fact, the next time
we meet you will ask *me* a question. If it is not the right

question then they will be the last words you speak. You see, if you are really from our friends then the question has never changed. Until you are tested, you will be our restrained guest. You will not be beaten or tortured, but you still can die. You intrigue me. It would be a shame if that happened before you are given the chance to ask your question."

What question? A bag was thrown over his head and his hands were tied behind his back. He heard a trapdoor opening, then he was led down some cold steps and into endless twists and turns, finally to a room. His bonds were cut and the door slammed behind him.

Pulling off his hood, Jason tried to get a look at his dark and musty cell, but there was no light anywhere. Feeling around in the dark, he learned that the cell was small and empty except for a tin can. The walls were made of sandstone and rock. The door was iron with a small slat at the bottom. There was no light anywhere. He made a pillow out of the hood and sat down. He reasoned that the cell was most likely bugged.

"Anybody hear me?" he whispered.

Nothing. There could have been a number of reasons the Party didn't answer—all of them bad. Things didn't look good, but there was a bright side to it all, he was still alive.

Examining himself, he gave his shoulder a better assessment. It hurt, but that was the least of his problems. He was going to need all his wits just to hold it together, look for clues, escapes, anything!

He was on his own again and in another precarious situation that he had no control over. Jason shook his head. "Why's this shit always happen to me?"

Things could've been worse. True, he was naked. But he wasn't cold or wet. He didn't have to be anywhere at the moment. And his balls weren't hooked up to any electrical torture device. No one was beating the hell out of him. So far he'd been treated fairly well, but by whom? Taliban, al Qa'eda, some warlord; there was no way really to know.

His head began to swim. *Damn! They drugged me again. I gotta be careful about everything that goes in my mouth.* It was the last conscious thought he had before the lights went out.

•

CHAPTER 19

0330 MONDAY / 1 OCTOBER 2001
HINDU KUSH REGION / AFGHANISTAN

President Bush says that time is running out for the Taliban to hand over bin Laden.

WAR PLANNERS ALREADY CONTEMPLATED THE enemy's escaping through the Northern Alliance lines and heading into the high mountains—they needed to know where the escape routes were and what kind of caves they might use. With most of the enemy out of the lowlands, targets were becoming more difficult to locate and assign priorities to.

The No Name Guys were ordered to continue observing, locating, and pinpointing known or suspected enemy strongholds. That meant that now they had to range farther and farther from camp, and they had to go higher up into the surrounding mountains. More spec ops teams were arriving in-country daily, ready to direct joint attacks with the Northern Alliance on D-day.

Everyone dismounted at the base of the Hindu Kush Mountains—Kush translated to "slaughter" in English.

Looking up, they were already at eleven thousand feet and the mountains towered still another ten thousand above them. Somewhere in those massive snowcapped mountains and across deep ravines, countless enemy fighters could be waiting and ready to do battle.

The plan was to follow the more worn trails and see where they led. They had detailed maps and the latest satellite reconnaissance photos from the space operators working out of Prince Sultan Air Base, Saudi Arabia, but nothing that could give them any definite proof that the holes and shadows on the pictures were actually caves, enemy encampments, or just shadows.

Low tech was edging out high tech. The Predator operators discovered that when the enemy heard the noise of the UAV, the enemy could just cover themselves with their blankets and blank out on the infrared imagery. They needed eyes on the ground to ferret out the enemy locations. They needed what Dar carried.

"Rene, I got something that might cut down our own exposure time," Dar said. It was time to pull the rabbit out of his hat.

"Oh?" inquired Rene. "Go ahead, I'm interested."

Taking out a securely wrapped package from the saddlebag, Dar found a spot away from everyone and unwrapped it.

To the onlookers it looked as if Dar keyed in a few notes to a Palm Pilot. Then he held out a tube and pressed a release latch. Out popped out a pair of wings and Dar tossed it into the air. The rover sailed away while Dar looked at the Palm Pilot screen. He showed the Palm Pilot to Rene.

"Whoa!" Rene was looking at himself from fifty feet above. Looking up he neither saw nor heard anything. He then watched with amazement as the screen showed in real time what was over the first ridge crossing, another higher ridge dotted with visible cave openings. The rover mapped the caves' locations, then turned around and retraced its flight path.

A high whine filled the air as the rover hovered, then gently touched down in front of Dar. "I have the GPS cave locations stored in this Palm Pilot. I can upload all the data into your laptop computer."

"Damn, Air Force, that little flight saved us at least a day's ride!" Rene exclaimed.

"It's *Sergeant* Garo, sir."

"Right. Just what in the world is this rover?"

"It's a Remote Operated Vehicle Reconnaissance, rover, sir."

"But how does it operate and fly? What's its power source?"

"Classified." Dar smiled.

If he could tell, Dar would have had to explain that the rover flew on microjets powered by a pager-sized pulsed abnormal glow discharge reactor (PAGD). It was the most radical stuff of cutting-edge technology. Dot-sized pellets made of lead styphnate fed the micro reactor. Every particle of the fuel was used to power and turn the main propeller, microavionics, mini optical cameras, and six stamp-sized microjets. Utilizing the PAGD technology, there was theoretically enough fuel to fly the rover for months.

Suddenly Dar's value on the team increased a thousand percent.

2030 HOURS
THE PARTY / FLORIDA

The fact that the Global Hawks were back on-line did very little to improve the morale of the Party. Their operator was missing and they felt as if it was their fault.

With all their specialties and knowledge, nothing

counted but the loss of a man thousands of miles from where they sat.

Every asset available had been called in for a secret search. It'd taken only a few phone calls and faxes, but soon two Predator uninhabited air vehicles were sending the Party near-real-time overhead images of Kabul and the surrounding areas.

The Party was not staffed with intelligence-trained assets. These were talented men and women who'd quickly learned a basic fact of signal intelligence (SIGINT): No matter how good or clear the overhead imagery was, it didn't mean shit without human intelligence (HUMINT) on the ground.

Reconnaissance pictures couldn't tell you who was inside of buildings, or what those people in the rooms were thinking or saying.

Mike Gorsline sat in his chair, mesmerized at the imagery of Afghanistan, trying to will out the hidden location of tons of opium. If they couldn't find Gomez soon then he would have to go straight to his DEA chief and clue him in to the operation. The turf war would be bloody. There would be hell to pay by everyone involved. But he would do it if it meant keeping the heroin off his streets.

He glanced over at the stone figure of Cadallo. He was a big man but Mike had taken on bigger. The DEA was only a phone call away. "How long will this game go on?" Mike asked himself.

SOMEWHERE IN THE AFGHANISTAN MOUNTAINS

There was a little light in the cell. Jason rubbed his face and wondered how the drugs that they kept slipping him were affecting his senses. *How long have I been here?*

The cell door was ajar. Jason crouched and slowly peeked out the door. No one was in the tunnel. The light in the tunnel came from a candle in the recess of a carved wall. It was just above a stone table. On the table were some kind of shorts, food, and a jug.

The first thing Jason did was down the whole jug of lukewarm tea, not caring if it was drugged. Thirst quenched, he had no idea what he ate because it was gone too fast. Examining the shorts, a length of cord fell from them. The cord was about ten feet long. The shorts were barely enough to cover his goods, but it was better than being naked.

It had to be a test of some sort.

Jason took a deep breath and tried to reason out and choose his best options. Really, there were none. Whatever Nazari was up to, it beat the hell out of sitting alone with his thoughts in a dark cell, the kinds of thoughts that could drive a man crazy. Besides, if there were any hope of escaping he'd have to reconnoiter the surroundings.

The tunnel ran in both directions. It was just over his head. Stretching out his arms, he could about touch the sides of the walls. He mentally flipped a quarter and turned right. Picking up the candle and wrapping the rope around his shoulder, he felt his way, creeping low along the left side of the passageway.

The walls felt like the same sandstone his cell was made of, crumbly and grimy stuff. He scratched at his beard, feeling just as grimy as the tunnel he was in. He tried to control his breathing so that he could listen to anyone else with him in the creepy passage—there was nothing that he could do about his booming heart.

If it was a test, then it was an elementary one. Trip wires and deadfalls—all were easy to spot, then crawl under or step over. The only constant was the relatively straight, endless passage he was in.

He figured that he was moving through some dried-up underground river. It was tight and musty. Jason had no way of knowing how far it might go, where it might turn, or who else was in the tunnel with him. He took comfort in knowing that he was a tunnel rat. Kelly had taught him. *How I wish that you were here with me right now, buddy.* He silently thanked him for teaching him how to move stealthily in the dark.

He froze when he heard a faint scraping sound. Someone was moving somewhere in front of him. He carefully set down the candle and backed away into the darkness to wait for his quarry to approach. He didn't have long to wait.

It was a man wearing only a loincloth. His hair and beard were long and scraggly.

The man came up to the candle, eyes filled with fear, not rage. He was scared. A dagger trembled in his right hand. He didn't look like killer material and might turn and run if someone said "Boo!"

Jason waited until the man picked up the candle and, blinded by his own light, came closer.

The man never saw the foot coming. Jason struck him full force in the groin. Grabbing his balls and falling to his knees, he hollered in pain but didn't see the hammer fist rocketing to his temple.

Jason picked up the candle and looked under the man's left arm. No arrowhead brand.

The man started to stir. Grabbing the man's dagger, Jason had to make a fast decision—kill him, or not.

A beam of light bounced off the wall toward him. Jason ducked to avoid being spotted. Crouching as the light illuminated the tunnel, he could run, but where to? There was a small depression in the wall, possibly just large enough to hide a man. Jason blew out the candle and rolled toward the alcove.

The searchlight fell on a prostrate, naked, bound man with bulging, frightened eyes. The man couldn't cry out a warning because Jason had gagged him with his own loincloth.

A dark figure passed Jason and bent over to inspect

the bound man. Sensing someone behind him, the man stood and twirled around, but was too late.

Jason, bent low, grabbed the man's ankles and jerked him off his feet. He slammed the man headfirst to the ground. The man didn't move. Out cold, maybe for a long time. He tied up the man with his cord.

Jason took the man's loose-fitting trousers, robe, and sandals. "Hey, I'm downtown, now," he whispered to himself. Wearing clothes made him feel better and warmer, somewhat.

He picked up the flashlight and, using the light sparingly, continued up the tunnel. Now he had a small chance, maybe.

After an endless prowl, there was a turn. *Shit!* There were a lot of turns.

He finally came to an enormous cavern with lots of other tunnels. He'd arrived at Grand Central. But it was deserted. Frozen with confusion for a moment, he had no idea where to go.

Suddenly a red beam of light nailed him right in the chest. He backed into the tunnel he had just exited. The beam unerringly followed him as he backed away. He turned and ran back the way he had come.

Running for all he was worth, he could hear the heavy breathing of someone close behind him. *Run!* He heard a grunt, then a scream as the laser beam cut out. Jason didn't bother to stop and look around to check it out.

Now he could see lights coming from the way he was running. He skidded to a stop and ran back the other way. He tripped over something and landed with a thud. He scooted to the balls of his feet and got ready to sprint back toward Grand Central. He heard yelling and looked back the way he had come. Scores of light beams were coming from that direction. He felt like a picked-off runner in a baseball game, but there was no safe plate to tag. He was suddenly too tired to try anything, so he slumped over what tripped him.

He turned on the flashlight and found himself staring at the eyes of a dead man. His throat was sliced wide open. Something hung around the bloody neck.

Jason looked over the body and pulled the night-vision goggles from the head and looked them over. Big and boxy, they were Russian-made. They probably had all the night vision they needed.

He raised the man's left arm and saw an arrowhead brand. The lights became brighter as the yelling grew louder.

Breathing deep, he yelled, "Hey, Gul, how'd I do?" *Wait a second*. He smelled those flowers again, and now he knew the smell. Lavender.

Bodies swarmed all over him. Hitting and kicking, their blows were ineffective in the small and dark tunnel.

"You hit like women!" he yelled, then he started fighting back. Biting and kicking, it felt good hammering back. For a few victorious moments he held them back, but then he couldn't move. Once again his mouth was being pried open. "Come on," he mumbled, "I'll go peaceful. No more of that shit."

A hand pinched his nose, cutting off his breathing. There it was; the nasty drink. Well, at least it was fast-acting. Then the curtain came down.

CHAPTER 20

EVERYONE'S NERVES WERE BEGINNING TO FRAY.
Everyone felt a sense of failure. There was no read
from Cadallo. He locked himself into his dark
room, emerging only to issue a directive or browbeat
someone for an imagined infraction.

Tapped into every technological system focused on
Afghanistan, Jason was gone. While thousands searched
for Osama bin Laden, a far smaller number ceaselessly
searched for Jason Johnson.

It was just hours before the bombing campaign would
begin in Afghanistan. If he was in the wrong place, then
Jason would die under a barrage of bombs, and with him
any chance of getting back the 300 million dollars.

It was like looking for a particular grain of sand on an
endless beach. The Party was dedicated, but clueless. The
imagery was detailed and they used every asset they had
available, electronic, visual, and all the satellite imagery
that they wanted, but all of the wizard technology was
useless to spot their man. Nothing worked.

Tensions were stretched to the limit. Conversations were short and curt. Fear of Cadallo lessened—how could the big man call them all together just to blow the whole mission?

Soldiers stood in line and took orders, but there was an air of rebellion around Cadallo's civilians. They voiced their opinions and one opinion seemed to stand out. If Cadallo couldn't find some way to keep Gorsline shut up then his authority would be in jeopardy, and his plans would all fall through.

He tossed a top-secret folder on his control panel. The Party needed a diversion to keep them in line.

Cadallo hit the public-address button. "The bombs are about to fall. I want everyone up and on station to help fight this war."

1830 SUNDAY / 7 OCTOBER 2001
BAMIYAN PASS / AFGHANISTAN

The war began with cruise missiles. Washington war planners selected the targets and relayed encrypted messages to missile ships in the Persian Gulf. A good portion of the targets the guided missiles aimed for came from the No Name Guys, compliments of Dar Garo and his rover.

The sky then filled with the roar of jets, and contrails of high-flying jets appeared high in the sky.

The fight was on. The No Name Guys were cleared in hot to engage targets. With Dar's rover, they had relayed and confirmed enemy positions. As an incentive, the war planners gave Dar's team their pick of the best targets.

The mountains came alive with thunderous explosions as ground-support aircraft like Apache helicopters and A-10 Warthogs provided cover fire for allied Special Forces and their Afghan fighters, who were the tip of the spear against terrorism.

AC-130U Hercules gunships ripped through the enemy and quickly earned nicknames among those on the receiving end of their guns. Spitting Witch, Screaming Witch, and Hell's Fire—the flight crews called their warbird *Spooky.*

Waves of bombers dropped death while more high-flying bombers and jets laden with ordnance circled like deadly predators just waiting their turn in the feeding frenzy.

Besides eyes on targets from the ground, the Predator uninhabited air vehicles lent their thermal-imaging and synthetic radar capabilities to track the fleeing enemy. At the same time, thousands of miles in outer space, satellites gave crystal-clear images of a fleeing enemy and possible locations of Osama bin Laden.

Hundreds of acoustic sensors had been dropped from the air and scattered throughout the Afghan mountains. They gave hard evidence to mark human passage and provided valuable intelligence that the war planners passed on to ground teams, who searched for an enemy becoming more elusive as the days passed.

After the devastating air strikes, ground parties had to be sent looking for things of intelligence value, weapons, or any survivors to take as prisoners, and make the always sketchy body count. Sometimes it was an almost impossible proposition when whole mountainsides collapsed. The sheer angles of the faces of the mountains sometimes made climbing them virtually impossible.

The rover had more than done its job. Locating cave openings, it would land and "sniff" the air. Able to sense minute molecule-sized particles, it could sense humans, live or dead, explosives, even food. With the information, Dar's team mapped the area with hundreds of active targets and relayed the locations back to CENTCOM, located at MacDill Air Force Base, Florida. Without the rover they might've been there for months before accumulating information that the rover could gather in just a matter of hours.

They got moving so fast that there was no telling what kinds of terrain they would cross. Through icy canyons, over snowcapped mountains, across sand dunes, and even lush fields, Iblis still slipped and bitched every step of the way. But overall, they were kicking ass, so far.

The Barneys were learning the tactics taught to them and were spoiling for a piece of the fight. The MREs were getting low, but good water was plentiful thanks to a small portable water filter the team medic carried.

Enemy positions and cave openings plotted, they finally came across a fleeing force that was on the run to a cave that had already been surveyed. Now it was time to put it all together.

The horses were secure. They got to the high ground and had the enemy pinned down.

From his vantage point high above the cave, Dar looked down on the roads and all the activity. Firing mortars and small arms, the enemy knew that they were being backed into their holes and didn't like it one bit. There was no surrender, and everyone knew it. Hurling epithets along with their explosives, the Taliban tried to bring their tormentors in closer. They looked like hundreds of ants whose nests had been disturbed. Well, the giant with the Big Firecracker had lit his fuse.

A peculiar smell wafted in the air. He couldn't quite place it until he looked over at the Afghans. They were smoking hash. Dar was incredulous. What in the world were these guys doing getting high right before a battle?

"It's not our call, Dar," Vance said as he crawled next to him. "You know the British used to get bombed on beer and rum before they fought us in 1776. It helped them build up courage. Rene said to let it go and he'll talk to Ubu after this is over."

"Yeah, you're right that it's not my call, but I still don't like it."

The first attack was automatic. Dar had programmed the targets and times for the allies to drop their bombs. After that it would get real fluid. This was his first performance as a combat controller.

Above him he could see circling contrails of B-52s. His stomach started dancing wildly. As he glanced at his watch, the bombs were already falling, but only he knew. It was time to make a point. He stood up. Everyone looked at him with curiosity. Raising his right arm, then pointing with his left forefinger at the Taliban below, he cried out, "Taste the penalty of the Blazing Fire."

First there was the light from the bomb's impacts, then there was a concussion that almost knocked Dar over. The following explosions almost blew out his eardrums. "And the mighty blast overtook the wrongdoers." The blasts were blinding. It was like the hand of God had actually smashed the mountainside.

Turning, he saw that everyone, including the No Name Guys, were in shock. Never had anyone experienced such concentrated explosive power. It took several moments before rational thought returned.

"Well, you stoners, go get 'em!" Dar yelled to their fighters. The mountains echoed and the ground shook from bombs dropping on other enemy locations. The night sky flashed with deadly thunder. His brother combat controllers were busy at their work, calling in the aircraft stacked like cordwood in the sky, waiting for their turn to pickle their load.

First one fighter climbed on his horse and starting riding down the hill, then another. Soon all the Afghanis were whooping down the hill and yelling like madmen. Some waved scimitars over their heads. Space-age warfare had come to the stone-age warriors, or rather, *stoned*-age warriors.

"Nice work, *Air Force*." Vance grinned. "Right down their throats. I've never seen anything like it."

"You want to ride down there and get in on some of that, Rene?" Vance asked.

"No. It's going to be a massacre. You know how they are when the killing lust comes over them. I don't want to have to testify to anything but that we set up and executed an authorized killing box. Attack complete."

"Sergeant Garo, you want some of that?" Vance motioned below to the men gone wild with killing lust.

"No. I'm the one who delivered it." Dar was still stunned. It all worked, just as in training. But this time it was real. The death was real. The war was real. His radio transmissions had triggered the explosive power of the twenty-first century. Wide-eyed, he couldn't wait for the next attack.

> *Dear Rita,*
> *I've seen the lion. I am a warrior.*
>
> > *Love,*
> > *Dar*

2215 HOURS
CLASSIFIED LOCATION / MIDDLE EAST

The third and last C-130E Hercules landed and taxied to the hangar, where the first two planes were parked, then shut down its engines. The aircrew quickly grabbed their gear, got out of the plane, and got on the waiting crew bus. The crew bus then drove the crews to the waiting C-17.

In minutes the C-17 was airborne to thirty-five thousand feet. No record of the C-17's landing was made—it was never there. Neither were the three American C-130 crews—or their airframes.

Official records showed that three Air Force C-130E Hercules aircraft had been decommissioned, flown to the "Bone Yard" at Davis-Monthan Air Force Base in

Arizona, and cut up into scrap metal. The 781 flight maintenance records survived, but the planes would be reborn to fly for another country.

One by one, ground crews towed the planes in one side of the hangar. Inside the hangar the plane's American markings were removed and replaced with Pakistani Air Force emblems.

At the same time that the international marking switch happened, six cargo pallets piled high with weapons and explosives, and weighing a total of forty-two thousand pounds, were loaded onto each plane, plus a new flight record.

In a matter of a few hours a C-130 with Pakistani markings emerged from the other side of the hangar. They were towed to the tarmac and refueled. As soon as the planes were flight-ready, buses arrived with crews employed by the Pakistani Intelligence Service (PIK). Prepared to take off at any time, bound for Afghanistan, no record would be made of their departure. It was a very secret deal offered to the Pakistani government that they would have been stupid to refuse: Use the planes to deliver weapons to the Taliban, then get three free C-130s added to their air force.

The most surreptitious but essential part of the deal included two Meridian dialysis machines to be personally delivered to Mustafa Omar, a local leader of the al Qa'eda.

The Pakistani aircrews waited only for their destination in Afghanistan to be given, and they would be airborne.

CHAPTER 21

JASON FELT A LITTLE BETTER. HE HAD SOME CAN-
dles and a blanket that was warm—they let him
keep the bloodstained clothes. He had lost all sense
of time, but now it didn't matter. There was nothing he
could do about it. If he was past the deadline, then so be
it; now he was just trying to stay alive. But he still had to
try and figure out what in the hell was going on. Were
these guys Taliban, al Qa'eda, or both?

Time and again his cell was visited, a flashlight was
turned on, and eyes peered in. Something was going on,
but he didn't know what to think. *First they leave the cell
door open, almost inviting me to leave, then they watch
me like white on rice.*

Did they know who he was? Had he made any
progress with these guys? Was he passing their tests?
Who killed the third guy in the tunnel? And who had
kissed him? The lips had been too soft to be a man's,
right? Whoever it was sure smelled good.

He heard footsteps that stopped in front of his cell. A
lower flap opened, then a plate and tin can were passed

through. The flap clanged shut and the footsteps went away.

He picked up the plate. It was a small portion of warm rice with some kind of meat on it. Gingerly tasting it for laced drugs, he decided that it didn't taste half bad. It was probably what everyone else there ate, wherever *there* was. He was very wary of drinking the cold tea, but then he really had no choice. It wasn't bitter like the crap they forced down him. He quickly downed the food and drink, then stretched out on his blanket to sleep. He wanted to be ready for anything that came his way. Things couldn't be all that bad if the food was getting better.

He woke to the sound of his door opening and instantly jumped to fighting stance. He was surprised to see a blindfolded old man carrying a book under one arm, and what looked like a lit genie's lamp. The old man held out the lamp and Jason took it. The man then smiled, unrolled a small rug, sat on it, and laid the big book in front of him.

"Please come near. I speak your language. I am blind, old, and harmless. I am Imam Sinan Kon. I am told you wish to learn the ways of Islam, and the Qur'an. The Grand Wizard has told me about you.

"The sole reason you are alive, right here, right now, is because of what you have brought us. Very few, in hundreds of years, have joined the clan and become one of us. If your word to learn Islam is true, then I will teach you."

"Yes." *Damned if the stunt I pulled didn't work!* Now he had something he could work with.

The door opened and a black-clad person brought in a small tea set and laid it to the side of the imam.

Deftly feeling the kettle and two cups, the imam poured some tea and held out one cup. "I am commanded by the master to ask a few questions before we begin."

Jason took the tea. "Sure, as long as I can ask a few of my own."

"I may not be able to answer the way you want me to."

"I'll take what I can get. Go ahead, imam."

"In the tunnel, you let the first two men live, but killed the third. Why?"

Was it a trick question? He hadn't killed anyone. But *somebody* killed the guy. He had to be careful how he answered.

"Then the tunnel *was* a test."

The imam nodded.

"Is this another test I can fail?"

The old man cracked a toothless grin. "I only test the man who believes in the Hereafter. That man cannot cheat."

While earlier someone had cheated and helped him pass. *And probably saved my life.* Jason remembered something that stood out from the night before. "The first two men were not branded."

Sinan Kon smiled and nodded. "Correct. The one you killed in the tunnel was fully initiated. Only one with our similar traits would have known what to do. When one of the Order is tasked he must complete it to a final end, attain martyrdom and Paradise, or forfeit his soul to hell."

Who were these guys? The old geezer seemed nice enough, so he might try to get some answers to his questions. "Now me. Where am I?"

"You are in the stronghold of the Nazari, an ancient family clan."

"Who is your leader?"

"You already know him. Enough. Now we study."

It was easy to play dumb, but be interested enough to keep the old man talking. Jason had bought an English translation of the Qur'an and read through it enough to be familiar with the suras and the more important passages that his young Khobar mullah had taught him.

He watched in amazement of the old man's ability to

feel the Qur'an by touch and point out and read from memory the exact sura. Of course, it was all in Arabic so Jason didn't have a clue what it said. The old man could've been doing a con for all he knew. With nothing to lose, Jason would play along.

Jason feigned ignorance, but knew to ask "enlightened" questions, or include incisive comments at the right time. His attitude brightened up the old man and led him to believe he was an inspired teacher. The imam left, telling Jason that he was a most apt student and that he would return a few more times to complete his lessons for indoctrination.

Indoctrination? Did they expect him actually to convert? But it didn't really matter one way or the other— he'd do whatever it took to stay alive. *Hell, I'd sign on with the devil if it set me free.*

Jason sat in his cell feeling better than he could remember. The Islam charade seemed to be working. He wasn't too hungry or thirsty.

Things were looking up a little. "I'm in a private suite. No one's kicking the shit out of me. No one's screaming, getting tortured or raped, especially me. So far, so good, just a little banged up." He spoke not just to himself. He hoped that his transceiver was still working somehow.

Make the most out of any little victories. I ain't goin' nowhere, so go back to sleep. It was a technique taught at the many survival schools he'd been to—sleep and eat whenever you can, there's no telling when you'll get your next chance.

2330 TUESDAY / 9 OCTOBER 2001
IN FLIGHT OVER AFGHANISTAN

The crew had "sanitized" their flight suits, pulled off all the Velcro patches, turned in all their personal possessions to the search-and-rescue vault, but kept their military ID and dog tags. They reviewed the information on their search-and-rescue cards, in case they got shot down. After drawing their weapons, body armor, night-vision goggles, and flight gear from Life Support, last, they got their Combat Talon ready to fly.

Most flyers would not admit to it, but they are a superstitious lot. Stopping the flight engineer before he opened the engine start checklist, a person might discover a lucky coin in his flight sleeve. The pilot could be carrying a note from his mother. The navigator taped a picture of her son, Cody, over the radar at the navigator station.

"Thirty seconds to slowdown," the navigator, Colonel Jackie Powell, said.

The loadmasters snapped on several chemical lights tied to the load they were airdropping.

"Slowdown checklist complete," acknowledged the primary loadmaster.

The C-130H Combat Talon II cleared a ridge at fifty feet and dived into a river valley pushing 250 knots. The specialized plane could just about fly itself, but at that moment the crew was busy working together. The supply load was small, two thousand pounds, but it held essential items for the team on the ground: ammunition, MREs, and radio batteries. And it also had gifts for the Afghan allies too: boots, lighters, and camouflage uniforms.

The navigator plotted the point of impact at a particular spot just north of the Kabul River. Not once during the forty-five-minute modified contour flight did she look up from her station. There would be nothing to see—it was pitch-black. Airspeed, altitude, timing, heading, and radar were all that she needed to do the drop. Lose any one of those, and the guys on the ground were shit out of luck.

Flying so low and fast in the night, the crew had little chance of getting nailed by a man portable air defense missile (MANPAD). But everyone stayed alert for any kind of offensive small arms or a lucky shot that could permanently cancel the mission.

This was their fifth event of the night. They had already dropped leaflets for psychological operations (PsyOps), infiltrated operators to blacked-out landings, done midair refuelings for Black Hawk and Chinook helicopters, and one other previous airdrop. They were exhausted and nerve-frayed, but still focused and working hard.

The pilots flew on night vision and pure adrenaline. The engineer kept his eyes glued to the instruments, ready to detect and react to any malfunction.

Two loadmasters hung on to the ramp behind the load, waiting on the checklist to do their part for the airdrop. Thrown and tossed, they had to have trust in the pilot to keep them off the razor-sharp mountains.

THE PLANE WAS MINUTES FROM THE DROP.

Dar looked at his watch and keyed his radio, calling in the blind to the Combat Talon. "Winds calm. You are clear to drop."

"FIVE SECONDS TO SLOWDOWN. SLOWDOWN, SLOW-down, now," said the nav.

The pilot leveled out 250 feet above the ground. The loadmaster opened the ramp and door. The opening ramp pulled the bungee cords on the load taut.

"One-minute warning," the nav said, then timing the approach, she said, "Ready, ready, cut!"

The loadmaster cut a strap holding the load to the plane. The bungee cord slingshotted the load from the plane.

The MC-130 turned sharply, up and away, disappearing into another valley.

DAR HEARD THE ROAR OF THE C-130'S ENGINES AS IT flew overhead, but never saw the plane through the darkness. When he looked through his night-vision goggles, infrared chemical lights appeared in the sky, rapidly falling to the ground.

One swing from the stabilizing parachute and the two-thousand-pound bundle struck the ground with a thud and rolled to its side. It was like Christmas. The biggest surprise, however, was over the case of beer that the loadmasters brought over with them from Florida and added to the load.

"God bless those zipper-suited flight gods," Rene said as he stood over the beer. "Now you guys know no booze is General Order Number One in this theater. But since Dar here is the only one who has to follow that order"—he laughed—"Dar can't have any."

They rode back to camp and split up the beer. Rene gave Dar a couple of cans anyway. A guard rotation went up. For two hours, each man on the team was able to lay down his weapon and take a short break from the war.

Dar finished his beer in just a few swallows—it never tasted so good! He then covered himself with a pattus in his fighting hole. He popped in both of his earpieces. A little beer buzz, fresh batteries, and he was ready to hear the rest of Rita's CD. After listening to it, he would start it all over, again and again, until it was time to go home. What a treat! *Relaxation*.

Explosions still happened, but Dar had adapted to the life. He could recognize the sounds of outgoing as well as incoming munitions. The crackle of gunfire sometimes sounded like firecrackers on the Fourth of July, but it wasn't a celebration of freedom, or was it? These people were passionate about whatever they did.

They quit calling their Afghan fighters "Barney" after witnessing their fighting sprit. Dar realized that no one would ever dominate these people. Even when they were down on ammunition, or even out of bullets, the Afghans would continue a charge. The battles had become bloodier as the encounters escalated, both sides giving as good as they got.

Without the team doc there would've been no medical aid for the Afghan wounded. But the Afghans didn't care; they said they would, to the last man, die to drive out "the Saudi."

They always seemed to know whether they were fighting Taliban or al Qa'eda. The Taliban would sometimes surrender when pressed—many of the prisoners they captured were from the same tribes. The al Qa'eda foreigners knew of the Afghan hatred for them and would fight to the death—martyrdom.

Sometimes the enemy would turn and suddenly be on the attack, then the team would quickly find cover and let Dar go to work bringing down airpower.

Dar had every intention of giving the enemy their reward in Paradise, but *first* he was actually going to try to feel normal, if for just one night.

CHAPTER 22

SOMEWHERE IN AFGHANISTAN

JASON, BLINDFOLDED WITH HIS HANDS TIED BEHIND his back, was led on a long walk. He was stopped and the blindfold was removed. Two monsters clad in black stood next to him. They pushed him to his knees. A basket was in front of him.

He was in a huge chamber of some kind. Strange designs on the ceilings looked to be carved from solid rock. The walls were black and white, hung with tapestries woven with intricate and colorful mosaics. There were several halls and doors, but no windows or anything to indicate where he was.

"It is time to ask your question, messenger," Gul's voice called out.

Jason was bent over until his head was just above the basket. He heard the taps, then saw the polished boots.

"The last head that filled the basket beneath you belonged to Alex Gomez," Nazari coldly announced.

Jason glanced up at the giant man next to him holding a scimitar. The blade was long and thin, but with a wide head, not like the huge scimitars he'd seen in the movies.

There was no doubt in his mind that the blade was especially made for lopping off heads. The man slowly raised the sword until he looked like he was ready to hit a baseball.

Think. Think, fool! But there was nothing to ask. He knew it wasn't about the drugs. What could it be? He looked around the chamber filled with black-clad men. Taking in every detail of a doomed man. One thing stood out, a hooded man wearing a white robe and thumbing amber worry beads.

Jason almost laughed. Maybe this was really a Klan rally. He zeroed in on the beads and remembered the first time that he saw them. Suddenly it all became so clear and so simple. If Bishop McFadden had steered him wrong, then it was all over. He took a deep breath, then asked, "Who are your grandfathers?"

The sword was lowered and Jason faced the man wearing a gold arrowhead on his turban. The veil covering the man's face fell away. It was Gul Nazari. Next to him, the man flipping the amber veil drew his veil below his chin and slyly grinned through a mouthful of gold teeth. How did the old bastard set him up? And why?

"The first cause is the Word of God!" a deep voice boomed off the walls.

Everyone knelt but Jason and Nazari.

Gul spoke in a loud English oratory. "The Word came forth from the Sacred Fire. Then came the Arsacid, and then the Sasanian. From the heat of the Fire came the Nazari devotees of the true ta'lim. But in A.D. 632 of the Christian calendar the Nazari were labeled heretics and forced to take refuge in the kingdom of Daylam and the fortress Alamut.

"Da'is missionaries from the Alamut served the Shi' and followed the will and word of God. The da'is gathered knowledge from all parts of the world: literature, art, astrology, mathematics, and forbidden works, then brought them back to the Alamut. The Nazari fathers were charged to become the *Assasseen,* guardians of the secrets.

"Our grandfathers' influence reached all corners of the Islamic empires. With our forbidden knowledge we silenced our enemies with our fedayeen. Our grandfathers became the *first* true martyrs for God.

"From A.D. 1033 until today, we have fought the Crusader ceaselessly, as we have fought our archenemy. Our fathers were hated, despised, and persecuted by many in the Faith for our beliefs and power. It was then that the infidel Templar, and Maltese knights became a part of our circle; the enemy of my enemy is my friend. Our grandfathers financed them, nurtured them, and controlled them. They did not hinder our beliefs.

"Still, the grandfathers faced the Crusaders until our blood mingled together on the sand. But we were betrayed by one of our own. Our queen, Riza, was captured by Baldwin, but ransomed to the Templars. She was held for many years until she became unwell. Delivered to the Maltese Hospitalers, our fathers made a secret alliance with them, and Queen Riza was returned to our clan. From her issued our true line. We owe *kindness* to the Maltese."

Gul then went into a song, naming all the leaders of the clan since A.D. 1130.

As he spoke, Jason's bonds were cut and he was led to a large, well-lit chamber.

"Before the destruction of the Alamut in 1256 we moved our source here among the isolated mountain Nuristani clans. Only the fully initiated may leave this center breathing."

Jason saw that he was in an immense library. It was modern and ancient at the same time, books, VCRs, and old rolled scrolls stood side by side. Tapes ran, showing men in black demonstrating killing techniques. It was a treasure trove of death.

"The Nazari of our tongue are the masters of potions. We teach the Taliban and al Qa'eda our methods in exchange for our ancient control of the narcotic, but they have never been here, even the Young Lion. We finance them. We nurture them. We control them. They do not hinder our beliefs or ways."

1450 WEDNESDAY / 10 OCTOBER 2001
HINDU KUSH MOUNTAINS / AFGHANISTAN

The team had just come down from an insane trail, and now they were in a wide river valley. It had been a cold, icy, and slippery descent. For the first time Iblis wasn't screwing around. He'd gotten the hint from two horses and one Afghan fighter that had fallen to their deaths. Dar got the message and got off, then walked Iblis most of the way down.

He had been in the middle of the line. A lot of the Afghan fighters wanted to, and tried to turn around, but three of the No Name team brought up the rear—they wouldn't back up an inch. Dar had looked at their faces through his binoculars—they were scared shitless too, but they had a job to do. Dar wouldn't have argued too hard if Rene had decided to turn around. But now they'd finally reached the base of the mountain.

Dar's range finder had it exactly ten miles to the base of the next crazy and insane climb. He mounted Iblis and pulled ahead to launch his rover.

Dar didn't know what to think when he first saw them. It was weird to see thousands of blue, gray, and yellow stumps. Getting closer, he saw that the colored stumps were women covered in burqas sitting on the cold ground.

They all sat on the ground, going nowhere. Hundreds, if not thousands, of children sat next to their mothers and stared wide-eyed at nothing.

He dismounted Iblis and walked toward the mass of people. No one moved. Thousands of eyes, zombie eyes, watched his approach. Iblis pulled back on his reins, not wanting to go farther. "Chicken." Dar dropped the reins and kept walking.

Before he got too close, he instinctively brought his rifle to the ready. The children looked starving, ready to die—but there were thousands of them.

It was drizzling and muddy. Everyone sat without moving in the muck. He saw tiny bundles stacked in several small mounds. He gasped when he saw tiny hands and feet sticking from the bundles. He couldn't go any farther. He pictured Rita and grasped the sonogram in his pocket.

The sounds of Ibilis's braying and hooves brought him out of his trance.

Several Afghan fighters suddenly rode into the women and started yelling and pushing everyone around. They shot their rifles into the air and rounded up the old men.

After herding their captives together, the fighters punched and kicked several of their captives.

Vance jumped off his mount and started yelling at the troops, pushing and shoving them until he had them separated from the camp. Vance argued with Ubu and his men for a few minutes longer. Then the Afghan fighters sulked back onto their horses and began riding toward the other end of the valley.

The team had circled on Dar and waited until Vance reached them.

"Our guys say that they don't know them, they may be Taliban or al Qa'eda family clans. Our guys didn't know what was true and were going to kill a few of the men to find out. Some of them insisted that they were enemy clans and wanted to kill everyone."

"Fuck that!" cried Dar. "I'm not here to kill women and children. And I'll tell you what. No one else here is going to either. *No one.*"

Rene surveyed the scene before him, then looked down at Dar. "Don't overreact, Dar. No one's going to kill anyone here; they're already dead. You know our mission. I got my orders. We got to make it over the next mountain before nightfall." He reined his horse and turned around.

The rest of the team followed.

"Hey, Rene," Dar called out. "We can't just leave them like this."

Rene stopped and looked over his shoulder. "We can't? Just what do you propose to do about it?"

Dar stood silent, thinking hard, then answered. "Airdrop! We can airdrop food to them."

"We can?" Rene looked interested.

"Yeah, if you'll let me."

"As long as it doesn't delay our mission."

"It won't."

"Then by all means. Do it."

"What if what our guys say is true and they are enemy-related?" Vance asked.

"Can you tell me who they are?"

"No."

"Are you willing to let women and children starve if Dar doesn't help?"

"No."

"Neither am I, whoever they are." Rene turned around and continued to ride.

Dar pulled out his keypad from his radio, punched a few numbers, and started talking. He picked up AWACS and asked about the C-17 humanitarian airdrops Intel had briefed.

The missions were conducted above twenty-five thousand feet. The purpose was to airdrop tons of packaged food to isolated groups and refugees caught in the cold mountains and deserts.

AWACS confirmed that the airdrops had been going on for three days.

Dar pulled out his map and located his position, then backed it up on his GPS. "You got something close to drop at..." He read his location.

AWACS said that a drop at his location was possible. "Are you requesting a humanitarian air drop?"

"Affirmative. Roger that!" He gave exact coordinates. Triple-checking his location to make sure everything was exact.

The team rode slowly, waiting for Dar to finish his call.

Dar put away his radio pad and trotted back to the people. "Anyone here speak English?"

A few moments later one of the frightened men nodded. "A little. My name, Abdullah Hadar."

"Very cool." Dar smiled. "Listen, Abdullah, when you guys pray to your God, look straight up, you're going to get food from the sky. Manna. They're from America. USA. Got that?"

Abdullah looked a little confused then gave a quizzical smile. "Food. USA?"

"Right!" Dar quickly shook the man's hand and trotted back to Iblis. He got on and rode away.

Dear Rita,
    Have I got a story to tell you when I get home!
                                    Dar

SOMEWHERE IN AFGHANISTAN

Jason smelled the familiar aromas of a trauma room: urine, disinfectant, and blood. It was some sort of hospital room. Several men lay in cots. They had all sorts of wounds and injuries.

"These men are not of our clan," Gul said. "They have been brought to us. The American bombs have taken a heavy toll on the Taliban and al Qa'eda. They are looking to us for medical aid. Our own physician was killed when he went out from our fortification to help them.

"This will be your final test. The Maltese have always been known for their healing ways and methods. I do believe that you are their messenger; this is why I have shown you our deepest heart—show the others here that you are a healer, or I will stick my own dagger into your heart. Tell me what you need to start."

They walked into the next room.

Jason walked around the room, mind racing. It was well lit and tiled with drains on the floor. A realization hit him. *The war's started, and must still be going on.*

A metal operating table was at the center of the room with a huge operating light over it. It was a state-of-the-art operating room. Jason had put in countless hours in trauma centers to perfect his field skills. It was like being asked the million-dollar question, and knowing the answer. *I'm gonna milk this for all it's worth!* "Well, Gul, I wouldn't want to infect anyone here with my infidel germs, so the first thing I need, is to be CLEAN!"

Alone in a scrub room, he formulated a lot of plans while he washed himself with a piece of soap from the bucket of warm water. Few were worth a promise. The transceiver still wasn't working, he had no idea where he was, or knew of any escape exits. Besides, there was still a good chance that he was getting closer to sealing the deal with the *assassins*.

Had everything he'd seen and heard been right, or real? What was it that Gul had said? "Assasseen, guardian of the secrets." Assassins by any other names were still stone-cold killers.

"Fuck me, these doper-killers are *ancient* thugs." He'd had his run-ins before with nutzos, but this took the cake. These were serious nutzo killers. "Dope-dealing nutzo killers training nutzo fanatic terrorists." He laughed to himself. "But at least I'm still breathing."

Scrubbing all the grime off him, many things were still

dark, but a few things did become clearer. His life was more than ever in jeopardy. No matter how they treated him, he was still their prisoner and under their control. He still hadn't located any escape exits, made contact with the Party, and the opium deal wasn't done. Now what about his captors? They were an ancient clan.

Everyone seemed to have some kind of lineage but him, the Maltese. Man, even the assassin thugs had a lineage. It was their land. They had been at this jihad struggle thing a lot longer than he, *a lot* longer.

The most obvious plan was to go along with Nazari, expecting to be tricked and betrayed at any point. But getting initiated into the assassin clan might open up more escape options and might even help him complete the mission.

He rinsed off and just stood, his mind aimlessly wandering.

They believed that he had intentions of becoming a Muslim, not that he would, and was about guaranteed to ace a test to become part of an ancient criminal elite. Killer ancestors. *Shit, I don't have any ancestors I can call my own.* Maybe that was why he couldn't connect to anyone's struggle. Maybe that was the reason he couldn't find what he was after. He was baseless, nothing to anchor on, without anything to call his own. No tradition.

The only tradition he'd ever had in his life was the pararescue brotherhood. Standing where he was, his body turned cold as an epiphany seized him.

It wasn't that true that he had no lineage. It wasn't true at all. He did. His ancestors went back as far as the first time a pararescueman laid down his life for another human being.

His brothers' heroic acts were legendary, historic. There was the Medal of Honor winner, William H. Pittsenbarger, and other mythic and noble guys like Rick Smith, Mark Judy, and Jason Cunningham. And the list went on and on. In the carnage of war or relative peace his brothers continually fought to maintain life, not destroy it. While the assassin's compulsion was to strike at life, the PJ's passion was to preserve it.

Treachery and illusions had no place beside the nobility of man's spirit.

"You come now!" someone called into the room.

"You bet! I'm right with you."

Jason stepped into the trauma ward a new man. Ready to continue playing the game, the second half was about to start. He would play by Nazari's rules, ready to make a few of his own when the time came.

Several of the men had gunshot wounds, others bled from missing limbs. Without emotion and calling on all his training and skill, he went on automatic. Using a standard triage, Jason called out orders while someone translated his words. A few slaps by Gul's gunmen got everyone not wounded to pitch in and help.

Medical help was needed. Jason figured that he was helping the enemy, but what could he do?

He was a PJ. He knew field medicine. If he didn't do something, then a dagger in his heart would be his reward. Taking charge, he methodically began to address the wounded.

Jason lost track of time until no one else was brought into the blood-covered operating room. He walked out of the room and dropped onto a carpet, exhausted. He lost count of the patients he worked on, perhaps fifty or more. Some had died on him while on the table. He didn't care; they were the enemy. Most would live. He just prayed that none of them he healed might one day go out and kill any Americans.

Gul Nazari sat next to him. Smiling with open admiration, he clasped Jason's shoulder. "Alice, you are truly from our old friends. And you are now a friend and guest of the Nazari. Soon you will be family. I am the Grand

Wizard of our clan, and it is my decision that you receive our brand."

Jason shuddered. He didn't want the mark of killers on him if he could help it.

"I will hear your true message now," Nazari said.

Jason raised his eyebrows and leaned back against a wall. "It's never changed. I'm here to buy your opium and deliver you arms."

"I believed this from the first."

"So why did I have to go through all this crap?"

Nazari sighed. "It was necessary to test you."

"Fine. So where am I and how much time has passed?"

"You are in our fortress of Samar. Only the Nuristani clans abide in these highlands. For over six hundred years, an outsider has never penetrated Samar and lived. You have been with us for a little more than two weeks. The Golden Horde has the Saudi kitten on the run. The Americans are now bombing the al Qa'eda and Taliban day and night. They are desperate for help, *our* help. They will pay anything for it. They both will get a measure of assistance from us, but not enough to be a threat to our ways.

"Cut off the head of the hydra and another, stronger head will take its place. This time the Afghan hydra will have a neck of steel, Nazari steel."

Jason was stunned. He quickly calculated that it must be the middle of October! He thought he'd been captive for months. It was the first time he thought about the world outside. *What is going on out there? Where the fuck is Ben?*

"You are tired. You will rest, then we shall initiate you. After that you and I will complete our dealings as family. You see, the Taliban actually believed that they were in control of this country. But they depended on us for many things—training, arms, and money. At this moment they are running for the mountains.

"They have discovered what every other invader has. This land may be occupied, but not held. Our order has been here for hundreds of years and will be here long after they, and any other foreigners, are gone. Come."

He led Jason through well-lit tunnels and caves. Several of the chambers looked well-appointed. Veiled men dressed in the same black or white clothing came and went, leaning forward and touching their hearts as they passed. Samar.

Jason caught glimpses of the night sky as they crossed several overpasses. He had a couple of things figured out by the time they went through an open gate and over a drawbridge. He was in a castle cut out of solid rock. It was a very ancient fortification.

The Nazari fortress, but no Westerner had probably ever even heard of it. But none of that mattered. With enough guile there just might be a way out.

They came to a row of rooms and Gul showed him to one of the chambers. "This will be yours. It will not be locked. You are here now on your honor." He peered closely at Jason. "To break that honor will be fatal. We will come for you soon. Do not wander too far from your room."

The chamber was a simple affair. He stood on a small prayer carpet next to a soft-looking pallet. A kerosene lamp lit the chamber and a Qur'an lay open on a reading rack. The only other things in the room were a washstand, a cup, and several cylindrical pillows. The pallet and pillows looked too inviting to pass up.

He had barely gotten comfortable when the door opened and Imam Sinan entered his room. "Are you ready to declare your belief?"

"I don't understand what you're asking."

The imam reached out until Jason took his hand, then he pulled himself close to Jason. He took off his blindfold and felt Jason's jaw, then gently guided him to his face. The imam had the eyes of the blind. It was no trick.

"I am a lifetime guest of the Nazari. I do not take part in their affairs. The Ismali library is all I require." He let go of Jason and sat down cross-legged on the carpet. "As for you, my friend, before you can go any farther you must declare your belief."

"What? To be a Muslim?"

Imam Sinan composed himself, and said, "At all times of man there have been good and righteous men, women, and children. They belong to God. It will always be that way. Alice, by definition, *all* of them are Muslim.

"Alice, are you a good and righteous man?"

"Yes." Jason wanted to come clean all the way, but kept his mouth shut. If he had spoken the full truth he would've told Sinan that he was good, but not *that* good. And he would've told him that he was only *technically* righteous. His friend Mac had said that he did a righteous job as a PJ. The only reason he was going through the deal with the nice old man was to keep his skin. *Oh well.*

The imam slowly got up. "It is time to declare your belief. Please stand."

Jason got up. "And how do I do that?"

"You will say, 'There is no deity but Allah, and Muhammad is His Prophet.'"

Jason did as he was told.

Sinan smiled. "You have given up all false gods. You have declared the Prophethood of Muhammad, peace be upon him." He shuffled toward the door and opened it. "With your admission you must believe in God, His angels, His revealed words, and life after death." The old man tied the blindfold back on and stepped into the hall. "It is done. You are a Muslim. All that remains is for your initiation into our clan."

"I'm a Muslim? That simple? I didn't even get dunked."

"Our ways are not like the People of the Book. Now

you are one of the Believers; only a believer may become a guardian of the secrets."

"Oh, okay. Now what?"

"You meet the clan. We go."

Jason followed the blind man, a little bewildered. He never thought that he would get snatched into the enemy's lair, just to emerge as one of them!

CHAPTER 23

An employee of NBC contracts a skin form of anthrax.

DAR WAS EXHAUSTED, BUT NOT YET READY TO rest. His eyes drooped and bobbed in unison with Iblis's gait. If he concentrated hard enough, he'd probably be able to fall asleep in the saddle. He'd already seen some who had fallen off their horse from sleeping. It was a funny sight.

Following their guides, the team crisscrossed ever more into high passes, always on guard for the ambush or the lone sniper covering a pass.

The day just didn't feel right to Dar. Even Iblis seemed more pissed off than usual, which was saying a lot. He heard the snaps over his head, then saw dirt geysers flare up around him.

"Oh SHIT!" It felt as if a bat whacked his helmet, then hit his back. He pitched sideways off Iblis and was out before he even hit the ground.

"Dar, Dar! Hey, Air Force, wake up!"

Dar opened his eyes to see Vance's concerned face looking down on him.

"What happened?" Dar tried to sit up, but a stabbing pain jabbed his back and he had a headache that felt like nails had been driven into his head.

"Stay down," Vance cautioned. "You got shot, but you ain't bleeding anywhere."

A firefight raged around them.

Dar kept his head low but watched as the Afghan fighters acted as one unit to try to ferret out whoever tried to trap them in a kill box. They fired for effect until the scene was secure. The Afghans fought as one; they were learning their lessons well.

Iblis stood totally oblivious to the battle blazing around him and grazed on nothing.

As soon as it had started, it was over. Whoever it was had made only one attack and vanished.

Dar's Kevlar helmet was creased; it had saved his life.

The best that Vance could figure out was that Dar took a second shot in the back as he fell from the horse. Once again technology saved his skin; the bulletproof vest had taken the round, but left a nasty welt that promised to bruise blue later in the day.

"I'm glad that you're alive, Dar," Rene offered. "Without you we'd have to get another combat controller."

"Thanks." Dar grimaced, Rene was not that interested in him as part of the team, just his talents to put bombs on targets.

Dar could almost swear he heard Iblis guffaw as he tried to grab the reins. It hurt like hell to sit in the saddle. With Dar's helmet damaged and bulletproof vest shattered, the mangy horse seemed to want to give extra bounces just to add to the aggravation.

"Dar," Vance said, riding close. "I think that you were pinpointed for death. The ambush looks like it was just concentrated on you. I think that someone among our

Afghan allies *ain't* a buddy. I think that they gave you away. What you've done to their land is making you, and that radio of yours, a priority target."

A chill came over Dar. Until then it hadn't occurred to him that someone would actually want to kill him. After all the years of training, knowing that his job only happened behind enemy territory, he never figured that engaging a foe could become personal. The first rule of war was to kill or be killed. There was nothing he could do but try not to be a stationary target.

Thoughts of his pregnant wife grew great in his mind. What would happen to her and his child if anything happened to him? Fear crept into his mind. Suddenly in his mind he saw snipers everywhere he looked. He wanted to find the traitors among the group and kill them, anything to keep from getting killed.

Another set of thoughts hit him harder than the bullets: Up until then he hadn't really thought of his enemies as human beings; they were just targets, almost like something in a video game. But they had to have families too. How many families had he destroyed? He learned a valuable truth. There was no glory or honor in war.

Someone actually *wanted* him dead. These people had been ritually killing each other forever. And then here he comes, this dressed-up kid with a combat radio and space-age technology to ruin their ceremony of death. They resented him for taking away their manhood, beliefs, and God.

To the Afghan men he had brought an atrocity of war. What did he know about killing?

Pulling Iblis's reins, he looked the horse in the eyes. A better relationship would begin. "See, horse, you keep me from getting killed and I'll give you the best care you've ever had. You don't, and I'll shoot you myself, do you understand?"

Once again, Iblis conveyed his immediate concerns by letting go a load of turds.

2125 HOURS
ABOARD A C-17 III GLOBEMASTER THIRTY-FIVE
THOUSAND FEET OVER AFGHANISTAN

The cargo compartment lights were set on red. The air-drop light was on red.

"Cabin altitude checklist complete," Loadmaster Rich Duke said. He'd been wearing his oxygen mask for the past couple of hours, breathing pure oxygen with the rest of the crew to decrease the amount of nitrogen in their bodies.

Without prebreathing 100 percent oxygen, the five-person crew stood a good chance of getting decompression sickness.

"This sucks," Duke mumbled.

The inside of his oxygen mask was dripping with sweat, but there was no way he'd disconnect from his helmet to dry it out. They would have to scrub the mission and they had come too damn far just to turn around and go home because he was a little uncomfortable.

They had taken off eight hours earlier from Ramstein Air Base, Germany, with over seventeen thousand yellow packs of individual humanitarian daily rations (HDRs), blankets, and all kinds and sizes of winter clothing. The food contained in the HDR packets was vegetarian: beans, rice, and dried fruit, over two thousand calories per meal.

Packed in forty-two refrigerator-sized cardboard boxes called triwall aerial delivery system containers (TRIADS), the boxes were rigged to fall from his C-17 and disintegrate in the slipstream, leaving the lifesaving food and material to flutter to the ground.

Safely harnessed to the cargo floor, and standing at the ramp and door controls, Duke gave the physiological technician a thumbs-up, to continue on with the drop. The pilot depressurized the plane.

The pilot took the crew through the slowdown checklist and dropped the flaps as the loadmaster opened the cargo ramp and door, letting in the minus-sixty-eight-degree, oxygen-depleted weather.

Duke grimaced in his mask. The temperature in the cargo compartment instantly dropped. Now he wasn't just claustrophobic in his mask; he was cold too, even through his winter flight gear. Through all the effort and dangers combined with flying over hostile territory, he smiled—there was no other place he or the rest of the crew would rather be. Starving lives were about to be saved.

All the defensive electronic equipment and missile warning systems were on and ready to react automatically to any ground attack. Flares, chaff, and infrared countermeasures would confuse and break the lock on any missile trying to get a shot in their direction.

The loadmaster looked for a nod from the second loadmaster, then finished the slowdown call. "Check completed."

All restraints but the aft strap had been removed. The static lines were clear and attached to the anchor cables. The drop was on. Duke nervously rocked back and forth on his feet. Sweat poured down his helmet in the frigid air. He was ready to react to any malfunction. It was up to the pilot to finish the airdrop. Duke's job was to react quickly to any malfunctions.

The pilot maneuvered the plane to a nose-up attitude. The TRIADS, sitting on rollers, strained at the aft restraint. He followed the navigation screen to the drop. Someone on the ground had given the coordinates. He hoped that the coordinates were good. This was a blind drop.

It was the copilot's turn. "Five, four, three, two, one, green light." He hit the jump light switch that automatically released the aft restraint.

It sounded like a freight train as the entire load raced

off the plane and came apart in the slipstream in less than eight seconds.

The two loadmasters walked out onto the ramp and pulled in any straps that might keep the ramp and door from closing. The loadmaster then buttoned up the tail end and the cargo heaters came on full blast to pressurize the jet's interior.

Duke didn't have time to savor what he and the crew had done until he completed the postdrop checks. The plane pressurized, bringing the cabin back down to a safe condition.

Cleared to go off oxygen, Duke disconnected his oxygen mask and pulled off his helmet. "Ahhhh." He sighed, scratching his head and wiping the sweat from his jaw, enjoying the freedom of movement.

The C-17 did a lazy left turn to begin its long journey back to Germany. It would take one midair refueling and another eight hours before they could get into crew rest.

Tired, but satisfied, they had another seven hours of flying before they would touch down back at Ramstein. It would be a long trip, but by not having landed in another country they wouldn't have to waste valuable crew rest clearing customs. After crew rest they were scheduled to turn around in twelve hours and do it again.

2130 HOURS
CHARIKAR VALLEY / AFGHANISTAN

The evening prayers were over. Abdullah Hadar tried to believe in the American's promise, but he held little hope. Miracles came from angels and genies, yes, but from American strangers? No. He walked among the women and children, trying to tell them that God's will was for them to live, if just for one more day.

He was tired. Out of food, there was nowhere left to go. The Taliban had entered their villages, taking away the men and boys who were old enough to fight. They drove the women and children before them as hostages until they reached the base of the Slaughter Mountains, then abandoned the women, children, and old men to "God's will."

It would take over fifteen days to walk back to their villages. They would all starve to death before they made it. If starvation did not stop them, then the cold, freezing wind and rain would undoubtedly kill them as surely as if the Taliban had.

He looked up and thought it was raining. Confused, he watched as the ground was peppered with small yellow objects. At first the people panicked, thinking that it was the notorious American cluster bombs.

A few gingerly touched the yellow bags—several kinds of land mines were colored yellow. Opening the bags, they found food inside, and then it was a scramble as everyone grabbed the precious packages. Blankets and jackets flitted in and around the mass of people.

"Life!" Hadar cried out. The American's miracle had come to pass. There was enough food and warm clothing from above to get them home again. His people would live. The family clans would hold together. The Taliban were gone. Now, God willing, they could get home in time to plant his fields, and they could continue to farm in their old ways.

Hadar started to call out orders; everyone had to work together, gather the food and clothes, then thank God, and go home. "Life! Life to all Americans," he cried out.

CHAPTER 24

JASON COULD BARELY OPEN HIS EYES. "OH SHIT, IS it bright, or what?" He grimaced.

Cupping his eyes, he rolled from his back onto his stomach.

Slowly opening his eyes, he stood, shaky, and tried to look around. Vibrant colors and strange visions met his eyes. There was no question he was on some sort of chemically induced mind screw. *Hell. Not again. Now how did they get me all juiced up again?*

And on what drug this time? It had to stop. What did they think he was, a junkie?

Things swam and flew in front of his eyes. Where was he? It was some sort of private hallucination.

Whatever he was high on, he hated it. "How do people get used to this psychedelic shit?" He had experienced enough drugs to last him a lifetime. Then he realized why he hated them so much—if he had nothing else going on in his life, he might actually get used to them. The same thing applied to booze.

Damn, what just flew over me? Angels? Genies? And they were good-looking too!

No. They weren't flying, *he* was. He was on some sort of magic flying carpet. It was kind of like being on the Peter Pan ride at Disney World, except that he was on a carpet flying over endless lush gardens. Fountains sprang from turquoise-blue lakes.

Flying low over one garden he could see women lounging on the green, green grass.

The women were gorgeous, incredible.

Passing over the lovely ladies, they waved to him as the carpet headed toward a series of towers. Getting closer, it looked like they were castles of some sort; amazing palaces right out of a story in the *Arabian Nights*.

The carpet flew through a Moorish arch, then softly landed in a courtyard. He got up and started to walk around. This time he did not want to escape. His mind and body were reeling with pleasure. But what was he seeing?

It was like an oasis in Paradise. Was this a hidden garden? Colorful trees surrounded him, and he actually knew the names of them, persimmon, pomegranate, and more. There were carpets everywhere with incredibly intricate mosaic patterns. For a moment Jason thought he'd get lost forever in bliss, amazed by the beauty of the magic carpets.

A violet-and-amber sunset slowly turned the sky to a dark blue, but floating lights turned the garden into a nighttime wonderland.

And then he saw the moon and freaked out! He had to be insane. It looked as if the moon were smiling at him, a crooked but very loving smile.

Turquoise streams flowed. Waterfalls spilled into gentle pools with spurting fountains.

He was stoned on some really hallucinogenic and metaphysical shit.

She came to him like a dream, veiled in violet silks from head to toe. It was her dark eyes that captivated him. They almost looked like the eyes of the wild cat that had disappeared into the Florida Everglades, but this cat had desire in her eyes. He *wanted* to tangle with her.

She dropped her veil, and Jason realized he *had* been transported to Paradise.

Wordlessly she held his head and drew him close. He could smell lavender perfume.

She kissed him. "Hello, Lost Soul. I am a Lost Soul, too."

They made love.

It had been so long since Jason had held a woman in his arms that his chemically induced passions drove him way, way over the edge with lust. Still, this woman outmatched him in the lovemaking world, driving him ever higher to pleasures he had never known before in his life. She was everything he had ever missed, it was all his. After all the gorgeous women he had passed in his life but never got a simple "hello" from here was a love he could grab on to and hold. But was it real? Who was this woman who had to be a goddess?

"Who are you?"

"I am your illusion, desire," she seductively smiled. "I am your beloved. I am your lost heart. I am your delivered relief. Love me now, and your memories will be sweeter than honey. Touch me once, and I will be yours forever."

If this was his last moment alive, he wanted to remember every feature of the beautiful smile on the face in front of him. Her smile was for him alone. He kissed her again and again. She returned his passion with even more intensity.

All his emotions broke like a dam. She held him and he entered the Garden of Bliss.

Like a drunk who'd lapsed into a stupor, Jason was aware that his senses had returned to normal. Looking around his room, he was alone with the scent of lavender perfume.

His head hurt. He sat up trying to regain his senses. Had he even left the chamber? Things seemed back to reality. Did he really make love to an incredible woman, and feel the way he had once with a woman in a Bosnian cave? Was it just another part of his private hallucination? Where did she come from? Where did she go? She had to be real—that, or his mind was totally blown.

Who was she? If she was an illusion, nothing in his life ever felt more real, even stoned on some spacey drug. This had to be what he'd been searching for.

"What is her name?" he whispered.

1300 SATURDAY / 13 OCTOBER 2001
THE PARTY / MELBOURNE / FLORIDA

They had given up. He was gone. There was no mission, but Cadallo wouldn't release anyone from the building. Where the Party started out as a force, it was now a prison. Their cubicles were cells. No one could get in and no one would be let out. All the arguing from everyone was for naught. Cadallo made it clear that the only other place they could go, if they chose, was a federal cell in solitary until he said the mission was over.

They could sit all day and night in front of a computer, or look at crystal-clear imagery of any part of Afghanistan, but what for? All the millions spent on high-tech electronic gadgets couldn't do jack shit to find the one man the Party was dedicated to support. They lost him and it was their fault.

Ben Cadallo learned that there was a *big* difference between civilian and active-duty subordinates—civilians had a tendency to talk back and question orders. The uniform and spit and polish might've worked a few weeks ago. It counted for nothing now. His credibility had taken some major hits.

Everybody else had seemed to lose hope of or interest in ever finding their operator but one person.

"Gomez, can you hear me?" Bri Lopez sat for hours at her station, endlessly changing frequencies, making calls and listening for a voice that she had committed to memory the first time she heard him resist the situation he was in. At the same time she would check in to the line tap connected to the Vatican.

She planned on sitting at her station until they made her leave the Party. Gorsline and Ibrahim would relieve her. Bri believed that Gomez, or whoever he was, was a fighter. He'd show up somewhere. He *had* to.

CHAPTER 25

1845 SUNDAY / 14 OCTOBER 2001
HINDU KUSH MOUNTAINS / AFGHANISTAN

Bush rejects the Taliban's offer to hand over bin Laden to a neutral country in return for stopping the bombing.

DAR GARO WAS ON THE CHASE, DRIVING IBLIS FOR all he was worth. The rover circled overhead, shadowing the Taliban's retreat. It was definitely a fighting retreat. Without airpower, the struggle might've resulted in heavy casualties, or even turned into a counterattack.

It was hard for the jet fighters and bombers to hit the moving and fleeing targets from their high altitude. Command had restricted them from going lower. The bombs that they dropped were often ineffective as they bounced off the deep ravine's insane angles.

Apache Longbow helicopters became instant stars, providing air cover by launching their 6.5-inch rockets, trying to keep foes' heads down and on the run.

It was a concert of chaos and levels of death. A new order of battle was evolving.

From a god's-eye view, spy satellites in space defined the area of direct military interest to the out-of-theater commanders, thousands of miles away from the action. U-2s and Global Hawks above seventy thousand feet transmitted the details below to target planners in Florida and Saudi Arabia.

Big reconnaissance jets like the AWACS, JSTARS, Nimrod, and Rivet Joint flew at assigned levels between thirty and fifty thousand feet. They carried air traffic controllers, linguists, and a host of specialists relaying and conducting battle.

EC-130 ABCCC Hercules jammed, tapped, and over-rode enemy communications. Commando Solo planes dropped leaflets and did psychological operations.

Fighters and bombers overhead above fifteen thousand feet stood by, waiting to get into the action while AC-130U gunships at five thousand feet wasted any enemy firing at the choppers or troops on the ground.

Just above the action uninhabited aerial vehicles relayed battle-damage assessment in near real time. In several secure and classified rooms, concerned viewers watched as space-age soldiers used ancient battle tactics to try and kill a force with martyrdom on their mind—there would be no surrender.

The enemy was on the run, horses, all-terrain vehicles, twisting and turning while they fired on the ground to get in their best shot as they headed ever higher into the mountains that had triumphed over every conqueror who tried to subdue the ferocious Afghans.

Time was beginning to jumble together for Dar. They had started out working only at night, stealthy and secret, but now they fought at all hours, day and night. He'd learned to instinctively act, then react, to the tide of battle and be able to know which way the bullets and mortars were flying. He was The Man when it came to calling in and pinpointing the Big Drops.

Several times the team rendezvoused with the Chinooks

for supplies and incoming Dagger and KA-BAR personnel inputs. Dar would pass on his information to arriving CCT and, at the same time, get more batteries for his radio and the latest changes.

Back in focus and surveying the scene, if he could get to high enough ground he'd be in the perfect spot overlooking the far ridge, where the enemy had collected to make a stand. He had to get to the high ground, then he could rain hell down on the enemy.

It was nonstop action since the first bombs dropped. The Taliban and al Qa'eda were fierce fighters, better organized than the Afghans, better disciplined. Rarely did the enemy willingly surrender. They'd dig in or disappear into countless mountain caves.

Airpower permanently sealed them in, and most of the locals believed that Dar was God's hand that did it—they were afraid of him, and some hated him.

Once riding through the results of one of his calls, he was horrified and awed to know he was the one who'd pinpointed everything. Everything burned. The vehicles were melted, tossed off the roads like child's toys. The only thing he could recognize were body parts, no whole bodies.

The sounds of destruction were replaced by silence.

Like zombies and vultures, people started appearing from nowhere, stripping the body segments and taking anything of value, including shattered wood to use as fuel.

It was war. It was what he'd trained for. Power. It was supposed to be sweet. Well, it wasn't anymore. It was scary, a nightmare. He would do his job, but he'd always remember the awesome power that he had learned to control, and the death that it brought.

The special operators had finally accepted him as one of their own. Some of the Afghan fighters would do a small bow and touch their hearts as he passed. Others stood back and stared at him through their dark eyes as if he were some sort of evil apparition.

There were still a lot of things to learn about the locals. The part of Afghanistan that they were in was peopled with basically either Pashtuns, or Tajiks with some kind of clan loyalty to one warlord or another. Everyone looked and talked the same to Dar. Sometimes even the locals got confused, unless they flew their flags. "Gang rags," as Vance called them.

Be what may, Dar was getting *good* at calling in air attacks and the one he was trying to set up next would snuff out about ten truckloads of enemy fighters.

He could've used the rover to find the best vantages, but that was too easy. His only addition to the little flyer would be a laser targeter. But then it could spell the end of the CCT job. That was something to think about later. A battle was quickly developing. If he could just get to a near, high ridge it would give him the optimum position to call in air.

He drove, cajoled, and cursed Iblis up the side of the mountain until the horse refused to climb any higher. Jumping off the animal and looking down the valley, he saw that the trucks were just minutes from reaching the base of the mountains on the other side. The Afghans on horseback were hopelessly outdistanced. Where he was at was just as good as any to go to work.

When he checked in he was quickly voice ID'd by a pack of F-15s.

"Whatcha' got for us?" the flight leader, Jeff "Powder" Hannold, queried.

"You see the scene in the valley?"

"Tally," Powder said.

"You see the trucks?"

"Got 'em."

The Taliban was about to cross a bridge over a river. Bridges, power stations, mosques, schools, hospitals, and any other infrastructures were off-limits to bombing.

"You see the guys on the horses?"

"Roger."

"Kill the guys in the trucks. The ones on the horses are the good guys."

"We're crashing this party," Powder confirmed.

"Right with you," his wingman keyed.

The Taliban seemed to understand the rule of leaving bridges intact. They rallied beneath a major bridge and began to put up a fierce stand like a cornered lion.

Powder wasn't having it. He dived below the hard deck and made his pass over the bridge. "DRB."

"Yeah," answered Dirty Rat Bastard, Powder's wingman.

"Let's do the standard play we use at Cope Thunder, you know the one?"

"Roger."

"Mind if we run this?" Powder queried Dar.

"Go for it," Dar answered.

Powder went vertical and disappeared into the sun as Rat Bastard dived supersonic toward the bridge.

Dar had to cup his ears to keep them from bursting when Rat roared down the valley just feet over the bridge. The ear-shattering noise frightened and enraged the Taliban.

DRB then made a couple of passes in front of the bridge, creating a horrifically loud sonic boom, drawing small-arms fire that would never reach him to do any damage.

On the third pass, huge portions of the dry riverbed beneath the bridge exploded from the other direction, sending men and vehicles flying into the river.

Powder came in zooming from the other direction. He released two AGM-65s and guided them in right on target, barely scorching the concrete pilings.

DRB used the Taliban's panic to roll over the bridge and let loose his own missile, firing it point-blank into the vehicles and enemy, creating a firestorm beneath the bridge.

The concrete bridge held, but the resolve of the Taliban didn't. They broke and made a headlong rush to reach the mountains.

Dar made rapid calculations with the intention of preventing the Taliban from reaching the base of the mountains.

"We got one laser bomb left between us," Powder said.

Dar reached into his pocket and pulled out his laser target designator. "I'm lasing the target. I'm trying to slam the door shut on them," he signaled Powder.

Dar waited until the bomb struck. Now the Taliban's exit was cut off. They were in the open and at the mercy of their pursuers. The fight was going to be nasty, but he had no intention of being anywhere near it.

"Thanks for the work," Dar keyed. "We got it from here."

"Our pleasure, really. Out." Powder and his wingman beat feet toward home. "Hey, Rat, go to private interplane."

Dirty Rat Bastard switched channels. "Yeah."

"Let's get back to base, fast. Tonight's steak and lobster at the mess hall!"

"Right on."

Dar was about to get back on Iblis when his eyes were drawn to the top of the ridge by a strange glow. It wasn't that far to reach, but way too steep for Iblis to climb. It was worth investigating, so he started out on foot.

Cresting it, he saw an unbelievably beautiful sight. Hidden under a giant alcove was a turquoise-blue mosque with two massive columns that touched together at the top, creating a Moorish arch. The whole place *glowed*. Stepping closer, he heard a rhythmic clapping sound.

He quietly entered through the front hall, ready to blast away at the first sign of the enemy. The place looked like something out of a fairy tale. The walls were solid marble inlaid with lapis lazuli Arabic writing. How could such a wonderful spectacle exist in the middle of nowhere, in the middle of a war? As he walked farther down the great hall, the music became clearer.

Some type of percussion accompanied the clapping, then haunting strings floated in the air, accompanied by a flute. He followed the music toward a white-and-red chamber.

The music had acoustical combinations that Dar couldn't identify, but was attracted to nonetheless. It had rhythm that was very alluring. He came to a huge room. He swept the room with his rifle, looking for any hostile intentions coming his way. There were none; as a matter of fact, everyone was totally oblivious to his appearance. A small band played on the far side of the room.

In place on the light blue marble floor, men in long white gowns spun in circles, their gowns billowing out like a fan. It was a peaceful and hypnotic sight, until the staccato blasts in the valley shook him back to reality. The musicians didn't stop playing and the spinning men continued to twirl in another dimension.

"Hello, brother, welcome. You are on holy ground. All are welcome. You do not need your weapons here."

Dar spun on the balls of his feet, finger on the trigger of his rifle, ready to fire. The small man in front of him had a calm but bright look on his face.

"You do not need your weapons here. The Taliban and Saudi have left. They called us heretics and were violent. They killed many of our order. They would not let the Sufi perform the *sama*. But now, because of your aggression, we spin once again."

The small man wore a purple robe and bright blue turban.

"Who are you?" Dar asked.

"Brother, we are a tariqah order. Many call us Sufi.

And what you see in front of you are dervishes, followers of al-Rumi."

"Who?"

"The founder of our sect, al-Rumi. He was born very near, in Wakhsh, in the year 1207 of your time. This is the Mawlawi brotherhood of Islam. This is a place where we commune with our beloved. This is one place where we express our love for God in poems, music, dance, and song.

"The ceremony before you is our offering to God for His mercy on us all, peace and salvation from sin. Truth is here, in our movements, we are not separate from the *Divine*."

Dar shook his head and gazed at the effortless turning dervishes. "I don't understand, you're dancing for peace?"

"We dance for the unity of being. They are knowing God, seeing God, and uniting with God, functioning on love, they are reaching the highest level of intelligence for all salvation from sin."

"You're saving everyone from sin?"

He glanced down at Dar's rifle. Concussions from explosions in the fighting below shook the hall.

"If God were to punish the sinners, He would leave no creature on earth alive. We thank him for sparing our worthless lives. We spin to find Reality, peace. We are not Christian, Moslem, or Jew. We dance in triumph forever."

Dar was doing his own dance, and his dance partners weren't waiting on him. He smiled at the man; there was no war here. "I'm glad to have been able to help you all, but there's a war going on out there and I have to get back to it."

"War and peace, death and rebirth, it all happens in the creastic folds of our eternally crossing paths. American, I tell you for true, we pray every day for your Trade Tower martyrs who were murdered by the al Qa'eda

Saudi. It was a terrible, terrible act that bought freedom for the Afghan peoples."

"I don't follow you."

"Without that attack, you would never have come to our land to release us from our oppressors."

Dar nodded and backed out of the hall, dervish music fading in his ears. He slid down the scree back to his horse, surprised to see the animal still waiting. "See, you nag, our 'eternal paths' were meant to cross. So don't screw with me anymore."

As if Iblis understood, he laid out a long stream of steaming urine.

CHAPTER 26

0130 MONDAY / 15 OCTOBER 2001
FORTRESS SAMAR / AFGHANISTAN

The heaviest bombing raids occur in Afghanistan.

JASON FELT HIS ROBES. THEY WERE WARM, strong, and well made. The imam said that they were made from virgin lambskin, virgin material that symbolically represented an initiate of the order.

Checking himself out, he had to smile; he looked pretty good in the assassin getup. "Too bad I can't get a graduation picture of this."

He had shaved himself hairless from the neck down according to the imam's instructions, leaving his pubic hair untouched. The door was unlocked, but he knew better than to try an escape at this time—so close to being accepted, it was stupid to try and get out.

A man dressed in white robes and veiled face opened the door and entered, then silently motioned for Jason to turn around.

A blindfold was placed over his eyes. A hand was placed on his right shoulder. It firmly pushed him forward.

Light and sound came his way. The hand pushed him faster and soon he was trotting. Waves of heat, then cold, washed over him.

The hand pushed him faster and in no time Jason was running, following the lead of the hand. He had to trust that it would not guide him to, then throw him over, the side of a cliff.

Echoes, voices and music, bounced around him. It felt like he was running through caverns, then tiny tunnels that might bang his head. There was no stopping. Then he was sprinting and it felt like his heart and lungs would explode.

The hand gripped and pulled Jason to a stop. He bent over, taking in as much air as he could. He could smell kerosene and a burning odor, maybe torches.

Someone spoke, but he had no idea what was being said. He figured that it might really be another test rather than an initiation, then passing it meant life or death. He'd better pay attention or it was all over. He straightened up and listened to the words being spoken again, this time in English.

"Who comes to the Temple of Light?"

Jason stood for a moment thinking of the words the imam had coached him on. It was time to meet the clan. "One who wishes to know your grandfathers."

The blindfold was pulled away. Jason was struck dumb by what he saw. It looked very much like the Paradise in his hallucination. Peering closer at the walls and floor he saw the lights; looking up he saw the hand-painted sky. *Nice job. Real professional.* This *was* the place where he made love to a goddess, but instead of her, there were black-and-white ninja-looking people. *Okay, don't goof around.* These people were serious about what was happening. A screwup, or misstep, and it would be all over.

A ninja type with a golden arrowhead crowning his turban began speaking.

"Our grandfathers' time begins before the time of the Prophet, birthed by the Lord of the Flames."

As the man spoke he walked toward Jason with a strange-looking dagger. He knew that the Arabs were queer for daggers.

"This is the Jahiliyya dagger, your dagger. Your honor to the Nazari is loyalty." He reached out, took Jason's right hand, and sliced his thumb. The blood dripped into a cup an assistant held. "Your blood is now our blood, mixed with the sacred waters of Zam-Zam. You will share your essence with the keeper of the Furnace."

The cup was passed from man to man, who cut themselves and added their blood until it returned to the orator. He then passed the cup back to Jason and stood back.

"And who shall teach thee what Hell-fire is? It leaves not, spares not, and blackens the skin!" The orator made a motion for Jason to drink.

Jason took a deep breath, then took a sip from the cup and handed it back.

Once again it passed to each man, who also drank the pooled blood until it was back to the speaker.

The speaker drained the cup and held it over his head. "By Allah, he who drinks from our cup will become we, and we become he, together, forever."

A gong echoed.

The speaker said. "Hassan was beloved by the Prophet, peace be upon him. As a token of his love, he gave him a piece of his cloak. The Cloth of the Prophet was in the Nazari family until five years ago, when it was stolen." A miniature Qur'an was laid in front of him. The man opened it.

It was the green swatch in plastic that was in the Qur'an he took as a souvenir after killing a Muslim in Bosnia. *Go figure.*

A big ninja got behind Jason and pulled up his left

sleeve. He raised Jason's left arm and braced it. The brand that lay in the coals was red-hot.

A man took it from the coals and walked toward Jason. The tip of the iron brand he held glowed red-hot.

Jason steeled himself for what was coming.

The orator, standing next to Jason, spoke. "It is the poisoned arrowhead, mark of the assassin. Mark of the Nazari clan. Whoever bears this mark is your brother, body and soul.

"If God were to punish men for their wrongdoing, He would not leave on this earth a single creature." The orator dropped his veil. It was Gul Nazari, who nodded at the man holding the brand.

Jason's skin sizzled and he smelled his own searing flesh, but he didn't cry out. He'd taken worse, remembering how he stayed silent as he suffered under the insane bastard who beat him; these guys were just as nuts. No, they were zealot drug dealers. He'd taken worse.

"We are God's hand to kill the wrongdoer."

The veil fell away and he was looking at a smiling man with gold teeth. Jason wanted to kick his ass, but kept his cool as Gold Teeth touched his heart, then kissed Jason on both cheeks.

"Say nothing," Gold Teeth whispered.

"Fuck you," Jason mouthed.

One after another, the remaining assassin brothers did the same thing as Gold Teeth. Jason sniffed each person. No lavender scents.

Gul was the last person in the line and slipped the dagger into the front of Jason's sash. "Under the penalty of death, you will *never* reveal our existence to an outsider."

The initiation rite *had* to be over. He was an assassin, and looked on as family of the Nazari. He was an Islamic ninja.

Jason was now a keeper of the secrets. But what secrets, Jason didn't know.

He was guided to a small chamber, where Gul sat waiting on a thick carpet. He touched the side of the rug, indicating where Jason was to sit.

"And now, Alice, your message," Gul said.

"Well, you stole my thunder when you found the Qur'an on me. That was it. I was bringing the cloth as a token."

"From who?"

Jason looked directly into Gul's eyes. "The Maltese," he lied.

"YES!" Gul clapped Jason on his shoulder. "That explains all. Only the Maltese could deliver to me the most sacred and holiest icon of all Islam. Its true value is beyond estimation. Now I have the mandate to rule not only Afghanistan, but all Muslims!"

Jason was in shock. The look in Gul's eyes showed something close to rapture, or madness. *Damn, am I glad I brought that sucker with me!* He could have left the little Qur'an in the corner of his closet. Treachery and illusions; he'd unwittingly pulled a fast one on the Gul Nazari, Assassin Grand Wizard. "Right, but I'm still here to buy all your opium." Jason wasn't stupid. He needed to play whatever role Gul had cast him in.

Gul waved his finger in the air. "Alice, consider it done. But that is a matter for later. Tonight we celebrate your joining our clan. This is a special night. Only those who have reached the eighth level of our clan may attend. You, because of your tests, and the fact that you come from the Maltese, progress to this level."

Gul suddenly grabbed Jason's chin. "You have seen, heard, and learned to become one of us. Now hear the truth. There is nothing true; it is all treachery and illusion. All is allowed. There. In one sentence I have advanced you several degrees, which takes a lifetime to achieve.

"Maltese, you have become one of us, and as their

emissary, now you are bound to do your first assassination for the clan."

"What?"

Gul suddenly slapped him on the back as if he were making a joke, but he wasn't. "You must know of our tradition of reciprocation. There is one man who stands in the way of our transaction, but with your skills it is a minor obstacle.

"He controls the passes where we will carry your opium. He refuses to allow our load through. He has molested one of our own. He has insulted and robbed our Order of three loads of narcotic. This is an insult to our honor and we must have our satisfaction.

"We of the Nazari cannot purge his influence as he is under Saudi protection. But an unknown, someone such as you, can do the removal. You have the honorary degree of an eighth-level assassin. But it is not a free honor. Do this for me and it will seal our relations."

"Whatever it takes." He was positive that he had been suckered, but there was no way he was going to call Gul a liar.

"Come. It is time to celebrate!"

This time the hall was full of clan by blood and eighth-level assassins, and no women. They sat on the floor at small tables. A small band played festive music as the men dropped their veils and twirled their worry beads around on their fingers. The smell of hashish and opium coming from the several hookahs was almost overpowering. Wine, vodka, absinthe, and Iraqi gin bottles were passed from hand to hand.

Jason sat next to Gul, watching the impromptu dances and returning stares of curiosity or hostility—being a favorite of the number-one man had its advantages, but pissing off any of his protectors was a guaranteed disadvantage. At least his moves had taken him this far to keep the deal working, so there was no reason that he couldn't take it to the final act, as long as he didn't screw up and wind up dead.

ASSASSIN MOUNTAIN FORTRESS SAMAR / AFGHANISTAN

She would come to Jason like a whisper.

At first they only made passionate love, then she was gone. Later she would stay longer and they would quietly talk.

"What is your name?" was Jason's first question.

She frowned. "I will not tell you, then you not tell anyone. Understand? I cannot leave this place alive." She smiled. "Anyway, we may not live long. We have just now. I am lonely, and you are here. I will make love to you, but we can be friends, no?"

Jason nodded. "No names, then." In his mind he would call her Lavender, after her scent.

At times they would just hold each other saying nothing. At other times they would whisper made-up stories of dreams and fantasies.

She had memorized the *Arabian Nights* and entertained Jason for hours with ribald Eastern tales.

With the mystery woman Jason wished that the world and its problems would just go away. He wondered if this was just another test of Nazari's, or another way of holding him prisoner.

0800 HOURS
SAMAR FORTRESS / AFGHANISTAN

Jason entered the small room. Gul was seated at the head of the room warming his hands from the flames of a lantern next to him on a carpet. He was on his own, and free to roam the stronghold, but knew that his every move was being watched. He'd figured out ways to escape Samar, but then what? There was nowhere to go; besides, his nights with the mysterious woman had become worth staying for.

A feast of lamb and fruits was spread out on a tray.

Jason sat on the carpet next to the assassin and began eating. After a few handfuls of food he asked, "What're the terms?"

"Terms?" Gul smiled. "Why, nothing's changed; 300 million dollars, and included in the deal is the weapons shipment. We will deliver the narcotic to Pakistan. Alice, I am very interested in how a clever person such as you will make all of this happen."

Jason held up his hands. "You make it sound way too easy. I didn't go through all your *tests* just to give away big bucks; I know that if I give it all to you up front, I'm probably dead."

Gul feigned a look of astonishment. "Impossible! You are now one of the clan, one of us. How can you consider this?"

"Past history." Jason wanted to tell Gul all about his dealings with the Doors, but would only let on to the wisdom he'd gained from them. "Then, as clan, you won't mind me covering my own ass. Here's the deal: I'll give you one hundred now, one hundred when the shipment crosses the Pakistani border, and the last hundred when the Falcon organization takes possession of it.

"The weapons I'll give to you now. Just point out the airstrip that you want it delivered to." Jason tried to sound as calm as possible, but his mind was racing. This was his only chance to get a message to Ben. All he had to do was remember the codes and follow the pattern the bishop had shown him. "I'm sure that you have a bank account somewhere."

"Several." Nazari's eyes gleamed. Like magic, a satellite phone and map appeared. Gul spread the map before Jason.

Jason was shocked to see that it was an American military map. "There." He pointed to a spot on the official National Imaging and Mapping Agency (NIMA) aviation chart of Afghanistan. "Right there, deliver the weapons tomorrow, at noon. Now you make your call and I will tell you what account to transfer the money to." He covered Jason's hand. "No tricks."

Jason nodded, then punched in the numbers and waited, while Gul pulled out his own phone to monitor the conversation.

Gul then handed Jason a paper with the name and account number of his bank.

"Yes?" a metallic simulated voice answered.

"Hello, I am calling for a voice-verified confirmation transaction," Jason said, then waited.

"Please continue."

"There is a fly in my milk."

"How may I help you?"

Jason was elated. "I would like to make a transfer of funds."

"How much?"

It went back and forth until the transfer had been made.

"The transfer is complete. May I be of further service?"

"Yes." Jason then gave a time, date, and location of the planes to land.

"Anything else?"

Gul shook his head.

"No, thank you." Jason turned off the phone, handed it back to Gul, and nonchalantly went back to eating. There was no way Gul could decode the code to gain access to the rest of the money. The Party *had* to have been monitoring the call. Jason also knew that people running supercomputers were alerted and already tracing the electronic trail from a 100-million-dollar wire originating from the Catholic Church's Peter's Pence Collection.

Gul's phone rang. "Yes." He listened for a moment, then smiled and stood. "The transfer is complete. Come, assassin, I have something to show you."

Jason followed Gul through the stronghold, memorizing every turn and possible escape route. He was surprised at the lack of people around. Anyone they passed was fully clad in either black or white. It was like being in a black-and-white ninja movie or something. But when he was taped up like a mummy, the mystery woman's sweet voice had told him that it was all treachery and illusions. Maybe Gul was trying to give him false impressions and information.

Lower and lower they descended in the bowels of the mountain fortress. *Fuck me,* Jason thought. There was no way in the world that anything short of a nuclear bomb was going to get to these guys; and he was one to know, having planted an underground nuke.

The smell struck him like a blow. It was like ammonia and chocolate, lots and lots of it. They turned a corner and were in a gigantic cavern. Burlap bales were stacked as far as he could see. It really would take a nuclear to blow all the dope in front of him.

"These are the tears of Allah." Gul's eyes were glazed. "The narcotic is yours after you eliminate our obstacle."

"How are you going to be able to move all of this out of here without attracting every bomber flying over the country?"

Gul grinned from ear to ear. "You let me worry about that; just be ready to transfer more cash."

0100 HOURS
THE PARTY / MELBOURNE / FLORIDA

Lights came on everywhere.

"GET UP!" The general's voice bellowed over the intercom. "Get to your stations. We're back on-line."

Mike Gorsline rolled out of his bed, unconsciously reaching for his pistol that was not there. Something was happening.

The halls filled with people as they raced to their stations. In minutes the computers were up and running and all ears listening to Cadallo.

"Here's the situation, 100 million dollars has been moved from the Peter's Pence Collection. We're already tracking it from the source to wherever it goes. Three C-130s are about to take off from Peshawar, Pakistan, to Afghanistan. The flawed weapons have homing devices in the load. We have a Predator UAV and AWACs ready to shadow and monitor the flight the moment it gets into Afghan airspace."

"How do you know this?" Ibrahim asked.

"Brianna," Cadallo's amplified voice answered. "The moment she heard it, she woke me up.

"Our operator has surfaced. I want all of you ready to identify him and where he's at the moment you get a trace of him."

The cheering and clapping were spontaneous. All the derision against Ben was gone in an instant. Everyone raced to their stations. The Party was back on.

CHAPTER 27

**1545 WEDNESDAY / 17 OCTOBER 2001
FAIZABAD / AFGHANISTAN**

Thirty Senate staffers test positive for traces of anthrax.

DAR SILENTLY CREPT TO THE RIM OF THE CANYON and peeked over the precipice. Scanning the collection of caves below, he was surprised to see another group of men on the crest line across the small valley. They all wore sand-colored cloaks. If it had been day the black-and-white clothes that they wore would've stood out like a target silhouette, but now they removed their cloaks and blended into the shadows cast by the mountains.

"Do we hit them too?" Vance whispered to Ubu, the headman.

"No," the Afghan chief answered, violently shaking his head. "We should go. We should not be here."

Dar looked at the men through his binoculars. Their horses were tied up just behind them. One of the horses carried a black standard with a golden arrowhead at the center. They were the same chumps that the Afghans refused to engage before. "Who are those guys?"

Vance translated Ubu's words. "Whispers of death. To attack them will bring death on my men, our families, and our family's family."

Dar saw that with all Ubu's bravery and courage, he and his men were scared shitless of the men on the other side of the valley. Nonetheless, the target was assigned and would be hit regardless of the Afghans and their superstitions.

"Okay, this is as far as we go. If those guys see us and try to attack, then we strike back." Rene decided. "The show's all yours, Dar. You call it, then we go home. Do it."

"THERE, THAT IS HIM, HIS NAME IS ARMAN," GUL Nazari said, handing Jason a pair of binoculars. "Kill him and the road to Pakistan will be ours. He is the one who is blocking the clan from moving our narcotic. He controls the high pass into Pakistan. There is no other way around this. He must die."

Jason peered through the glasses. "Which one is Arman?"

"He is the one wearing the green jacket."

"Yeah, I got him. Is he the one wearing a blue turban, too?" Jason nodded. Handing back the binoculars, he then raised an AK-47 with a mounted sniperscope and began to plot the shot.

Jason was dispassionate. It would be a straight kill. When he was done he would go back to Samar and be in the company of a most beautiful woman. The target environment picture was just about set.

But before he could squeeze the trigger one of the men near Arman appeared to answer a cellular phone, then yelled to the group of men. The target jumped up and ran a short distance with his men into an open cave.

"Shit," cried Jason.

"You *have* to go get him," said Gul. "He can't get away. I have already contracted and made a payment to the Nuristani to load and move the narcotic. This is too big a venture to have the passes blocked."

Gul made a signal and someone produced an old Russian Makarov pistol crudely fitted with a silencer, and handed it to Gul.

Nazari put the gun into Jason's hand. "We cannot get close to him. He knows who we are. You are not known. You must go into the caves and kill him."

It amazed Jason how relaxed he felt about the thought of doing the killing for Gul. "You wait here. If I don't come out you'll have to go in and take him out yourself."

Handing the rifle to Nazari, he stood up and ran in the direction of the cave. Racking the pistol slide as he ran, he wasted no time scooting to the entrance of the cave. Hesitating for only a moment, he snapped on his flashlight and entered.

DAR WATCHED ONE OF THE "DEATH WHISPERERS" EN-ter the cave. He didn't care. "He's going to be a *dead* Death's Whisperer soon."

1600 HOURS
FIFTEEN THOUSAND FEET OVER AFGHANISTAN

It had been a three-and-a-half-hour flight and two communications-out midair refuelings for the two F-15E Strike Eagles to make it on station over the Afghan mountains. It was time for the Bold Tigers to make their strike against the Taliban.

Major Hugh Funk, flight lead pilot, was ready to go to work. Silently praying, he asked, "God, please don't let me mess this up." Getting tagged by an enemy missile didn't bother him as much as his peers seeing him screw up on tape. That *really* made him nervous.

"Ready?" he asked his backseat electronic weapons officer.

"Take me to the hunt," Donnie Rouse answered. "Let's get this party started."

Glancing down to his right, Funk picked up his wingman some thousand feet below him.

The big cats were on the prowl.

JASON JUST FOLLOWED THE CROWD OF MEN THROUGH the twisting tunnels. The target was hot and he was jazzed. An assassin was on the hunt. The only two questions he had were if the gun even worked, and was it another fucking test? It didn't matter; his dagger was sharp.

"THIS IS BIG CAT. I RECOGNIZE YOUR VOICE," FUNK said, verifying the CCT man on the ground. "And I'm ready to drop the hammer."

It was a clear contact. Dar quickly assessed the target and knew the weapon that would close the deal. "Are you packin' bunker busters?"

"Rogo. I've been wanting to unload one of these babies for a long time."

"Gottcha. Do you see the cave just below the ridge?"

"No joy. You got it?" Funk asked his wingman.

"It's all looking the same to me," Rouse answered.

"Damn!" Dar muttered. There was just too much junk between the target and him to lase it. Calling off the hit was the last thing that he wanted to do.

"Ground Party, this is Spooky 13. We are in your area. Are you looking for assistance? Do you voice authenticate me?"

"Affirmative Spooky 13, affirmative!" It might be just the act he needed. He'd worked with the gunship a

few nights before and knew that now they were a god-
send.

JASON FOLLOWED EVERYONE TO A HUGE CAVERN. HE COULD
see clearly through his night-vision while they crowded together. Slowly moving in the shadows, he spotted his man.

THE AC-130U GUNSHIP CIRCLED OVERHEAD AT FIVE
thousand feet above the closest obstacle.

Dar was elated. "I got you. Do you see the cave opening about two-thirds down from the crest line on the far
slope of the mountain?"

"Got it."

"Mark it with white phosphorus."

"Willie Pete on the way."

Skeletal fingers of fire reached out and hit the cave,
creating hot crucible at the front of the cave.

"You see it?" Dar radioed to the F-15.

"No joy," Funk responded.

JASON MOVED IN FOR THE KILL, BUT STOPPED WHEN HE
heard the thuds. Everyone in the cavern huddled closer.
Something deadly was going on outside and he wondered
about the wisdom of his decision to enter the tunnels.

"SPOOKY 13, CAN YOU MARK THE WP WITH YOUR MINI-
guns? They got tracers?"

"Watch the show."

Tracer fire shot out from the left side of the Hercules
gunship. The red flame shattered the cave's entrance.

OH FUCK ME. JASON KNEW THAT SOUND AND THE
weapon that made it. A gunship was making passes and

racking up some trigger time, but for what? He had to get the hit done and book feet!

Pushing through the mass of terrorists, he neared his target.

"YOU SPOT IT?" DAR ASKED.

"We see the flames, but still can't make the mark. Spooky 13, can you blast the son of a bitch with your 105 howitzer?" Funk asked.

"Give us one minute to come on-line."

"Spooky 13. Target your munitions about fifty feet above the mark. Big Cat, that'll be your target," Dar instructed. He looked down at the black-clad men. They were holding their horses to keep them from scattering from all the noise. He grinned. Things were about to get a lot louder.

Jason slowly raised his pistol to the back of the mark's head and pulled the trigger. It went off with a big flash and loud bang. Arman dropped. Everyone saw Jason standing with the smoking gun in his hand.

"Ooops," was all Jason could say.

The ground shook and rumbled. He dropped the pistol and took off, running for his life as everything began to rumble around him.

FUNK SAW THE EXPLOSIONS AND POINTED AT THE TARget. His backseater nodded, plotting and inputting the target solution. Using the targeting pod, he relayed the target solution for Funk to fly.

RUNNING FOR HIS LIFE, JASON PRAYED THAT HE wouldn't forget the way out. Yells and shouts echoed in the tunnels. His pursuers were close. The concussions and explosions of the howitzer grew louder the closer he got to the entrance. He didn't stop running. It was either chance getting out between the explosions, or face a certain death chasing behind him.

"PINCH-HIT! PINCH-HIT! PINCH-HIT!" THE EWO CRIED out. Funk's targeting pod had blanked out at the worst time.

"I'm on it," Rouse called out, instantly taking over the targeting for lead. "Stay on the run. I'll get you through to the target solution."

Seconds later he gave the pickle squawk to Funk. Funk hit the release on the GB-28 and sent the bunker buster on a direct path to the smoking hole just above the cave entrance.

The bunker buster punched through the ground at the speed of sound, penetrating into the earth for over a hundred feet before five hundred pounds of TNT lit off. The violence of the compactness from the dirt and rock surrounding it amplified the blast, collapsing tunnels, caverns, and killing everyone caught under its malice.

JASON FELT THE HEAT AND SAW THE FIRE OF THE BURNing cave exit. He flew through the flames and dived out into black space. Suddenly he was spinning and rolling in the air. He slammed onto the scree and slid to a stop as a tremendous explosion rocked the valley. Holding his head close to the ground, he heard wet thuds falling around him.

Slowly looking up and around, he saw body parts landing everywhere. He didn't bother waiting around for any battle-damage assessments. He stood up and took off. "Anyone picking up my signal?"

Nothing.

SCANNING THROUGH HIS NVGS, DAR COULDN'T BE-
lieve the Death Whisperer's luck. He went in, and made
it out. The son of a bitch had incredible timing! Suddenly
he heard someone talking over his radio, but couldn't tell
who. He had no time to waste and cleared in Funk's
wingman.

THE BOMB STRUCK THE TOP OF THE MOUNTAIN, CREAT-
ing an avalanche of rocks and rubble that collapsed the
entire side of the hill. Anyone caught under the onslaught
was buried without any possibility of escape.

THE ASSASSINS STOOD IN SILENT AWE. JASON PUSHED
past the assassins and grabbed the reins of his pony,
jumped on, and rode away. Pissed, he knew that it had to
have been another test. "Hell yeah, I can kill," he said to
no one. "And I'm *sick* of it!" It suddenly hit him that he
was the perfect assassin. Unknown, but highly trained,
he could pass anyone's trial. He started wondering if his
mysterious lover was just another test.

DAR AND THE SPECIAL ACTIVITY TEAM WAITED UNTIL
the black riders were gone before they mounted and rode
away in the opposite direction.

1030 HOURS
THE PARTY / MELBOURNE / FLORIDA

The trace on the 100 million coming from the Peter's
Pence Collection to an Arabian bank was mind-boggling.
"Thank God for the Janus program to keep track of it,"

Ben said to himself, reading the trace report. There were still millions left.

The moment it went into the Saudi bank account all of it automatically went back out to private banks around the world. Money wires commingled with other bank accounts, bank funds, and bonds—shells within shells.

Further investigation revealed that there were no clear client profiles. Even though there were clear laws on the subject, the banks never questioned the source of the funds.

The biggest share of the money went to the Hawala. These were moneychangers in the Middle East who worked on scraps of paper, phone calls, and handshakes. There was no tracing it. It disappeared.

Ben initialed the report to up-channel the intelligence report. He didn't add any extra notes, like where the source money originated, or that there was another 200 million still waiting to follow or disappear.

He went back to manning his center. Everyone was looking for Gomez everywhere, on all channels. The general was elated. His man Jason had proven him right. He *could* stay alive. No one at home station would dare challenge his authority now. No one. He flicked on the intercom switch. "Listen, everyone. Be ready for anything from our operative. Look for something out of the ordinary, and our boy will probably be right in the middle of it."

0830 THURSDAY / 18 OCTOBER 2001
FAIZABAD / AFGHANISTAN

It was a clear blue morning as three Pakistani C-130s flew over the airfield. The runway was made out of corrugated metal. Once a Soviet airfield, the abandoned

Soviet aircraft had been picked to the bone, littering the field with aviation carcasses.

They touched down one after another on the worn and rusted landing strip, then taxied to a dirt cargo pit near a huge crowd of vehicles, horses, and donkeys. Hundreds of men anxiously waited.

The ramp and door of each plane opened, then the planes taxied back toward the runway. As they moved forward, pallets full of weapons and munitions rolled off the ramps.

In minutes the pallets were off and the planes were back in the air.

**0400 FRIDAY / 19 OCTOBER 2001
FORTRESS SAMAR / AFGHANISTAN**

The celebrations over Arman's assassination and the C-130s' delivery of the weapons and munitions went on all night. Jason just stayed in his room. Lavender, the mystery woman, never showed. Jason convinced himself that it had to be a ruse anyway. He chuckled over his ability never to be able to get laid, and when he did get into something amorous, it always was in the worst possible places, and at only the worst possible times.

Someone knocked on his door. "Come in."

Gul came stalking through the door, smiling and full of cheer. "Everything goes well, assassin. I am impressed with all your capabilities. The Nuristani have prepared the narcotic for movement. Once you have crossed into Pakistan one of my men will give you a satellite phone for the next money transfer."

"Okay," Jason agreed. "When Falcon's people take over the load I'll finish the deal. But I've got a question. Just how will you get so much of the opium to Pakistan without attracting any attention of, say, bombers?"

"Illusion. No one will attack us. Every kilo will be

safely delivered." Gul cocked his head at Jason. "I know that *you* wouldn't do anything to hinder the rest of our dealings, would you?"

"What do you mean?"

"Nothing. I am, as you say, just covering my ass."

Jason was instantly on guard. "How?"

"A very lovely woman has been visiting you, has she not?" Gul saw the surprise in Jason's eyes. "Yes, I know all about it."

"And?" Jason instantly was on guard.

"And should the load not reach its destination, be hijacked, lost, or anything that stops the next two money transfers, the woman will die."

"What? Why would you do that?" Once more Jason looked for the trap and the way out.

"Insurance. I'm protecting my investments. I always do. Just in case something happens that the load is lost, how will I get paid the rest of my money? If you do not care for the woman, then I will have no reason to ensure that the load will get through."

"Damn! Man. I've been cool the whole time, doing your dance. Now you pull this on me." Jason glanced around the room, sizing it up for a fight.

"Go ahead, make your move. We can see just who is the deadliest; either way, the woman would be dead."

Jason dropped his attitude. "So what's the deal?"

Gul's happy smile returned. "You just do your part of the deal, that is all."

"And the woman?"

Gul's eyes burned. "You may never have her. She is promised to another. You have had your time with her. Now you must leave with just your memories of Samar." Gul pointed his finger at him. "You complete this deal, transfer the moneys, and you may even be invited to return back to Samar's Garden of Bliss. Perhaps the woman will meet you there."

Jason didn't want anything to do with a doper's high.

Now he just wanted the woman to be free from Gul's promise.

Gul opened the door, then turned around. "But for your heart, you could be an excellent assassin. Now be ready to leave in the next hour."

"Wait. What is the woman's name?"

"Oh, she did not tell you? Mya. Her name is Mya."

CHAPTER **28**

The ground war in Afghanistan "officially" begins.

JASON LOST COUNT OF THE NUMBER OF GAS
tankers, trucks, and all the vehicles that tried to pass
as trucks that had come from the base of the mountain. One after another, how many? They were all stuffed to the bursting point with opium. It was like seeing a modern-day Ali Baba cave. He'd quit watching the trucks and turned his attention to Gul's men admiring their new desert uniforms.

The weapons arrived the day before. Among the pallets of munitions was a pallet of military-style uniforms.

Everywhere Jason looked he'd seen happy assassins dressed in the same uniforms.

They left Samar at dawn. Jason climbed onto the bed of a rickety truck that was toward the end of the convoy. It reeked of the sharp, acrid-sweet smell of opium.

Committing to memory every turn and twist of the dirt road and all landmarks, he had every intention of making it back to Samar. He had to hand it to Gul, he'd planned the move to be out in the open the whole day— show the false, hide the real.

All the trucks were marked with the Red Cross emblem and the Red Crescent. They even flew white Maltese humanitarian flags. The opium Jason bought was under the protective symbols of international aid. Under the Law of Armed Conflict, recognized humanitarian convoys were strictly forbidden targets.

There was no way to get a message to Ben. He had to hope that the Party would somehow be able to discern the ruse and hit the load. That, and he had to find his way back to Samar and rescue Mya before word of the destruction of the convoy got back to Gul.

His mind ran at the speed of light trying to figure out some way to stop the massive load, but nothing was illuminating.

At first it was just static, then it was unmistakable. Someone was speaking English.

"This is a ground party. Is anyone hearing me?"

Master Sergeant Jean Fawcett, Airborne System Communication Operator (ACSO) aboard the EC-130E Airborne Battlefield Command and Control Center (A-B-Triple-C), was surprised to hear someone speaking over her shortwave frequency. The Hercules was there to jam enemy transmissions while a PsyOps bird broadcast shortwave news and information to the radios of Afghanistan in Pashtun and other ethnic languages. The mission operators aboard the plane also told the listeners where to get medical aid and that the Americans were there to help the Afghanis rid their land of the Taliban.

In addition to eavesdropping in on and jamming enemy transmissions, they also were recording top al Qa'eda and Taliban voices and triangulating their positions. Then they worked with the war planners to insert CCT to put bombs on targets. The war had gone so rapidly, that the

A-B-Triple-C mission moved on to its next phase, population control.

How was it that she had picked up someone transmitting over her frequency? Alerting her mission commander, and knowing the identification procedures, she opened her channel. "Ground Party, identify yourself. What is the word of the day? Five."

Jason was elated that he might be talking to an American. "I don't know what the code words are today, but it was Chump and Four on September 20 when I went in. Check it out, quick!"

In seconds the crew had queued in on the radio's transmissions. The Airborne Close Air Support Coordinator (ACASCO) backed up and confirmed information for Fawcett.

In less than a minute Fawcett's voice came back. "It checks, now I got to ident *you*."

"Listen, there's no time for that; besides, I still don't know who *you* are. Just keep it simple. If you have the capability, I'm FLASH ordering you to contact CENTCOM and tell them to establish me a contact link with the Party. Tell them that *Alice* is making a collect call. Did you get that?"

"I think so. Ground Party, can you give your location?"

"Nice try. We've got to establish a little trust first. I need air support for a fast-developing target. You just do what I told you."

In a matter of ten long minutes Cadallo's voice came on-line in Jason's ear.

"Talk to me."

"Listen, I'm in a huge humanitarian convoy, but it's not. It's our vile package. I think that I'm somewhere in northern Afghanistan, headed for Pakistan. Pick it up now on any imagery you got. Hurry!"

"Roger that. Ground Party, that's a Law of Armed Conflict (LOC) prohibited target."

"Who's on this freq?" Jason asked.

In the time it took to establish the link, Fawcett triangulated Jason's approximate location and had CENT-COM send a nearby Predator to the coordinates.

"I'm a Predator pilot. I'm over your signal, and that's a Notice to Airmen (NOTAM) humanitarian convoy."

"Well, Mr. Predator. It's a *trick*!" Jason had to work and quickly explain his situation. "Radio. Can you keep this frequency secure?"

"I don't know, sir. I'll try."

"It's Alice, not sir. I don't know who you are, but you gotta know to keep this line open, and keep everyone else not in this, out. Ben, verify with the Red Cross that they ain't got nothin' to do with this.

"Listen, everyone at the Party, feed in on the Predator and anything else that you got to get this shit whacked. Ben is my primary communicator. And don't *nobody* fuck with me while I'm running this thing. How soon can we hit this load, and with what?"

"It's two weeks after the coordinated attack," Ben said.

"What were you going to hit it with?"

"We had two Combat Talons lined up to drop a couple of Daisy Cutters."

Jason whistled. The power of the BLU-82 was awesome, and times two? "Not enough."

"What?" Ben exclaimed.

"This convoy is too long and linear. Two Daisy Cutters would only cut off segments. We gotta hit it somewhere, like at the base of a valley, a place where they'll be more concentrated. This is a gigantic load, Ben."

0500 HOURS
THE PARTY / MELBOURNE / FLORIDA

Everyone was opening up computer programs, making calls to bring up the gazillion things they had come up with a lifetime ago.

"Got him!" Ibrahim cried.

Almost instantaneously the Party brought up everything about the area Jason was in.

1015 HOURS
TALOGAN PASS / AFGHANISTAN

Jason put his fingers in his ears, thinking he could listen better to the transceiver.

"You're in the Hindu Kush Mountains, about eighty miles from the Pakistan border," Ben said. Information and images lit up on his computer screens. "I can see the procession. I'm told that there's a valley twenty miles ahead. It angles close enough that it almost turns back on itself. That might do it." Ben was a machine, processing information as fast as his eyes scanned it. "The Blu-82 mission is still on alert. The Air Force never turned it off!"

"God bless Big Blue," Jason said. "Hit it with the two BLUs, then use the heat signature to fry it with any conventional bombs we got in the air. When will the Talon birds be here?"

"I'm told they can be overhead in less than an hour."

"How far am I from the ambush?" Jason looked at the motorcycles weaving in and out of the caravan.

"The Party estimates that, from your forward speed, you'll be there in about an hour and a half," Ben said.

"That'll be the place then." He looked at his watch, grateful that Gul had the sense to give him back his medallion, rings, and watch—even Gul Nazari knew the significance of talismans, but he kept the ten grand and mini Qur'an.

"Alice, this is the radio operator. I do know of a Special Forces team with a CCT less than an hour from your point of impact."

"Great!" Ben cried. "Patch me through to them.

Alice, I'm going to get them to pull you out after the attack."

"It's not gonna happen like that. It's better that you just get the CCT to call the drop and the rest of the strikes. But that's only *after* I clear the convoy. Got it?"

"Why aren't you linking up with them?"

"Unfinished business."

1020 HOURS
HINDU KUSH MOUNTAINS / AFGHANISTAN

Rene brought the team together. "You guys aren't going to believe this one." He waited until everyone was quiet. "We've got to attack the Red Cross an hour northeast of here."

He waited until everyone stopped laughing. "It's true. The Red Cross cover is a fake. I'm told that it's the Taliban, or someone's smuggling a load of something massive."

"What if it is the Red Cross?" Vance asked.

"I got official word that it's not."

"But *what if it is*?" Peyton questioned.

"Look. We're going to take it out. Orders. I will not question them. They come directly from headquarters." Rene looked at Dar. "The ball is in your court."

Dar slumped in his saddle. "Man, if we're wrong, if it is to keep people alive, I'll never get over it."

"Dar. I'm ordering you to make the tasking happen. The responsibility is on *me*. I am the leader here. You are one of my tools. Do you understand me, *Air Force*?"

"Yes, sir."

"Is there anyone here that questions these orders?"

Silence.

"Then I'm the one who will burn for this if it's wrong." Rene turned his horse. "Vance, translate to Ubu that we will leave everyone here and only take the scouts. We got a lot of riding to do."

1230 HOURS

"Jason, can you see the road where it cuts back into the valley?" Ben asked.

"Uhm hum," Jason said as he scanned the sky, looking for the Predator, or any other airplanes. He saw nothing.

"We've passed the spot to the CCT. They plan to strike the load dead center of the bend with the Daisy Cutters. The team is on station right now. Once he calls it, you got exactly five minutes to get out of where you are because the whole convoy's going to go up at once."

"Oh shit." Jason jumped off the slow-moving truck and rolled to his feet. Dusting himself off, he flagged down a motorcycle. The rider got off to help. Smiling and shrugging as if he'd fallen, he chopped the biker across the throat, then punched him square in the mouth.

The man fell in confusion and pain.

Jason grabbed the man's AK-47 and jumped on the motorcycle. It was a little one, but it started and away he went, leaving behind astonished Nuristani drivers and assassins.

1245 HOURS

Dar watched, then calculated the location of the attack. He passed the information to the incoming MC-130s. He watched as a lone motorcycle emerged from the tail of the caravan and sped back in the opposite direction. That must've been the one that they said had to get clear. "You are clear to drop," he keyed to the MC-130.

Looking through his binoculars, Dar saw that it was

going to be close if the fleeing man was going to make it out of the concussion kill zone.

1250 HOURS

Two MC-130H Combat Talon IIs scooted over a distant ridge. Jason heard the droning engines before he saw the planes. He twisted the throttle of the motorcycle wide open; he knew what was coming. Pockets of dirt geysers erupted around him, only inspiring Jason to will the motorbike to move quicker. The assassins were shooting at him, but they would quit soon enough.

The MC-130Hs roared six thousand feet over him. Jason turned his head to see the ramp and door open. They were on slowdown.

The assassin guards fired their AK-47s at the plane, ineffective, as they were unable to find range. An extraction chute flailed from the ramp, then popped open, ripping from the plane a fifteen-thousand-pound bomb filled with a GSX slurry of ammonium nitrate, aluminum powder, and polystyrene soap.

A huge stabilization parachute deployed and the bomb gently and unerringly descended toward the convoy.

"OH SHIT!" Jason pointed the motorcycle to a culvert, jumped from the bike, and rolled himself into a tight ball, waiting for the fuse extender to touch the ground. He knew the destructive power of a Daisy Cutter.

The blast produced an overpressure of over a thousand pounds per square inch. Anything that was remotely in its blast area was immediately vaporized. Anyone close had their lungs and ears exploded.

Jason cringed, expecting the worst, but it wasn't so bad. His ears rang like never before and his nose bled. But other than that he was still breathing. He sat up and looked back at the convoy. Everything burned. One shot. One *big* kill. The Combat Talon flew in a lazy arc, viewing the damage assessment as a second bird made its bomb run.

Jason curled up once more and waited for the next explosion.

Just about addled, Jason sat, trying to regain his senses. The heat of the fires made him hurry and get the bike back onto the road and away from the incredible inferno. The lines of fire looked like the Highway of Death.

"It's dead." He remembered the promise he gave to the spirits of Khobar. Two fifteen-thousand-pound bombs on a load of narcoterrorist dope still didn't feel like payback enough for the loss of good friends.

Fires slid down the mountainside.

But the mission was complete as far as Jason was concerned. "It's over," he said.

Nothing came back over his transceiver. Either his ears were damaged, or the Kissiah transceiver was busted during the blast.

It didn't matter. The Party couldn't help for what he had to do. He had to get back to Samar and free Mya.

1300 HOURS

Dar watched with horrified fascination at the inferno in the valley. Bomb after bomb sent the trucks flying into the air. The fire raced up both sides of the mountain trails, burning any remnant of the huge convoy.

He could see people running from the conflagration, many covered with fire.

A low estimation at two-hundred-plus trailers handled by three or four men each put a body count somewhere between five hundred and a thousand people.

"God forgive me if we were wrong," Dar prayed.

The team mounted to return to base.

Suddenly they were in the middle of an attack. Men and horses cried out as bullets and explosions struck them.

"Ambush!" Vance yelled.

They were caught in a high pass with no cover.

The last thing that Dar remembered was hearing the whistle of incoming artillery flying in the air.

0700 HOURS
THE PARTY / MELBOURNE / FLORIDA

Pandemonium reigned at the Party. The Predator had been too close to the blast and was blown to pieces.

The A-B-Triple-C bird was at least twenty minutes from the strike scene to be of any use.

What was a victory had quickly turned into a disaster. They had suddenly lost contact with both Jason and the CCT. They had been given a taste of how the Party was supposed to work, and once again, in accordance with Murphy's Law, they crashed.

2215 HOURS
FORTRESS SAMAR / AFGHANISTAN

The sun was just beginning to set. The secret entrance to Samar was well hidden to anyone not familiar with the treacherous area.

Jason dumped the motorcycle to the side of the trail, reached into his bag, and donned the assassin garb. All that could be seen were his green eyes.

He was unchallenged by the guards—the purple arrowhead above his brow identified him as clan.

Once inside the fortress his night vision really paid off. He quickly found Nazari's chambers. Rifle at the ready, he crept quietly until he had reached Nazari's inner sanctum and barred the heavy door behind him. Creeping farther into the rooms, he froze.

Nazari held a knife at Mya's throat.

"Let her go, Gul. If you kill her, I'll shoot you."

"Good, Alice. *Very* good. I have just received news that my load is burning. I knew that it had to be you, and here you are, just as I am about to make good on my word."

"Gul, don't kill her."

"So you do care about this woman? Is she the one who convinced you to destroy my load?"

"No. Not at all, she, she . . ."

"Ah, you have feelings for her. How?"

"It doesn't matter." Jason could hear the banging and shouting of men outside Gul's barred door.

"Ah." Nazari smiled. "She came to you on your night of Bliss. My daughter comes to you, and you betray me like this?"

Daughter? "I didn't know it. Besides, I did only what you assassins yourself consider the highest attainment: treachery and illusion. I fooled you into thinking I was one of you, then I turned on you." Jason tried to laugh. "Come on, isn't that worth something?"

He froze when he saw Nazari push the tip of the dagger into Mya's throat, drawing a trickle of blood. Her eyes were filled with terror. "Hey, I'm the one who brought you that cloth, the *messenger*."

Gul almost laughed. "Fool. I have it now. So?"

"Look. I'll give you the codes worth 200 million dollars if you let her go."

Gul sneered. "You think I'd settle for measly millions when I could have *billions*."

"What?"

"Yes. You thought that burning the opium was your idea, don't you?"

The confused look on Jason's face made Gul's eyes light up. "You Americans are so gullible and stupid. You really think that you are fighting a war against terrorism."

"We're not?" He had to do something to save Mya before Gul killed her.

"No. It is the oil, and more."

Jason could only stammer.

"Before all *this* began, the oil companies sent their geologists here. Besides natural gas and oil, they discovered gemstones like emeralds, lapis, and rubies. You see, while the people are poor, the natural resources are rich.

"They tried to make deals for billions, but the Taliban was stubborn and stupid; they didn't understand the West and their kind of greed. They did not understand that the West's god is the god of money. They had to be replaced. As you say, they became their own worst enemy. We assassins understand these things. We've mastered the intrigue. We made a deal with the oil cartel to protect the territory of the oil pipeline that will cross Afghanistan, but they wanted an example of our power."

Mya's neck seeped blood.

"The *parochial* oil consortium wanted proof that I could stop the opium trade, then they would pay me to guard the pipeline through Afghanistan and the gems we unearthed would be mine. When this is all over I will be the supreme warlord, thanks to you and the Blind Imam claiming my possession of the Cloth of the Prophet to the Islamic world. *All* Islam will be under my control!"

"And then?"

"I will be the power. Then we will not have to suffer your blond peril, your Golden Horde. I will eclipse everything the Young Lion has done. You, fool, have been *my* secret hand."

They could hear the shouts of Gul's men as they splintered the door.

"I have kept you here long enough. Only you know of the secret deal with your great American oil company." Gul gave Jason a wicked smile.

Jason jumped toward Gul, but it was too late. Gul plunged the knife into Mya's neck and ripped out her throat. Mya's gushing blood covered and blinded Jason. Gul swiped the dagger at Jason but missed.

Clearing his eyes, all Jason wanted to do was kill his enemy. Gul, seeing Jason's rage, ran yelling out of the room as Jason fired his rifle, barely missing him.

Mya's lifeless body lay at his feet, blood seeping into the dirt floor. There was nothing that he could do but try and get away from Gul's men. He quickly blew out the two lanterns in the room, plunging it into darkness.

Jason sprinted past the men pouring into the room and made his way out of Samar without a hitch. He grabbed the motorcycle and roared away with the intention of hooking up with *any* friendly forces in the area. With Mya dead there was no longer reason to stay.

CHAPTER 29

0555 SATURDAY / 20 OCTOBER 2001
HINDU KUSH MOUNTAINS / AFGHANISTAN

Northern Alliance soldiers move in close to key cities.

DAR WASN'T SURE WHERE HE WAS, OR HOW HE
had gotten there. He sat up slowly and backed
away from a ledge. He was only inches from a
thousand-foot drop. "What happened?"

The last thing that he remembered was that he was
doing something in, in Afghanistan. It all came back in
an instant. The team had been ambushed. He tried scooting farther up the crumbly slope, but something was
wrong. His left leg was in incredible pain.

He slowly examined it through a mental fog. The knee
was possibly shattered.

"Damn!" Whatever exploded about stripped him
naked. The rover was gone. He sighed with relief when
he felt Rita's CD still in his pants pocket. He rolled to his
stomach and began a long, painful crawl to the top of the
ridge.

It was almost dark when he pulled himself back to

where he had called in the air strike. The convoy they had attacked still burned below in the valley.

Everyone was dead; worse, the bodies had been stripped and mutilated. Dar was instantly on guard. He pulled out his pistol. With great difficulty he stood and hobbled to the first body. Dar threw up. The headless body was hacked up beyond recognition. The rest were in the same horrible condition.

From the looks of the scene, somebody had known their location and ambushed them. He guessed that it had to be someone in the Afghan group. He wanted to kill all of them.

His radio was gone and there were no other radios anywhere to be found. Dar fashioned a crutch from a broken pole, then tried to scavenge some gear and set out to hook up with allied forces. He had to report the ambush and murder of an elite secret commando squad to someone.

Following orders, he had never even asked who the team really belonged to, so who would be responsible for the recovery? The only thing that he did know was that anyone else in the area besides him was looking to make sure that no survivors could say anything to anyone.

He used the crutch and tried to figure the best way out. Hobbling away, he was shocked when he saw the familiar figure of a horse, on its back. It was dead. Getting closer, he shook his head. "Well, Iblis, it looks as if you made good on pitching me over the side of a cliff. And you saved my life. Thanks."

Upon closer inspection he saw that the horse was missing a leg; it looked as if someone had cut it off for food.

1620 HOURS

Jason crept up on a lame man who was trying to skirt the side of a cliff. At that moment everyone was an enemy to

him. He threw himself at the surprised man, grabbed him
in an arm bar, and forced him to the edge of a thousand-
foot drop.

The man struggled with all he had. It was a broken
arm or death.

Jason had the leverage and had the man inches from
going over.

"Hey, I'm going to kick your ass!"

Jason pushed him over, but just as quickly pulled him
back. Now they were both about to go over the edge.
Jason heaved with all he had and they were back on level
ground. "You speak English."

"That's because I'm American."

"So am I."

"You are? You don't look it."

Jason raised his eyebrows. "Neither do you."

"Yep, I am."

"Hey, were you with all those guys dressed in
black, then got out of the convoy attack on a motorcycle?"

"That's me."

"I'm the one who called in the air strikes."

"You're a combat controller?"

"I am."

"Holy shit! I'm a PJ. What are you doing out here?"

"The team I was with got ambushed and killed. I got
to get back and report who did it. What're you doing
here?"

They asked each other questions about their training, places, and people that they both might have in common.

Satisfied that Dar was the real deal, Jason said,
"Look. It's great shooting the shit with you, but I've got
a problem. You asked what I was doing here; go have a
look over that ridge."

Dar peered over the ridge, then stood in utter amazement. In the valley he saw something out of *Lawrence of*

Arabia. Every horse, camel, and donkey that carried riders was headed his way.

"Guess who they're after?"

"No."

"Oh, yeah. I had a motorcycle and was about to outrun them, but I ran out of gas. There wasn't a gas station close by. And think about what's going to happen when they find out you're the one who whacked them."

"Uh-oh."

"Yeah, I think we better get moving."

Dar pointed to his leg. "I can't move so fast."

"Then I'll help carry you."

Up ridges, down mountainsides, and across valleys they went until they were at the base of a mountain. A river cut through a flat valley. It looked to be about a mile from where they were. They could try and make it to the river, jump in, and float away, or go up a *very* steep and bare mountain. They faced an almost impossible free climb or certain hypothermia in the river.

The sun would be up in less than an hour. With Dar's bum leg holding them to almost a crawl, they reasoned that they would be spotted on the mountain, so they opted for the river and started to move out in the open marsh.

Several mistakes were made. The first mistake was evident the moment the sun rose over the peak. It shone on them like a spotlight. "Here we are, bad guys."

The second mistake was thinking that the marsh wouldn't be a problem to cross. Jason could barely drag Dar through the knee-deep muck.

Another screwup was estimating the river to be a short distance. Now it seemed like a thousand miles.

"Jason, look," said Dar.

He turned around to see where Dar pointed and his heart sank. They hadn't lost the assassins; as a matter of fact, they were all coming. If they didn't get to the river quicker, it would all be over in a matter of minutes. Already sighted, he could see muzzle flashes of the more excited and overeager pursuers. Jason turned and tripled his efforts.

"Damn, damn, damn!" Dar yelled through the pain.

Reaching the river, Jason dropped Dar, then fell to his knees and scooped up handfuls of water. Drinking deeply, not caring about any of the potential hazards it might've contained. He then threw some water on his face and sat on his butt. He watched Dar pitch a fit, while he just laughed to himself. "Hey, Dar, we tried."

Jason stood up and walked in the ankle-deep water. It was that shallow, all the way across. "Come on. Let's just keep going."

Dar was frustrated. "To where? It's just open sand on the other side."

"Well, I'm not staying here, waiting for them to catch up to us. That sure as hell won't do us any good. Let's go. I'll carry you on my back."

Jason stumbled many times over the sandy mounds.

"I had a horse just like you," Dar said.

"What happened to it?" asked Jason.

"Someone ate it."

"Oh." Jason used all the energy he had left to try and make it to the other bank. The game was about over.

They made it to the other bank. Jason stopped and set Dar down. Sweat poured off his body; his nerves were on edge. Thoughts of leaving and distancing himself from Dar tempted him. *Let them catch Dar first.* It would slow them down a bit. Shame stopped him. He just couldn't leave a brother behind.

"Jason," Dar pointed. "Do you see the rise? That berm?"

"Yeah." The small mound was about a hundred yards

away. Pockets of dirt sprayed near them—they were almost in range of their pursuers' guns.

"We should go there. The sun will be in their eyes. Maybe a few shots from us will stop them from overrunning us."

"Fat chance." There was little else to do and Dar's plan seemed to be the only course. He picked up Dar and continued carrying him piggyback, moving in a zigzag toward the only shelter in sight.

Now the bullets were snapping over their heads. The moment the assassins figured out that they were overshooting, it would all be over.

"Here, take my rifle and shoot back," Jason said.

Dar grabbed the rifle and looked over his shoulder. "It won't work. We're moving so much that I won't hit anybody. Besides, I'm a bad shot. I haven't fired a gun since I've been here."

"Great! Hey, Dar," Jason wheezed.

"What?"

"Are you searching for something?"

"What?"

"I mean, are you looking for something in your life?"

"Are you crazy? We're about to get whacked, and you want to know if I'm looking for meaning in life?"

"Yeah, I am."

Dar sighed. "No. I don't think I am. I've already found it. I'm in love with my wife, Rita." He took a slow breath and looked at the ground. "I wish you hadn't asked me that. I don't want to lose her this way."

"Okay, I'm sorry I asked. I still haven't found what I'm looking for," Jason said. He could now hear the rifle fire. Lead would start getting closer. But then he heard some loud pops and he saw some of the rifles misfire and explode. He started laughing with understanding. They were part of the load of weapons that the C-130s brought in. They were all defective. And now Jason understood why the load came in the first place; if the Taliban's Pakistani collaborators couldn't be trusted, then who could they turn to for help?

But that only made the situation more desperate; once caught, it would only make them want to torture Dar and him even worse. Ricocheting bullets pinging off the rocks showed that the assassins were getting too damned close. Almost at a run, Jason heard a smacking sound and was pitched forward to the ground. He turned over to look at Dar. Dar clutched his chest.

Dar tried to get up. Dark blood poured out from his back.

Jason grabbed Dar's pattu and began tearing it into bandages.

"Get outta here, Jason!" Dar gasped.

"No. I'm gonna plug you up and carry you."

Dar's wound looked bad, fatal.

"What? Are you stupid? Carry me to where? It won't work. It's too late. You know that. I feel so cold all over that it hurts."

Jason shrugged. "I know. Then I'll stay with you anyway."

"Why?"

"Call it whatever you want, they'll get me anyway. Why not shoot them with what we got, then save a couple of the last for us?" Jason grinned. "See, I've been there before. When you've done all that you could, you'll *know* when it's time to quit the battle, one way or the other."

"No surrender?"

"Not today."

Dar's breathing became shallower. Pink foam mixed in with the blood pouring from his back. He began to cough up blood. "Yeah. I just didn't think it would happen like this to me."

"Well, we gotta pay for the choices in our life." He

hefted Dar over his shoulder and stumbled toward the little shelter some fifty eternal yards away.

They reached the berm as the lead shots were getting more accurate.

The sun was up and it was a bright sunny day. Jason saw that the assassins were slowed by the muck he had been in, but some were already racing across the river.

Setting Dar down, he knelt and checked the few rounds he had remaining in his rifle. He checked Dar's wound and assessed that it was probably fatal. Without immediate medical treatment he would quickly bleed to death. "Hey, Dar?" *Keep him talking.*

"Yeah?"

"I've been meaning to ask you, what does your name mean?"

"Dar Garo...means...Giver, of Life." He was fading fast. Dar slowly reached into a pocket and handed a CD to Jason, his mouth moved but no words came out.

The first wave of killers reached the other side of the bank. Screaming and yelling, they were about to annihilate their prey.

Jason knelt and took careful aim at the closest man. From behind he heard the unmistakable sound of an M-60 machine gun racking to fire.

"I think y'all better duck," a Southern voice drawled behind him.

Jumping around, he peered for a moment and saw a slit in the berm. The barrel of a machine gun protruded from the slit. It was a camouflaged machine gun nest, an *American* gun nest.

"We saw y'all comin' our way. We was gonna open up on ya until we heard y'all talkin' American."

"Yeah, those guys are after us."

"So who y'all want us to kill?"

Jason glanced back at the river. "All of them."

"Can do."

It was a slaughter. The enemy was caught in the marsh and on open land. The battle line of Marines opened up with everything they had. The assassins turned to flee, but Harrier jets materialized and quickly made hamburger out of the enemy.

Jason was oblivious to the battle, holding Dar in his arms. It was too late to do anything for Dar, who had a frightened look on his face.

"Rita, Rita," he whispered.

Jason sat with Dar's body until a Marine captain knelt next to him.

"Can you tell me how this all happened?"

Jason shook his head.

"Who are you? Who can we call?"

"I'm, I'm Senior Master Sergeant Jason Johnson, pararescueman, and this was Dar Garo, a combat controller. He told me that the Special Forces team he was with got betrayed and wiped out. He took a bullet that had my name on it. He saved my life."

CHAPTER 30

Front lines form around Kabul and Mazar-e-Sharif.

ED DELEON SAT AT THE HEAD OF THE STAGE IN THE commander's auditorium. The rest of the Party filled the room. They were excited that their man had surfaced, unharmed, and was on his way out of Afghanistan. The massive load of opium was no more.

"General Cadallo is not here."

"After his money," someone said.

Everyone laughed, even Ed.

"Right." He held up a stack of envelopes. "These are your plane tickets and monthly checks, plus a bonus from the general." He laid them down.

"Where is he?" Gorsline asked.

"He is on his way to pick up his agent."

"You mean *our* agent," Ibrahim corrected. "And he probably *is* going after the money."

"Of course." Ed chuckled. "He asked me to tell you about the great job that you did. Now you can all go home." He became serious. "You know the Party rules, once you leave you may tell no one what happened here. You will not contact each other. This party never happened. You've signed your names to these rules."

He stood up. "But before you get the hell out of my building, I invite you to a celebration party you will always remember. It's in the next room."

Bri, Gorsline, and Ibrahim sat together watching everybody leave.

Bri smiled a little and started crying. "I'm really going to miss you guys."

Gorsline put his arm around her shoulder. "We did make a pretty good team." After the superbust, he wasn't quite ready to go back to the nickel-and-dime busts. But he would go back to the DEA knowing that he'd done his part to stop a tidal wave of drugs from washing over the country.

"Did you ever find out who Alice is?" Ibrahim asked.

Gorsline looked around the room, then winked at Bri and Ibrahim. "Let's go party. We have a little more time to talk about what's what."

2025 HOURS
CLASSIFIED LOCATION / KUWAIT

Jason stepped from the Spanish C-130 and walked in the light rain toward the waiting van. The look on his face told Bobby Creel to say little. He handed Jason back the pouch containing his identification and other personal items.

"You did it. Congratulations." Creel held out his hand.

Jason weakly shook it. "Cadallo?"

"The general is on his way."

"Late. Nothing new."

"We'll stop in at Intel for your debrief before the general gets to the base."

"Creel. I ain't going to no fucking debrief. I'm going to catch the next flight outta here."

"I seeee, then I guess you aren't interested in what's happened to Gul Nazari."

"What?"

"The Northern Alliance overran what was left of his clan and captured him. He paid them off, and now he's a part of the alliance. He's been pegged for elimination."

Jason fell back in his seat, his heart hammering in his chest. "Who's taking him out?"

"That's Cadallo's call. That's all I know. I'm going back to the Treasury Department in a few days."

The van slowed in front of the Intelligence building, but Creel waved off the driver, directing him instead to the Operations Center. He handed Jason his room key. "It's the same room as when you first passed through. I'm going back out to the flight line to pick up the general. His plane is just now descending. Pick any room to talk with him."

Jason just nodded, got out, and walked into the Operations Center. The noise and chatter stopped, but no one tried to challenge the hairy man with haunted eyes. Picking an empty room, Jason looked at the major behind the main desk. "You tell General Cadallo that the man he's looking for is in here." He stepped in and closed the door behind him.

Jason didn't bother to stand when General Cadallo entered the room.

"Congratulations. Where's the money?" were the first words out of Ben's mouth.

Jason coldly smiled. "Why don't you try 'Bitch, where's my money?' It was all about the money, wasn't it? You planned on me screwing up the deal, but getting out with the account alive. I *always* come back, right?"

"Well, where is it?"

"What are you talking about?"

"I know that you only transferred 100 million. Where's the other two hundred?"

"That was a great song and dance that you did on board the *Dark Secrets*. Wait." Jason saw clearer. "Man, you are a master. Either way it turned out would've worked for you, money or more power. Now the load is whacked and now you want the money too. What do you want to do? Fifty-fifty? Well, fuck you, Ben. You ain't getting it. I'll turn the whole thing over to the IRS first."

Ben's eyes narrowed. "Remember who you're talkin' to."

"Oh, I do. I really do. So you think I got money that belongs to you." Jason stood up and looked at Cadallo nose to nose. "I told you to kiss it good-bye when you lost me. What're you gonna do? Jump bad on me? After *all* the bullshit I've gone through for you to make the mission work. And you want the money too! Go ahead. See if you can beat it out of me. Give it your best shot." He had no idea what Ben was going to do, and he didn't care anymore. "Can't you see how bad the greed has got you?"

Ben blinked, then backed up, nodding. "You're right. I didn't mean to do that. I can see that now."

"Well, if you can, then you can also see that I got the upper hand here, so now you're playing by my rules."

"All right. You've earned it."

"I'm on the operation to take out Gul Nazari."

"Jason, this is over for you. You've just completed this mission. The follow-on isn't a Party assignment. It's Doors."

"So? Do you really think that you can deny me this?"

"No. I just didn't have you in mind for this. I figured that you would want to go home after this."

"Wrong. I'm going to do the hit. I'll be straight. While I was there I was searching for something of my own, but

I lost it, dead. Thanks." He got closer to Cadallo. "I'm going to tell you something."

Cadallo took an involuntary step back. There was a look in Jason's eyes that he'd never seen before. "What?"

Jason wasn't angry or vengeful. His words weren't accusing or damning, but they were cold, and that's what made Cadallo sweat. "You forget about the money, and you forget your power for a second. You never forget the people you've used to feed your *power,* especially me.

"*Me?* I just wanted to save lives. I was willing to lay my life down for my fellow man. I came from nothing, dreaming of becoming something. That dream carried me through to become a pararescueman." He poked Cadallo's chest. "You. You'll do anything to get that power you want so bad, even if it turned my dreams into nightmares."

Jason sat in his chair and gazed at the American flag on the wall. "Power. People like you exploit fools like me to keep your power, all the way to the top. You cloak your words in patriotism and *the greater good.* Then you turn loose killers like me to do your dirty deeds." Steel formed in his eyes. "I love my country, am willing to die for the cause as a dog of war. Until now I never gave any thought to the dog handlers. I never thought that they might use us to their own ends. *That's* why you called on me."

Jason turned over his right hand and looked at the scarring on his thumb. Then he looked at Cadallo, piercing him to the core. "With all your power, you don't even have a real clue, do you? No matter who you think you are, you're a dog too. Tell me something, who's *your* handler? I can't live with my ghosts any longer, can you?

"I know what this is all about—money and power. Well, I'm going on that mission. I'm going to finish this thing." He stood up again. "You know what, sir? When this is over you and your *power* are going to do something for me. You're going to cut me loose, from everybody." He looked at his right hand. "Because of being connected to you, I've killed more people than I can count. Now only one more person has to die, and I'm the trigger.

"So right now I want this fuckin' bug out of my ear. Then I will go back and kill Gul Nazari. Do you understand?"

Ben wordlessly nodded. "You've got quite an amazing picture in your head, can you deal with it?"

"No. I don't want to. Right now I'm going back in. How do you have it figured?"

"A sniper team makes the hit. Chopper in. Chopper out."

"Are the Brotherhood the snipers?"

Ben nodded. "Two trained members you haven't met. The team's already on a plane bound for here. Your pick and calls. You're the leader now. You can use the shooting range for as long as you guys need. You got three days before you go in." He put his hands on Jason's shoulders. "Are you sure that you want to do this? Maybe I can put the Party back together."

Jason shrugged off Ben's hands. "No, it'll be just the Brothers and me. And when this is done, sir, don't ever contact me again."

"And the money?"

"Still greedy?"

"I won't be a general forever."

"When you retire, come back and we'll talk." Jason opened his reclaimed personnel bag and took out his checkbook. He wrote a quick note, then wrote out a check, then put them both in Dar's CD and handed it to Ben. "I listened to her voice and it fucking broke my heart! I'm doing this for a friend. The wife's name is Rita Garo. Make sure that she gets this. And, Ben, I'd *really* appreciate it if you personally delivered this."

Ben nodded, then turned and left the room.

Back in his room Jason looked at himself in the

mirror. The damned beard was the first thing coming off! He was going back into the war as a clean-shaven soldier. The next mission started forming in his head. He stopped for a moment and stared at his reflection. He took a deep breath and sighed. All he ever wanted to do was be a PJ, not the vengeful killer that he was.

"Mya." *His own daughter, how could he do it?* Picking up a razor blade, he narrowed his eyes. "I'm coming to kill you, Gul, and this is for real."

Clean-shaven, he could not sleep, even on the soft mattress. So he got up and wandered around the small, dark base.

"I'm always the loser," he said to himself.

The moon was full. Jason looked at it. Only a short time had passed since he first left Patrick. A lot of things had happened. The search, if it was for love, was the worst thing that could've happened in his life. He let out a big sigh. "I could've loved her forever. Man, I'm *tired*!" The search would never end.

Suddenly sounds of cheers and bright lights drew him toward a crowd of people near the command headquarters.

Normally, raucous crowds, the cheers and yells, made him go in the other direction, but tonight his thoughts were the last thing he wanted to be with.

It was a boxing match. Clumsy and gangly, the two combatants slugged at each other. It was charming and funny, bringing to Jason's face the first smile he remembered in a long time. He climbed the bleachers and found an open spot to watch.

The fight was over and a young airman was declared the winner.

The ring announcer called out the final contestants for the last, the heavyweight, battle. The Main Event.

The packed crowd of airmen cheered.

Jason almost fell over when he saw his own PJs carry out Major Clay Grizwold, a combat rescue navigator, on a litter. What were his boys doing there? What was Clay, an old guy, doing boxing?

He heard a roar and saw an entire section of his squadron cheer for their hero. And leading the cheering was Mac Rio!

He sat there extremely amused and confused at seeing his mates in the middle of a boxing smoker. They had to have been doing time at the base. But a boxing match?

There were "Ooohs" from the crowd when Clay's opponent stepped into the ring. He was a sleek, finely muscled young black man. And he had moves, shuffling and throwing shadow punches at blinding speed.

The people surrounding Jason laughed derisively, making jokes at an old man trying to take on a hot stud. Placing imaginary bets on the obvious outcome. He found it funny too, until he remembered that Clay and he were both the same age. If it was for real, it was going to be a massacre.

While the young man continued flexing and swiping at the air, Clay stood wide-eyed, looking like a man about to take his last walk. Jason empathized with Clay. What in the world had inspired him even to think about entering a boxing ring? Was this some sort of joke? It had to be. Then he thought about his own acts. *Damn, we old guys just don't know when enough is enough!*

The announcements made, a shapely young woman carried the first-round card of a three-round fight and the crowd geared up for the slaughter. The bell rang and the contestants came out of their corners.

As expected, the stud gamely circled the old man with frightened eyes. Bobbing and weaving, the stud tried throwing several combinations but Clay quickly stepped back, then, out of nowhere, caught the young man with a left jab that snapped his head back.

At the same time the crowd let out a high-pitched "Whoa!"

Then Clay threw two more jabs that connected and a hard right cross. The stud looked completely taken by surprise as Clay tied him up.

As fast as the crowd was behind the young man, they shifted their allegiance to the "old man."

The referee separated the boxers and let the fight continue. Now the young man was more cautious about his opponent while Clay stood flat-footed and dared him to get closer. Fists flying, like a flash, Clay nailed his man with an uppercut. The crowd went wild as the bell sounded.

Clay sat on his stool, still looking around like a condemned man. Then he threw his PJ cornermen a sly smile. Jason grinned ear to ear—it was all a ruse. Clay, despite being older, was a skilled pugilist.

Another curvaceous woman strutted around with the second-round card and the bell sounded. The round went pretty much like the first.

Something began to dawn on Jason. Sure, he was "over the hill," but maybe not quite *over*. He had been in the shit many times, and once again he was still standing. Watching Clay duck and elude the frustrated muscled and sweating boxer, Jason realized that he too used his skills to outsmart a stronger opponent—Clay fought smart.

The third round came and the yells of the crowd grew to a frenzied level. Clay was tired and only a knockout would win the fight for his opponent. Clay stayed just out of reach of the man's flying gloves, taking only minor jabs. Ten seconds from the end of the match Clay walloped the man with a right cross, making a statement.

Moments after the referee raised Clay's victorious hand the PJs lifted him on their shoulders and carried him around the ring. Outside the ring, true to PJ fashion, they were in every picture taken of the victor. It was going to be a great night of celebration at the Planet Jaber Recreation Center, sans alcohol.

Jason sat there as the bleachers emptied. Once again he had been so down on himself that he had forgotten that he was a warrior, one of the best—an *old* navigator had reminded him. He vowed that would go back to kill Nazari, not because he sought vengeance, but because he was skilled. He *was* a war angel.

Mac walked across the square. Jason stared hard at Mac's head. Mac frowned, slowed his walk, and looked around until he saw his friend.

"Hey! Nice tan. You look good, kid." Mac stood at the bottom of the bleachers. "Find what you're lookin' for?"

"Had it, but lost it. Nothing new for me, right?" Jason found his way to the bottom and hugged Mac with all he had. "It's good to see you."

"Well, man, at least it's great to see you *alive*." Mac peered closely into his friend's eyes. "You've been through hell again, haven't you?"

Jason smiled, nodded, then laughed a little, pulling out his medallion. "I think that maybe this helped a little. I need it to serve me just a little longer."

"What? You're going back?"

"I got some unfinished business to attend to, one final deed."

Mac looked hurt and sat down. Jason joined him.

"It's okay, buddy." Jason put his arm around his friend, a little confused that he was consoling his friend for an act that *he* was going to do.

"Man, I don't want you to get hurt, that's all. When will it be over?"

"I don't know. I don't know if it'll ever be over. There's some nasty egotistical people out there who would enslave us if they could, and kill us if they don't."

"I know what you mean. We've been able to do a lot of humanitarian stuff here. They're people just like us." Mac set his jaw for a moment. "You know, I learned something on this deployment; we're not slaves of God. We're God's creation."

They sat silently for a long time watching the crowd disappear until they were the last two at the boxing smoker.

"Hey, you cash my check?"

"Yeah." Mac lit up. "Hey, I'm rich now, thanks to you!" Then he became somber. "But what good will that be if you might not be around to see me styling like a Big Pimp after this is all over?"

"I'll be there. As a matter of fact, I'll probably get home before you do."

"Promise?"

"God willing. Listen, I got to get going. Don't tell anyone I've been here."

"Yeah, I know the drill. Damn, this better be the last time we pass each other like this."

Jason stood to leave and walked back to his room in the comfortable darkness. Live or die, he really never had anything, so he had nothing to lose.

CHAPTER 31

Bombing raids on Afghanistan are intensified.

THE CAB PULLED UP IN FRONT OF THE DOUG EC-celston PJ building. His car was in the parking lot. Mac said that the keys were in his drop box. He paid the taxi driver and went into the building to get the keys. He looked around at the empty building—every PJ was deployed to the Afghan campaign. It was the last time he'd ever enter as an active PJ.

Gul Nazari was dead. The extraction went without a hitch. He caught the first jet out of the theater, then bought a first-class plane ticket all the way to Melbourne, Florida. There was no one to greet him, or offer a "Well done." But it didn't matter. He had done his best, and he was still standing. He'd escaped with just scratches, but he knew he had wounds that no doctor could heal.

It wasn't over, good men and women in uniform were in harm's way. When it was over they would hopefully return to the loving arms of their families; and that was good enough for him. And for him, a long, long sleep was all he craved.

He walked out to his car and got in, when someone stepped out from behind the building. There was something very wrong about his looks. He automatically reached under his seat for his gun and cocked the trigger. The man continued walking, so Jason opened the door and, using it as a barrier, turned sideways. "That's far enough, mister."

The man stopped and smiled. He had gold teeth.

"Shit. You again. How'd you get on base? And keep your hands in sight at all times."

Gold Teeth nodded toward the river. Three Skidoos were beached near the PJ boats.

Shit!

"Senior Master Sergeant Johnson, you cannot see them, but my men are here only to protect me in case you decide to do some harm to me." He slowly held out his right hand. "You did something of immense value to the Order, and we would like to give you a token." He slowly held out his right hand. In his palm was a gold Maltese Cross.

"I don't follow you and I'm not sure I want to. Besides, I'm sick of all you power-crazy mothers. You probably were in cahoots with Gul Nazari and had me blow him and the dope away to drive up the price of yours. Asshole, I just want to be left alone. Understand? This is over. I will kill you right now if you don't leave me alone!"

"Please, take this. It will be our last meeting. We would like to reward you for your act."

"What? Screw you. I'm sick of your kind! Don't you get it? I don't want the thanks of scumbag assassins. IT'S OVER!"

Gold Teeth smiled. "No. It is not the assassins who wish to thank you, but the Maltese."

Jason frowned, then took dead aim between the man's eyes. "Hey, Gold Teeth, just who are you?"

"My name is Bayan Zangi. I am one who secretly serves the Maltese."

"Oh fuck me." Now things were clearer, or worse. Spy versus spy, it was one of the oldest tricks in the book. Gold Teeth was a mole, and the guy would have let him die to keep from blowing his cover. Now he was here trying to kiss some ass. "No. Bayan, I don't want any of your blood money. I've got enough of my own. Besides, yours is probably counterfeit." He decocked, then lowered his pistol. He took the Maltese Cross and looked at it, four arrowheads touching at the center. If there were things beyond his understanding, then the politics of the cross that he held was one of them. Sure, he might've been an initiated Assassin, steeped in secrets and mystery, but he did it just to keep his skin.

"It is just a token; it is given to those who have served the forces of good. You must understand that back in the assassin stronghold I was the one who sent Mya to help protect you. I did not know that she would fall in love with you."

"Nice talkin' to ya, Gold Teeth. I'm outta here." Jason holstered his weapon. He pocketed the cross and shook his head, then got back into his car and started it. "I'll add it to my collection of lucky charms. And I'll lead a charmed life if I never see your gold teeth again, or anyone in your game. I mean it, too. Stay away from my ass, all of you!" Throwing the car into drive, he roared away, not looking back for any reason.

"What now? Where to?" he asked himself. "Who cares?"

It could've been argued that he was wiser for all he had been through, but he knew better. His search was for nothing. If it was for stopping the dope, the law of supply and demand just drove up the price. If it was for love, he had lost it again.

Love. Dar, a good man with a loving wife, had found what he was after. He didn't even know if his baby had been born when he was killed.

The road on A1A was closed to through traffic so he had to go out the South Gate. Security manned the gate with M-60s and heavy barriers. The war never stopped. Well, the war was over for him. He had had it. He'd done his share.

He didn't really want to go home, but his empty apartment had a soft king-size bed. Just then a bottle of booze and a long, long sleep seemed to be the best bet for the funk that he was in.

He had over twenty years of *searching*. "Searching for nothin'. Damn." He sighed.

Once again the missing part of his heart had been touched, then pierced. He loved a woman, one woman for only a short time. Her name was Mya. "Why can't it ever work out for me? And the wrong people always get killed!" He couldn't bear to think about Rita's pain at the loss of Dar.

It was useless getting mad. He stopped in at the Publix supermarket and grabbed a bottle of Verdi wine.

He inserted the key to his door and turned it. It gave with no resistance. Jason was on alert in a nanosecond. Sensing someone in his apartment, he pulled and cocked his gun.

The high-powered Surefire flashlight was on the coffee table. Picking it up, he moved slowly and quietly through the rooms, hitting the light and sweeping the room with the pistol at the same time.

His bedroom was the last room to clear. By now Jason was trembling with stress. Shit. If there was no one there, then he'd have to start questioning his sanity. He moved closer to the door.

A somewhat familiar odor, there *was* somebody in the room. Wait! The smell was like, what?

He turned on the light, leapt into the room, and was stunned. "Mya!"

Mya Nazari sat at the corner of the bed, hands wringing in her lap. "Hello, Lost Soul."

"You're not dead? How?"

"It was just an illusion of my father's."

"Oh, no." He turned on the light in the room.

"You are not happy to see me?"

"No. No, that's not it at all. I've done nothing but think about you. You saved my life several times. Why'd you do it?"

"Because I knew you were there to stop the evil; Bayan told me."

"But I saw your father *kill* you. Mya, I couldn't let that go unanswered. Mya, I went back and killed Gul."

"I know," she said. "My death was another illusion. I went along with it because if you tried to take me with you, you would have been caught. You had to get away, be free." Mya looked at the floor. "My father did not kill me because I was promised to another person."

Jason interrupted. "What? Marriage."

"Marriage I could accept. This was a feyadeen, martyrdom. I was to go to Palestine, train three hundred women suicide bombers, then be jihad's first woman martyr. My father sold me cheap, fifty thousand dollars."

Mya's eyes hardened. "I never have known freedom. I was a slave to my father's whims. What father would do this to his daughter?

"It was Bayan's responsibility to smuggle me to Palestine, but we came here instead and he let me go." She shyly smiled. "He even gave me a genuine green card to live here.

"Bayan told me that I was free." She gripped Jason's hands.

Jason was jolted by her strength and electricity.

"I may be bold, but I know that this life is short. I kill many, many peoples, in many different ways. For thirty long years I have been no more than slave, doing my father's bidding. I could not get out of the fate he decreed.

"I pray to God. 'Please, oh God, once in my life, I would know love, no more. Just once, before I die.' Then you come. I sneak in and come to you at your Bliss. God is great. How could I let you die? I went along to make sure that you live. In all my deepest secrets and hopes, and pray to God to ever be free, but, thanks God, and you, I am here. I come to be your woman, if you will be my man."

Jason sat on the bed next to her. He put his arms around her and gave her a hug.

All the pain, hate, and sorrow that was in Jason's soul vanished. Mya's tender, gentle touch healed a lifetime of deep scars. The ghosts disappeared. At that moment his eyes opened and he saw a brand-new world. It was a world full of color and dimension. It was a world full of possibilities and none of them involved having to kill anyone.

Looking into Mya's eyes, Jason realized that he had seen his last war. That mean old fucking world would just have to survive without him. He had served his time. It was over. The dues and all the astronomical interest were paid up in full. It was time to forget about all the killing.

Now was the time to collect, and cherish the advantages he'd earned: freedom to love a woman with all that he had. He had the right to start a family and pursue the privilege of becoming a husband and a father. He could share his love with his beloved. He had found the missing piece of his heart. One day his children's children could stand proud when they spoke of their grandfather's legacy, and grandmother's too.

The War Angel could now hang up his shield, sheathe his sword, and fold up his wings. He had done it. He had really done it this time! He had found what he had been searching for, and he held her in his arms. He was home, and he was finally free.

No one on the ground bothered to look up twice at the old Fairchild UC-123 Provider flying low and slow through the Black Mountains; any- and everyone flew them. Following the sharp contours of the mountains, the crew was buffeted and thrown around by updrafts and downdrafts until they were over a wide plain.

The navigator kept them on a steady course as he homed in on a small electronic beacon covertly placed the night before by a combat control team. "Five miles to target," he keyed.

"Roger. Spray checklist," retired Air Force Pilot Bill Scarboro said, pushing the yoke forward, diving toward the valley floor.

Scarboro felt great to fly Patches once more, his old bird from Vietnam. Completely rebuilt, it handled just like new. He was as excited as when he first flew the plane with the Ranch Hands of the Twelfth Air Commando Squadron.

"Drop altitude," the copilot said, verbally reading the

altimeter until they were a hundred feet above the ground.

"Slow down now," the navigator advised.

Scarboro eased back the throttles.

"One hundred twenty knots," the copilot said.

The navigator held a stopwatch, looking out the cockpit window. "Leading edge in, five, four, three, two, one." He pressed the stopwatch. "Drop."

Scarboro flipped a toggle switch on his yoke. "Spray on."

The nav timed for three minutes, thirty seconds. The vertical walls on the far end of the valley were coming up quickly.

Pumps in a thousand-gallon steel tank in the cargo compartment forced Pleospora through spray bars across both wings.

"Time," the nav said.

The pilot flipped off the switch and pulled back on the yoke, climbing up and over a valley ridge.

The Pleospora mycoherbicide spray landed on a poppy field as the lavender flowers were in full bloom. The growing conditions were ideal, rich sandy soil, twenty-five-hundred-foot altitude, and a twenty-five-degree slope for drainage.

In the normal growing cycle another month would pass before the poppy petals would fall and opium bulbs would form. The opium juice would then be ready for harvest. Small incisions would be made in the bulb and the tears of Allah would ooze from each bulb. This was but one poppy plot of thousands growing in the country.

Abdullah Hadar had already sold the farm's yield of opium to the opium buyers. His three wives and twenty-five children would gather the gum opium, then simply process it into small round balls each weighing about three pounds.

The drug was then collected by the opium traders and loaded on donkey caravans. Hadar's family saved the impurities, then pressed and extracted the oil to be used for cooking. Once the narcotic was removed the bulbs would be ground and used for livestock feed. It had been this way for the Hadar clan for over two thousand years.

Little did Abdullah know that in ten to twelve days the D-440 Pleosporum that Patches sprayed on his crop would turn the pretty lavender poppy petals a rust color, then black, and the entire crop would wither and die. A black furry powder was all that would be left.

Abdullah would be shocked and confused. He might pray to Allah for help, the same way he did when the American genie helped them return to their land. Or curse the Iblis, the devil, like when the Taliban stole their entire opium crop and drove them from the land. Either way there would be nothing he could do about it. The season was lost and his family would go hungry, and maybe starve.

Some of the Pleospora spray would leach into the ground. It would prevent poppies from growing on that spot for well over a hundred years. But that was only the beginning.

The black residue left on the plant would produce a fungus that would become airborne, searching out only other poppies on which to destroy the growing cycle.

The producers of Pleospora, a more deadly strain of Papaveracea, an opiate biotoxin, estimated that in less than two years the entire opium-growing region of Afghanistan would be infected with Pleospora.

Nowhere would it be reported that the West was the first user of biowarfare on a failed nation.

Dear Rita,
I know how much you loved your husband.
Dar was a valiant warrior.
Dar died fighting for what he believed in.
He gave me life.
There's nothing I can do but offer my sadness,
and this check to take care of you and Dar's child
for life.
Dar taught me something.
You were everything in his life.
This should not be a war against terrorism,
but a fight for love.
I pray that one day we may begin to feel
compassion again.
It's the first sign of humanity.
Your name was the last word on his lips.
Jason Johnson

ABOUT THE AUTHOR

MICHAEL SALAZAR is an Air Force loadmaster instructor with over nineteen years of service. He is considered one of the Air Force's most experienced persons in search and rescue. Currently assigned to the 920th Rescue Operation Group at Patrick Air Force Base in Florida, his primary mission is to provide combat rescue for fighter pilots. His group also acts as a rescue support for all NASA space shuttle launches, and he is regularly called on for civilian search and rescue.